The Fellowship of Kindred Minds

The Fellowship Of Kindred Minds

Stories Reflecting Love's Darker Mirror

Jonathan Bellamy

Jai Belami Publications

The Fellowship of Kindred Minds
ISBN: 979-8-218-82065-7
Library of Congress Control Number:

Published by Jai Belami Publications, Atlanta, GA

Cover design by Jonathan Bellamy
With design assistance from Phortune McRae

Printed in the United States of America

Content Note

This collection contains themes of child abuse, sexual assault (including familial abuse), addiction, and violence. Reader discretion is advised.

These experiences are explored with honesty and care, not for shock, but to bear witness; to survival, complexity, and the ongoing work of healing. Some readers may find portions of this book challenging.

Please read with discretion and self-care.

A Letter to Dr. Shirley Hodge Hardin

There are people who pass through our lives briefly and leave behind a lasting imprint. You are one of those people.

When I sat in your classroom at Valdosta State College in the 1980s, you were not yet Dr. Hardin. You were a young professor, newly married and starting a family, brilliant, energetic, and completely unaware that one of your students would carry your lessons with him for decades.

I don't remember every assignment. I don't remember every lecture. Time has a way of collecting details and scattering them into the wind. But there are certain things I have never forgotten.

I remember *Sailing to Byzantium.*

I remember your lessons on imagery.

I remember hearing the line, "An aged man is but a paltry thing, a tattered coat upon a stick," and realizing for the first time that words could do more than communicate an idea. They could paint a picture. They could stir emotion. They could linger in the mind long after the page had been turned.

More importantly, I remember you.

You often described me as smart, creative, and less than motivated. If I am being honest, I liked hearing the first two and did my best to ignore the third. Time has a way of revealing uncomfortable truths, and I eventually learned that you were right about all three.

Before your class, I planned to become an elementary school teacher. It was a respectable path and one I believed suited me. Somewhere along the way, your influence quietly shifted the direction of my thinking. I changed my major to Speech Communications and became fascinated with the power of language. I dreamed of becoming a political speechwriter.

That career never materialized.

Instead, life took me down a different road.

I spent years building a career, accepting responsibilities, navigating successes and disappointments, and learning that dreams often arrive wearing different clothes than we expect. Today, I write books. I perform spoken word. I tell stories. I help others tell theirs through ghostwriting. My words now live in places I could not have imagined when I sat in your classroom.

As I prepare this book for publication, I realize that some of those words trace their lineage back to lessons you taught many years ago.

This book is filled with stories about people who shaped my life. Some were family. Some were friends. Some stayed for years. Others appeared only briefly. Each left fingerprints on the person I became.

You are among them.

I don't know whether you remember me. The truth is, there is no reason you should. Professors teach thousands of students over the course of their careers. But I remember you.

I remember your passion for literature.

I remember your belief that words mattered.

And I remember the way you challenged a creative but unfocused young man to think more deeply than he had before.

For that gift, and for your influence on a writer you helped shape long before he knew he would become one, I offer my sincere gratitude.

You may not remember me, Professor Hardin. But I remember you.

And after all these years, I'm still chasing words.

Respectfully,

Jonathan Bellamy

Haiku

To Phortune

You are light unkept,
Rising where the shadows fall
God still calls you *son*.

Preface

Every story is a doorway. Some open into rooms filled with light. Others lead into corridors where shadows linger. This collection invites you to step into both.

What binds these pages together is not a single character or continuous plot, but a shared thread: the quiet complexities of love. Not the kind celebrated in simple songs or fleeting romance, but the kind that unsettles, hides, fractures, and sometimes refuses to speak its own name.

I am drawn to the unspoken. The pauses that interrupt a conversation. The silences that stretch between two people who know each other well yet cannot say what they feel. Those pauses often speak more honestly than declarations. In the space between what is voiced and what is withheld, love reveals its many dimensions: tenderness and recklessness, destruction and, at times, redemption.

That is why the subtitle names it plainly: *Stories Reflecting Love's Darker Mirror.* Each chapter offers its own reflection, not always flattering, but always revealing. Love here is not framed in absolutes of right or wrong, light or dark. It appears instead in shifting shades of gray, where longing meets fear, where connection coexists with loneliness, where devotion collides with betrayal.

You may find yourself unsettled. You may find yourself recognized. Either way, my hope is that these stories invite you to linger in the in-between spaces, to sit with their questions rather than rush toward easy answers.

Welcome to *The Fellowship of Kindred Minds.* May the voices within these pages keep you company as you gaze into love's darker mirror.

Contents

Chapter One

The Broken "O"

Carmichael Lanes sat on the edge of Vallotton Park in Valdosta, the kind of building you could pass without noticing if not for the sign out front. It did not read "Carmichael Lanes" in bright neon or polished letters. Just a tall glass, colorful sign with the word BOWL stacked down its length. The bulbs flickered unevenly, and the *"O"* had been half shattered by a rock, leaving it glowing like a broken halo.

Inside, the air smelled of smoke, grease, and lane oil. Pinball machines blinked in the corner, and the jukebox lifted the room with Earth, Wind & Fire's "September".

Foosball handles rattled, pool balls cracked together, and the steady thunder of bowling pins echoed down the polished alleys. Men leaned against the counter of the sports lounge, nursing beers while the Braves played on a single muted television.

To a twelve-year-old safety patrol boy in an orange vest, Carmichael Lanes was a kingdom. I wore my vest like armor, proud that traffic froze when I raised my stop sign, but here that power did not mean much. We had access to it all, pinball machines, the jukebox, the latest arcade games, and pool tables, but this was the crown jewel. Half-price weekday bowling, endless games, and the freedom to walk in like we belonged. It was louder, brighter, and wilder than anything I had ever known.

But I did not just wander into Carmichael Lanes by accident. For us patrol boys, it was the place we earned with honor roll grades and orange vests. Every afternoon after the last bell, we manned our posts and then mounted our bikes and pedaled two miles, our stop signs slung over handlebars. Carmichael Lanes was our clubhouse. It was our reward, our kingdom, and we believed it would always belong to us.

The school year had opened with celebration. My name carried through the auditorium more than once that fall, and each time the sound sent a rush through me. Honor roll again. Major scholastic achievement. Mom and Dad would be elated.

Then came the surprise—my name again. Not just for grades this time, but for something bigger. Safety patrol. A boy in an orange vest with a handheld stop sign, trusted to keep order where cars and children collided.

It felt like a badge of honor, almost prophetic. My parents did not hesitate when I asked for a bike that Christmas. No lectures, no second guessing, just a quiet nod, maybe a flicker of worry in their eyes. They knew I was sheltered, always under their watch, but now I had something official, something important.

The training was quick, little more than a meeting with Principal Greene and Officer Faison in the cafeteria and a demonstration outside. But when they handed me my vest and the bright red sign, I felt taller, stronger, and powerful. I could step into the street and stop traffic with one motion of my hand. The other kids lined up behind me, waiting inside the painted crosswalk lines, and for those few seconds, I was the man.

By the time spring of 1978 came around, I had been on post all year. My name was still being called at the end of year assembly for grades, but the vest and the stop sign had already shaped me. I was not just a boy anymore. I was a patrol boy, and Carmichael Lanes had become the place where we gathered, the kingdom we thought we owned.

Most days, I was steady at my post. Vest zipped, stop sign raised, feet planted like I was holding back the entire world.

But sometimes, when the cars had thinned and the sidewalks emptied faster than usual, temptation got the better of me.

A friend and I would cut loose, riding our bikes across town instead of home. The wheels hummed against the pavement, with the hot Georgia air rushing against our faces as we pedaled toward Carmichael Lanes. We were not supposed to go without permission, but the place had a pull all its own. It felt like we belonged there more than anywhere else.

That is where we saw him, at the pool table near the back. A skinny man, not much older than a teenager himself, chalking his cue and lining up shots like he was training for the pros. The balls cracked across the green felt, one after another, his voice easy and steady as he explained angles, spins, and bank shots.

He did not talk to us like kids. He called us little brothers and men in training, like he already knew who we wanted to be. We hovered nearby, half watching the game, half basking in the attention. For a sheltered twelve-year-old who had been told more about books than the world, his words felt electric, like he was letting us peek into a future we had not earned yet.

We stayed too long that afternoon, losing track of time. When he offered us a ride home, we shook our heads, pointing at our bikes. We had been warned better than that. But there was something about him, his grin, his easy way of talking, that made him feel familiar, almost safe. That was the beginning.

After that day, I kept finding reasons to drift back toward the pool tables. Sometimes it was just to watch him shoot. His hands were sure and practiced, the balls snapping loudly but cleanly against the padded rails. Sometimes it was the way he spoke to me, like I was older than twelve, like I understood more than I did.

He started small. A pack of peanuts, a soda, and a few tokens slipped into my hand when he won a game. Brother, he would say, or Lil Man, or Cuz. Names that made me feel like I belonged to something, like I was seen.

I had always been the sickly, sheltered boy. My parents' shadow trailed me everywhere, even when it did not need to. But at Carmichael Lanes, under the dim lights and the haze of cigarette smoke, I was somebody. Somebody worthy of a nickname. Somebody worth a smile.

At first, I was not alone. A couple of us would ride over together, still in our vests, laughing like we owned the place. But it did not last. One buddy's grades slipped, and he lost his spot on the squad. Another just stopped caring, his bike taking him to other hangouts. Before long, it was just me, orange vest folded in my book bag, pedaling hard toward the glow of that broken O.

So I kept going back. Once or twice a week, I would leave my post early, pedaling fast so I could lean my bike against the brick wall and slip through those glass doors. I told myself it was for the games, for the music, and for the chance to feel grown. But really, I was chasing something else. Attention.

It was enough to keep me coming back. The weeks took on a rhythm. School, post, patrol duty, then the slow pedal toward Carmichael Lanes. I knew the path by heart, the cracked sidewalks, the magnolia roots pushing up through the pavement, the dip in the road where rainwater always pooled. By the time I reached the parking lot, the broken O in the sign felt like it was waiting for me.

Inside, the routine was always the same. I would drift toward the pool tables, hover until he noticed me, then wait for the nod that meant I could stay. Some days he bought me a Coke or a bag of chips. On other days, it was just a few tokens for the machines. It never seemed like much, but the smallest things took on weight when you were twelve, a middle son fighting for recognition.

He knew how to make it feel like a secret club. A nickname whispered low, a joke told like it was meant only for me. Brother, he would say, or Cuz. Words that felt bigger than my name. At home, I was just the preacher's boy, sheltered and watched.

But here, under the buzz of neon and the haze of smoke, I was something else.

I told myself it was harmless. That it was just games and talk and the thrill of being noticed. But slowly, the talk grew bolder, the looks lasted longer, and the air around the pool table felt different. Like something was coming I could not quite name.

One afternoon he was working the table like always, lining up shots and talking easy, when he set his cue down and stretched.

"Come on," he said. "I gotta pee. We will finish when I get back."

I do not know why I followed him. Maybe it was habit. Maybe it was the pull of routine. Maybe it was that I had begun to move around him without even knowing it. The restroom was small, no stalls, just two urinals against the wall and a sink streaked with rust. The smell of bleach could not cover the sour aroma of smoke and sweat.

He unzipped and glanced over. "You ain't gotta go? It is not healthy to hold it in."

My feet felt nailed to the tile. My throat tightened. His body did not look like mine. I could not look away, but I could not move either.

Then came the gesture. A finger to his lips. Time for silence. I should have walked out. I should have said something. But I did not. My shirt stayed tucked, my zipper stayed closed. His hands did not stop. They wandered, sure and steady, as if this too were just another game he had been practicing.

Everything within me froze. The betrayal of my own body was that it would not run, would not scream, would not do anything but stand there while this new world opened.

When it was over, he zipped up, washed his hands, and walked back to the pool table like nothing had happened. The crack of balls against the felt sounded the same, but I was not. Something in me had shifted, and I did not have words for it yet.

The days kept coming, but I was not the same boy walking into Carmichael Lanes anymore. I kept showing up. Not for the bowling, not even for the games, though I told myself that is what it was. I came for the routine, for the nod at the pool table, the sound of my name in a voice that made me feel older than I was.

The snacks, the tokens, the nicknames had become a kind of currency. Payment for my silence and for my attention. Sometimes it was just a hand on my shoulder that lingered too long. Sometimes a whisper, a joke told low enough that I could not repeat it at home.

Before long, the pool table was not where things happened. The storage room became the place, the air heavy with dust and oil, the kind of quiet that made secrets feel safer.

At home, things shifted in ways I could not name. I laughed less. My eyes lingered on the floor longer. My parents noticed, I know they did. But they chalked the mood swings up to growing pains and the stretch between being a boy and becoming something else, up to adolescence.

They had no words for what they were seeing, and neither did I. So I wore the mask. I smiled at school, bowed my head at church, nodded through questions at home. And in the in between, I kept going back to Carmichael Lanes, chasing something that was already costing me more than I understood.

And then, just like that, he was gone. No warning. No goodbye. One week he was at the table, chalking his cue and grinning like always, and the next he was not. The pool table stood empty, the green felt littered with chalk dust, the surrounding space echoing with a silence I did not yet know how to name.

I told myself I did not care, that it was better this way. And in some ways, it was. Routine broke. Tokens stopped. The storage room remained locked. But the damage was done. My mind already crowded with images and impressions I could not shake.

The weight of silence pressed harder now, not lighter. I was twelve, and I had learned things I was not supposed to know, carried things I was not supposed to carry.

At home, life went on. My parents still saw moodiness and eccentricity, still thought it was just adolescence stretching me thin. I let them believe it. It was easier than giving them the truth.

In school, I laughed when I was expected to laugh, smiled for yearbook photos, kept my grades where they needed to be. But underneath all of it was a shadow I could not explain.

I never asked what became of him. Perhaps he left town or found someone new. It is possible that justice finally caught up with him. All I knew was that he was gone, and the silence he left behind felt just as dangerous as his presence ever did.

Years passed, quietly at first.

High school gave me new clothes, new classes, and a bigger stage, but underneath I carried the same weight. I laughed in the hallways, joined in on the jokes, and posed for yearbook photos with the grin everyone expected. On the surface, I looked like any other preacher's son, well-mannered, studious, and safe.

But I knew the difference. I had crushes like the other boys, felt the same rush when a girl brushed my arm or smiled too long. Only I kept my distance. I did not ask for numbers, did not push for more. The thought of closeness made me feel split in two, the boy they thought I was and the boy who had already been somewhere that had to remain a secret.

At church I bowed my head, lifted my hands when told, played the part of the faithful son. At home, my parents chalked up my silences to teenage moods. They did not see that I was carrying a secret I had no language for, a shadow that made me both cautious and reckless at the same time.

So I wore the mask. A smile that said I was fine. A posture that said I was obedient. And behind it, the echo of Carmichael Lanes, of the broken O still glowing in my mind, a reminder that a boy could look whole on the outside and still feel split in half.

By the fall of 1984, I had left Valdosta High behind and stepped onto a new campus with a fresh start. College was supposed to be freedom. Books, lectures, nights that stretched longer than my parents would have ever allowed. And in some ways, it was just that liberating.

But freedom came with categories I was not ready for. In high school, I could hide behind grades, church services, and polite distance. On campus, people wanted to know who you were, not just what you scored.

Labels hung in the air, whispered in dorm hallways, passed in the cafeteria. Jock, nerd, church kid, and freak were common labels. I did not know where to put myself.

I had crushes, and sometimes more than that. There were moments of joy, of reckless exploration, of tasting what it meant to be wanted. But every step carried a shadow, the memory of Carmichael Lanes, the silence of that storage room, the broken O glowing behind my eyes.

I told myself I was in control. That I could balance it, the mask for the classroom, the smile for the yearbook, the distance when things went too far. But the truth was I was still divided, trying to make sense of a self that had been fractured years before.

The grades kept me grounded, kept my parents proud. On the outside, I looked like any other young man, holding down a job, making payments on my first car, moving through life the way I was supposed to. But inside, the questions grew louder. Who was I really? What had that boy in Valdosta become?

By the summer of 1989, Valdosta felt too small to hold me.

A friend had whispered what I already suspected.

Atlanta is the place. It is full of brothers just like you.

That was all the push I needed. I packed what little I had, slid behind the wheel of my second car, a stick shift, the kind most of my friends still could not drive, and headed north with more hope than a plan.

Atlanta hit me like a current. The city pulsed with energy. Traffic and music and late-night lights that made Valdosta look like a faded photograph. Everywhere I turned there were people chasing something, degrees, careers, love, pretense, and escape. And for the first time, I could chase too, without my parents' watchful eyes on my every move. I was still going to church, not out of obligation, but because it had always been part of me.

There were jobs to be had, paychecks to earn, apartments to rent. There were clubs and house parties, spaces where laughter spilled loud and long, places where someone like me could disappear into the music and the spoken word culture.

I tasted freedom in flashes. A conversation that turned too close. A touch that lingered. A night that promised more than I had known before. But the shadow traveled with me. No matter how fast I drove up Interstate 75, the memory of Carmichael Lanes rode in the passenger seat.

Every new name, every unfamiliar face, carried an echo of the old ones, nicknames whispered too close, a hand that stayed too long. I smiled through it, kept the mask polished, told myself Atlanta was a fresh start. And yet, in quiet moments, I wondered if I was building a life or just learning how to hide in a bigger city.

Atlanta gave me years of motion. Jobs that paid the bills, apartments I could call my own, weekends filled with noise and laughter, and relationships that rose and fell like summer storms. Some brought joy, some regret, but all of them taught me something about who I was and who I was not.

I learned how to blend in, how to keep the mask polished, how to answer questions without really answering them. But I also learned how to stand on my own, how to pay rent on time, how to manage a car note, how to wake up and show up even when the night before had left me hollow.

There were moments when the past pressed in. Carmichael Lanes. The broken O. The smell of lane oil and smoke. The storage room. The silence. Those memories never disappeared. They just found new corners to hide in.

But brokenness is not the whole story. Somewhere between the echoes of that bowling alley and the hum of Atlanta traffic, I found my voice. The boy who once froze in silence became a man who learned to speak, to write, to perform, to stand on a stage and tell stories out loud. I became a poet, a spoken word artist, and a storyteller. Words became the place where I could take back what had been stolen.

So when people look at me now and wonder what my deal is, I do not rush to answer. Because the truth is complicated, and not everyone deserves it.

But know this. The boy who once stood frozen at a urinal grew into a man who commands a microphone. And even broken things can rise and speak.

Chapter Two

Sunday's Whisper

The summer heat in Lithonia always seemed to hang heavy over the pines past Evans Mill Road. Back then, it was country. Red clay underfoot. Two-lane roads stretching quiet. Fields that went on longer than they do now. Today, those same roads choke with traffic, lined with strip malls and subdivisions. But in the early eighties, it was still quiet, still a place where everybody knew whose yard you were mowing and whose mother kept an eye on you from the porch.

We were just boys then, fifteen, sixteen, seventeen, halfway between chores and dreams, playing ball in the street until somebody's mama called us in. That's when the talk would start.

Somebody would mention her name with a grin, and the rest of us would fall into laughter we didn't quite understand. Her name was Sunday.

She lived out on the edge. A churchgoing woman. Married, but mostly alone. Her husband was somebody nobody ever seemed to see. Her grass always needed cutting, her hedges always needed trimming, and somehow one of us was always willing to take the job.

It was a strange kind of secret, mostly because it wasn't hidden at all. Folks whispered, joked, even warned. Don't let your boy go over there too often. Yet nobody said much beyond that. To us, it sounded like luck. Like bragging rights.

The older boys carried themselves differently after a Saturday at her house. The rest of us listened wide-eyed, wondering when it might be our turn.

Sunday had grown up the daughter of a pastor, her name tied to the day she was born. Her father used to call her his Sabbath blessing, even though he knew the Sabbath stretched from Friday night to Saturday evening. To him, Sunday was the Lord's Day. Resurrection. Rejoicing. He preached that his daughter carried that spirit in her very name.

Her mother kept the house and the church together, the kind of woman who did everything quietly. Then one day her body surrendered. A brain aneurysm took her quickly. Her father didn't last long after that. Country folks said he died of a broken heart. She had done everything for him, and he could not live without her.

By the time Sunday turned eighteen, she was a mother herself. Twin boys born the very morning she crossed into adulthood. They grew into men who walked straighter paths than their mother ever did. One became a minister in Atlanta, carrying the family mantle. The other taught school in DeKalb County, content with the steadiness of classrooms and chalk dust.

Her husband was twenty years older. A man wounded in body and spirit. A work accident had left him disabled but compensated. One hundred and fifty thousand dollars and lifetime medical care. The settlement bought their house out past Evans Mill Road, where trees shaded the porch and gossip clung like moss.

His days stretched long, most of them spent sunk into a tan La-Z-Boy recliner, a plastic ashtray always within reach. His world was lit by the glow and sound of a floor model television. Wrestling on Saturday afternoons. Braves baseball in the summer. The evening news every night at six.

He loved the remote control, a small piece of power that let him command the world without rising from his chair. That was his kingdom. Four walls. The hum of the television. The click of a button.

Sunday moved around him like weather. Restless. Alive. The more he faded into that chair, the more she fed what was left of her hunger. The house held both energies. A man waiting out his days. A woman unwilling to wait for anything.

Sunday wasn't tall, but she filled a room. She was shaped like the women most of us grew up around. Thick thighs. A full chest. Hips that moved with a rhythm that seemed unhurried even when she was only walking to her car.

Her stomach carried the years, the children, the quiet gravity of time. It didn't erase her appeal. It made her seem real. The kind of woman you might pass at church or in the grocery store.

Inside the house, the silence pressed in. Her husband's television buzzed louder than his voice ever did. He leaned back in the recliner, shifting only to cough or reach for the ashtray.

Sunday moved around him as if she were invisible. Some nights she stood at the kitchen sink, staring through the window at the line of pines in the backyard, remembering her mother's hands moving through the same motions years before. Washing dishes. Folding clothes. Tending quietly.

Only now the house was hers, and the quiet was not a comfort. Her parents were gone. Her boys were grown. The man she lived with could barely look at her anymore.

She sang hymns under her breath while she worked. The same ones she sang in the choir on Sunday mornings. She wondered how long a body could carry longing before it broke open in ways that could never be put back together.

On Saturdays, the yards came alive. Push mowers rattled down driveways. Sweat streaked T-shirts. Boys rushed to finish so they could claim the rest of the day.

Sunday's house always needed something. Hedges trimmed. Gutters cleared. Tools carried from the shed. The work wasn't different from anywhere else, but what followed made it something else entirely.

From her kitchen window, Sunday watched them with a soft smile, hands busy at the sink or on a dish towel. She didn't have to say much. Her presence alone felt like an invitation.

The boys bragged later that she looked at them in ways no grown woman should. What they didn't know was how much of it came from her own loneliness.

Her husband's voice rarely rose above the television. When it did, it was only to ask for sweet tea or shuffle to the bathroom with a groan. The house had two currents. His stillness. Her restlessness. And on long Saturdays, the balance tipped.

We gathered at the liquor store on Covington Highway near Panola Road, not to go inside, but for boxes. Nobody bought boxes back then. You got them from behind the store. Liquor boxes were the best. Thick. Double-ply. Strong enough to hold a life if you packed it right.

That afternoon, Chick needed boxes. His real name was Corey, but nobody called him that. We called him Chick because once he got hold of a Kentucky Fried Chicken snack box and nearly buried his whole head in it, smacking and licking his fingers like he hadn't eaten in days. The name stuck.

Chick was also the only one of us with a driver's license and access to his family's GMC truck. That made him king. Two lucky ones rode up front. The rest piled into the back.

That day, he bent over the cardboard, acting busy. He'd already told us Sunday needed her garage cleaned out.

"You going over there again?" Kenny Man asked.

"Just helping her out," Chick said.

"Helping her out," Kenny Man repeated, dragging the words.

Marcus jumped in. "I'll help her out too."

We laughed. Chick smiled, shoulders squaring like he'd been crowned with something the rest of us hadn't earned.

To us, Sunday wasn't forty-five and married. She wasn't a pastor's daughter or a woman who sang in the choir. She was a story. A secret. A legend in her own house.

We loaded the boxes into the truck. Kenny Man claimed shotgun. Marcus and I climbed into the back, legs dangling as the engine coughed to life.

The wind rushed in our ears. Red clay dust clung to our shirts. We laughed at nothing.

"You know you ain't just cleaning out no garage," Kenny Man called.

Marcus slid the back window open just enough to holler, "She paying you with that thang, ain't she?"

Chick kept his eyes on the road. His shoulders told the truth.

One by one, we peeled off. Marcus near his aunt's place. Kenny Man at the corner. Finally, it was just Chick, driving toward Sunday's street.

I jumped down and watched as he turned slowly into her drive. The GMC crunched over gravel and settled quietly.

Sunday's house sat low and neat. Curtains stirred. The door opened.

She stepped out like she'd been waiting, wiping her hands on a dish towel. The garage door groaned open beside her. Not flashy. Just the way she looked at you, like you already belonged there.

Chick climbed out with the boxes. Her husband's truck sat in the driveway. From the street, it looked ordinary.

The garage door was fully open. Chick set the boxes down. The cardboard slapped the concrete. He wiped his hands on his jeans and followed her inside.

The door closed. The house went still.

That was the story. Cleaning out the garage. A reason. A cover. A way to make it sound like work. It wasn't the first time. It wouldn't be the last.

Sunday kept her smile steady. Her hat straight on Sunday mornings. Her alto voice strong in the choir. Mothers whispered. Fathers shook their heads. Boys got whippings for being seen near her yard.

Nobody said it out loud.

We thought it was about us. About daring and manhood. It wasn't. It was about silence. About what grown folks refused to name and what we were too young to understand.

If it had been the other way around, there would have been outrage. Instead, the worst kept secret stayed secret.

Her husband's truck stayed in the driveway. Maybe he knew. Maybe he chose not to.

Years later, the cost showed itself. Some of us carried it into therapy. Some cycled through marriages. Others chose singleness, deciding it was safer to walk alone.

As for me, I turned to words. Writing what I once only heard in whispers. Trying to make sense of the boy I was and the silence that shaped us.

And maybe that is the truest telling of innocence lost. Not the moment itself, but the echo it leaves behind, still whispering long after the doors have closed.

Chapter Three

Palindrome

My mother's name was Kamilah. In Arabic, it means "complete" or "perfect". For a while, she lived up to the name.

She could recite the alphabet before most kids could hold a crayon. By thirteen, she had already graduated high school and was taking college classes, a brown-skinned prodigy with a sharp mind and eyes that seemed to notice everything.

At age two, she spoke English and Spanish. Just a year later, she read scripture from the Bible and, thanks to her devout older cousin, passages from the Quran too. At five, she was solving sixth-grade math problems. Reporters wrote about her. Teachers bragged about her. Kamilah was not just a girl in the neighborhood. She was a headline.

And then there was me. Arora. Her son, given a name that would follow me like a riddle. The reason perfection became gossip and the story everyone told about her suddenly changed.

They, my mother and her cousin, created me in a way the family would never forgive.

I had not even arrived yet.

But once the whispers turned into truth, everything shifted. The genius they once praised became a warning. The girl they placed on a pedestal was now the girl they spoke about in hushed tones. Her name passed from mouth to mouth like a cautionary tale.

The cameras stopped rolling. The community closed its arms. Teachers who once stayed late to nurture her brilliance now turned away in the hallway. Family members who bragged about her test scores barely spoke her name.

She was still exceptional. But now she was something else. The one who let it happen. The one who brought shame.

And just like that, Kamilah disappeared from the headlines. Not because her light dimmed, but because people chose to stop seeing it. She was no longer a prodigy. She was a pregnant girl, a line from the wrong story.

Still smart, stunning, and special, but nobody wanted to say that out loud. Because now she had me.

So what is in a name?

Mine is Arora. A feminine name. A girly name.

My mother, brilliant even in her mistakes, told me it was Indian in origin, drawn from Hindu and Sikh traditions. She said persecuted people once called themselves A U R, meaning something else.

Over time, mispronunciation turned that something else into Arora. I have always found it ironic that a teenager gave me a name that foretold my story. Such foresight.

Even now, I look in the mirror and smile. I am something else.

Kamilah was born in 1980. I came along a little more than a decade later. Her pregnancy brought shame, so the family gave her money during my toddler years. Hush money, really, to keep their distance. By sixteen, she was out on her own.

She was still smart enough to figure some things out. But saddled with a child and no support, life got harder. My father, the family's dirty little secret, disappeared. Gone like vapor.

Years later, therapy gave me language for something I already suspected. Boys who violate, especially within families, are often replaying wounds they never learned to name.

So it was just the two of us, moving into a single room in a three-bedroom tenement. We shared it with the landlord, a young musician from Minnesota, part of the legacy of the Minneapolis Sound. He owned some cool things. He was peculiar.

I remember watching movies on his Laserdisc player, shiny discs the size of vinyl records. One film had a monologue I never forgot. A man warned that if you married someone foolish, the children would carry that same foolishness, the proof waiting at the front door.

Even as a kid, I thought of Kamilah when I heard that. She was smart. And in her own way, she was lucky. Our family had disowned us, but the landlord helped when we struggled. His help, of course, always came with a price.

As for me, I was a misunderstood introvert, misdiagnosed as depressed by untrained eyes. People threw affirmations at me like confetti.

"You're perfect."

"You've got so much to offer."

"Ordinary kids would sell their souls to be as smart and handsome as you."

Time did what it always does. It moved forward without resolving anything.

Maybe they were right. Maybe not. Today, I am about to receive my MBA. Back in high school, somewhere between skinny jeans and Obama's second term, I was a standout sprinter. An Olympic hopeful, they said. But it was not competition that drove me. Running just came naturally. I had talent, sure, but no love for the sport itself.

What I remember most is not the after-school practices. It is what happened afterward, the first time we showered as a team. This was the new millennium. Everything was open concept, even the locker rooms.

I walked in. Some glanced. Others stared. At first, I did not understand. We were all guys. But they were not really looking at me. They were looking at my body.

I did not understand it then, but I would later be told there was something about me that drew attention. I had never thought about it. I had nothing to compare it to. I had seen the landlord, but I had not paid close attention. It had not mattered to me. Not then.

But that changed fast. Rumors spread. Nicknames followed. I pulled away from everyone. They praised the way I ran, but they never saw the boy underneath the shoes and speed.

Truth is, sometimes I wished I were a girl.

So who am I now? A man torn between pride and shame, both wrapped up in her. Kamilah.

She believed in the bond between a mother and her unborn child. She said it was spiritual. Eternal. Maybe she was right. That bond shaped everything.

But what were we? Mother and son, or something else?

We shared more than blood. More than spirit. I do not know. Some days, I wonder if it was even sexual. I did not have the language then to separate love from safety, or closeness from need.

She was my first love. The first bond I mistook for something holy. The first face I ever remember seeing. I was her baby, yes, but she also called me her blessing. She is still my first dream girl. And I closed my eyes to so much.

The sounds she made when the landlord came into our room at night, the way she medicated her self-loathing with sex, the way we all pretended our family did not exist, each became its own language of survival. Sleep did not block it all out. Love did.

My next love, my first genuine love, was my best friend. We were inseparable. We played, fought, and protected each other. He was all boy. I was just all.

I loved him before I even knew what love was. When I finally understood it, I told him. I spoke my truth with a carefully crafted confession. He did not respond. He stormed off and never spoke to me again.

We were sixteen. I remember because the Trayvon Martin story was everywhere. The hoodies. The Skittles. The trial that split the country. I remember thinking he could have been me. For the first time, I felt like someone who had something to lose simply because we were the same age. And I had just lost my first real love, who happened to be a boy.

Years later, I heard he moved to Amsterdam. I stayed in the city. They say he is a father now, living with her somewhere far away. And me? I am just a friend. A former best friend. That is all I have ever been.

Eight years passed. Somehow, in the wake of shutdowns and Zoom degrees, I made it through. With an MBA in hand and a head full of questions, I stepped into the city that never sleeps. Gown, cords, and mortarboard tucked away in the closet, along with the truth I still did not know how to wear in public. I am still searching.

And then there she was. Perfectly designed. Well-spoken. Radiating confidence. What stood out most were her eyebrows, arched and elegant. She became the first love I chose for myself. My first virtual love affair.

In that eternal moment, I imagined dating her. Loving her. A girl, and me, the boy who never expected this. It did not fit my pattern. Buffalo raised me. My mother shaped me. My first love was a boy. And now this.

I approached her confidently. She looked at me, surprised, then turned away toward the subway. I followed without caution or fear. At the turnstile, she stopped and looked back.

"Arora?"

Her voice was familiar, impossibly so. She smiled gently.

"Sixteen was a crazy age for both of us. Your confession confirmed so much about my life. Not a day has gone by that I have not thought of you. Who I am now is who I was always becoming."

We boarded the train in silence. Together again. Just us.

The car lurched forward. So did my chest.

I am unapologetically Arora. A name with light. A palindrome. Every step forward, every step back, still the same direction. The right direction.

Chapter Four

Sons Of Thunder

The five houses that made up our corner of the neighborhood sat at the end of Pilgrim Street, tucked into a quiet cul-de-sac we called *The Mill Quarter*.

The Mill Quarter was a patch of land, what folks today might call a subdivision, full of rentals and working-class families. But our little circle at the very end? That was our world. Five houses in a row, close enough to borrow sugar without knocking.

Folks used to laugh and call our strip "shotgun row." Same open layout in every house. You could stand at the front screen door and see straight through to the back.

Just as I stepped into the house, I heard the engine of the pristine nine-year-old 1967 Chevrolet Impala rumble into our grassless front yard. I hurried to wipe the tears from my face with the edge of my shirt before Pops saw me.

I was the youngest of three. My two older sisters usually stayed out of the way when Pops came home. That left only me.

He was already on the front porch, so I had no time to compose myself. The porch was small and too open to escape his eyes. I turned my back slightly as he paused and bent down to unlace his boots. He placed them beside the rusty porch furniture, his usual spot. Then, without a word, he stepped inside.

I was used to hearing him call. Putting away his boots was part of my daily routine.

"Chris, son. Where are you?"

I tried to bury the tremble in my voice, pressing it down with as much low tone as I could muster.

"Yes, sir. On my way."

He caught it anyway. The thin shakiness in my reply changed his tone.

"What's wrong with you now?"

The *now* in his question wasn't just timely. It was fair. There always seemed to be something going on in the life of his youngest child and only son, Christmas Josiah Reynolds.

Before I could answer, my mother, hearing the irritation in Pops's tone, cut in.

"Chris, are you okay, baby?"

Pops shot back in her direction, his voice sharp.

"Woman, stop treatin' him like he's a baby. That's why he cries all the time."

He turned back to me.

"I asked you, what's wrong?"

I knew better than to be shy or soft-spoken at that moment.

"I got in a fight," I said, pausing before adding, "And I lost."

As I exhaled, he flashed a crooked smile and stepped toward me. With his thick hand, he lifted my chin and examined the faint bruise and slight cut beneath my eye.

He let out a low chuckle.

"Oh, he got you good under the eye, huh? And your nose looks a little swollen too. But don't worry, son. You can't win 'em all. You stood up for yourself. You held your ground. You didn't back down or let him bully you. I'm proud of you."

He walked off in a good mood, still amused. I let out a quiet sigh of relief, thinking I'd escaped any further talk about the fight.

Mom mumbled something under her breath as she headed back to the kitchen. I couldn't make out what she said, but I was sure it had something to do with her feelings about fighting, especially when it involved her only boy.

My relief was short-lived. Still in a playful mood, Pops asked without even looking my way,

"Who were you tusslin' with anyway?"

I didn't want to answer. So, I didn't.

"Was it Major Solomon?" he asked, like he hadn't just named the strongest kid in the neighborhood.

I wished it had been Major Harold Solomon, the neighborhood Hercules. Getting beaten by him would have felt like being noticed. He called us jitterbugs. Not out of cruelty, but the way rookies get named before they earn respect. Bugs too small to matter, but too persistent to ignore.

Did Pops really think I would pick a fight with the neighborhood Hercules?

Major Harold Solomon lived in the last house down in the Mill Quarter. He was one of the high-school legends. Athletic. Cool. The kind of guy we all wanted to be one day. Even his name sounded like a title.

He was nearly six years older than me and already living in a world that felt unreachable.

Every pre-teen boy in the neighborhood *knew* that one day, in his daddy's utility shed, Major and Irma Jean Marshall crossed a line none of us could fully name.

We didn't need proof. The story moved faster than truth ever could.

We didn't need to see anything for the story to harden into fact. The way Major emerged, the way Irma Jean didn't, told us enough.

And we loved her, in that dumb, bold way boys do. Not because we knew her, but because, earlier that spring, at the hour when day gives way to night, her presence had revealed itself to us once, quietly, through a bedroom window she never bothered to cover.

We were in the yard next door, standing still, knowing exactly what we were not supposed to see.

Whatever she noticed, she never let on.

The memory released me.

"No, sir," I said finally. "It wasn't Major."

My tone came out sharper than I intended. Pops stared at me without blinking.

Under that weight, I exhaled and said the name.

"Stefan Fillmore."

The room changed. Just like that.

"Stefan Fillmore?!"

Pops roared.

"That lazy ass Fillmore boy gave you a black eye?" he barked. "You gotta be kidding me. He's half your size and one of the sorriest boys I've ever seen. That sorry joker won't even shake a lick at a stick. He's the one who did this to you?"

This was exactly the response I had feared.

Stefan and I were the same age, but I had maybe an inch or two on him, and he was half my size in spirit. He wasn't a bad kid. Like me, he was a mama's boy. But unlike me, he was pretty.

The biggest difference was that he didn't have a daddy. And he was an only child.

Pops wasn't wrong about everything. Stefan had brains. He could outthink anybody in class, but outside, he wouldn't break a sweat to save his life. His mama never made him do any chores, not in the yard and not in the house. Still, there was something special about him.

He was one of the sharpest kids at school, and he could spin the funniest, wildest stories you ever heard. All of us liked him. Even the big kids laughed when he got going.

But with Pops, pride never stayed put for long. One minute he was smiling. The next, he came at me like I'd embarrassed the whole house. He stormed past me toward the only closet in the house and reached for his leather strap.

The sight of it broke me. The tears came fast, stinging as they mixed with the cut beneath my eye.

My sobbing pulled my mother back into the room, and she rushed in, trying to intervene.

By then, Pops was eye level with me. I didn't need to see it, but I did. He looped the strap once around his hand, pulling it tight until it formed a thick knot. Then he held his fist just inches from my face.

Mother gasped.

"You gonna go back out there and whup his behind," Pops growled, "or I'm gonna whip yours. Now dry your eyes and go."

I had my marching orders. I wiped my face again and stepped outside. The walk to the Fillmore house, just three doors down, felt like a thousand steps.

Stefan was still in the yard, right where I'd left him, surrounded by the same four boys who'd watched the first fight. They were getting ready for a quick game of pickup basketball.

I wasn't eager to start this again. But I was eager to finish it.

With careful steps, I crossed into their yard.

Stefan met me head on and said nothing. He just stared.

We stood there in silence while the ball bounced in the background, that hollow thump against hard Georgia clay. Then a voice rang out, quick and clear, breaking the quiet wide open.

"What y'all gon' do, man?"

One of the boys called out.

I clenched my fists and slid into my best fighting pose, one foot back, shoulders squared, my heart pounding.

In a low voice, just loud enough for Stefan to hear, I said,

"My pops sent me back. I got to fight you."

Stefan looked at me. Calm.

"You really want to fight again?"

"Of course not," I whispered.

He paused, staring at me as if he were trying to read something behind my eyes. Then he glanced toward his friends and said,

"I'll be back, y'all."

He motioned with his head.

"C'mon."

Without another word, Stefan led the way.

I followed, confused. I didn't know the plan. I didn't know if it was a trap or a new humiliation.

But the surprises kept coming.

He darted up the steps to my house, crossed the small porch, and started banging on the screen door like the place was on fire. Pops answered. Stefan stood tall, offered a polite good afternoon, and extended his hand for a firm shake. Then, in the most intelligent and colorful way he knew, he launched into a full explanation of what had happened between us.

"It started on the bus," he began. "My friends were praising Chris and teasing me. We were standing in the aisle, waiting to get off, and he was just ahead of me. When he stepped down, I gave him a shove. He fell and scraped his face on the clay bank by the road."

"When I realized I might have actually hurt him, I got scared, because I knew he could beat me up. So I ran home."

"When he showed up at my house just now, I thought he was coming to beat me up. But he said if I told you the truth, he would let me slide."

"So here I am. I already apologized to Chris, and I hope we can still be friends."

It was one of Stefan's most vividly imagined tales, and it instantly became my favorite.

Pops, surprisingly, seemed to believe every word. Maybe it was the way Stefan said it. Maybe it was the way he stood. But something shifted.

My father, just moments ago ready to whip me, now looked proud again. And for once, I felt both safe and seen. From that day on, Stefan and I were inseparable.

Our friendship, born out of confrontation and fueled by a shared appetite for innocent trouble, became something of a legend. Pops, who didn't even go to church, started calling us the Sons of Thunder, like the brothers from the Bible. We wore the name like a badge.

School let out about two months after our fight. The last ride home on the county bus was loud and full of laughter. We shouted our goodbyes through open windows, knowing most of them were temporary. Being country kids, our summers were always full of adventure.

The older boys, like Major, worked the harvests for local farmers, driving tractors, hauling produce, handling machines I was still too small to touch. I picked butter beans or cut okra instead. Three dollars and fifty cents for every hamper I filled.

Stefan's mother didn't require him to work. And on the days I didn't either, we walked the dirt roads barefoot and headed down to the lake we called the Blackfish Hole.

Most days, it was just about cooling off and clowning around. But on special ones, we made half-serious plans to catch a glimpse of Irma Jean, who, according to rumor, sometimes went skinny dipping at the far end of the lake we loved so much.

As the long days of summer stretched toward their seasonal end, Stefan and I were both a little disappointed in the results of our little missions.

Word around the Mill Quarter was that Irma Jean was moving to Detroit to live with her uncle and aunt. They had lined up a job for her at the Jefferson Assembly Plant, the one that made Chrysler cars and Dodge trucks.

Each weekday morning, my parents, Stefan's mother, and thirteen other passengers parked their cars at the local church and caught the community transit van. It carried them fifty-one miles from our little corner of Wilcox County to Robins Air Force Base, where they all worked Civil Service jobs.

Like twelve-year-old boys often do, Stefan and I saw opportunity in their absence. One particular Thursday morning, we slipped out early with our fishing poles, a few sandwiches, and a plan. We were ready for a full day of angling, swimming, laughing, and whatever else our young minds could talk each other into.

The fish were cooperative that morning. By ten o'clock, we had reeled in three bream and five catfish between us. After a couple of hours on the banks, we decided to eat part of our lunch, rest a while, and then go for a swim.

We each devoured two bologna sandwiches and washed them down with generous helpings of Mama's sweet tea, sealed in recycled mayonnaise jars. Then we stretched out in the shade of a Southern live oak tucked into the brush a few yards from the water's edge.

Lying on our backs, we stared up through the canopy, watching sunlight spill in streaks between the swaying leaves. We talked about everything that mattered to twelve-year-old boys. Comics. Baseball. Girls. And what we would do if we ran the world.

Lost in conversation, we didn't notice the shift in sound until it became too quiet. Not silent. Just wrong.

Faint voices echoed from somewhere in the woods. We froze, hoping it was just folks from town. But deep down, we remembered what the grown-ups always said about swimming at the Blackfish Hole alone. They said there were bears in the woods nearby.

We didn't know if that was true, but we weren't in the mood to test it. Without a word, we locked eyes, came to the same silent decision, and reached for the low branches. With the practiced quiet of two seasoned fugitives, we pulled ourselves into the tree.

Stefan looked down and motioned for me to follow him up to a higher limb, thick enough to hold us both and hidden just enough to feel safe. As I climbed, I glanced up at Stefan and saw it on his face. He looked spellbound. When I reached the wide, bench-like limb and settled beside him, my eyes followed his frozen gaze.

And there they were. On top of a worn blanket, in a clearing just beyond the tree, lay Major and Irma Jean. She was on her back. He was over her. They were both exposed, completely naked.

Without turning his head, Stefan slowly raised his index finger to his lips, silently commanding me to stay quiet. He didn't have to. I couldn't have spoken even if I tried. I was just as mesmerized as he was.

That moment, fixed in time like a snapshot, would shape years of misunderstanding between us and the world. For all the times we had whispered about "hunching," piecing together what little we knew from rumor and imagination, here was the living truth.

We didn't know what to feel. Our embarrassment nearly matched our excitement. Our eyes stayed locked, taking in everything. Neither of us spoke, and neither of us looked away.

At some point, without meaning to, our breathing fell into a matched rhythm. Absorbed by every breathy moan that escaped Irma Jean's raspy voice box, our admiration for Major only grew.

From our makeshift tree stand, we watched in silent awe. He moved with slow, deliberate thrusts. Every muscle from his neck to his ankles tense and sculpted. His frame seemed to swallow hers, eclipsing her thin but shapely body beneath him.

Then, without warning, his rhythm quickened. It was urgent and unrelenting. And just as suddenly, it stopped. Stefan and I held our breath, a shared gasp caught in both our throats.

Whatever ideas we had about hunching collapsed the moment they started. By now, we were lost. Just wide-eyed boys, watching something we couldn't name.

Then came the sound. A low, guttural grunt, not unlike the mythical bear we thought had chased us up that tree in the first place.

Major braced his hands outside the blanket, pushed himself upright in one strong motion, and rose to his feet. He stood there panting, looking down, then took a few steps to the side, leaving Irma Jean's body fully exposed to our stunned, unblinking eyes.

We finally looked at each other. The air felt different. Heavier. Like we'd crossed some invisible line. The surprise in Stefan's eyes was a perfect reflection of my own.

But as quickly as we turned away, we turned back.

We were drawn to her again, that girl who had been the source of our whispered fantasies ever since that spring evening when her silhouette appeared like a dream behind her bedroom window.

I'm not sure what kind of picture Stefan's vivid imagination had painted for him. But I knew what I saw. Irma Jean's relaxed, glistening body had seared itself into my memory, permanently. Her dark-brown skin, slick with sweat and perfectly even in tone, was now etched across my mind like a sacred mural.

And then there was the view between her legs. The part that my mind held onto the longest. Her flower, unveiled yet veiled beneath a rich layer of soft, curly hair. I was changed. A single moment planted a memory so deep it followed me into manhood, shaping me in silence and giving me a preference I never spoke aloud.

Major returned to her side, stood tall, and reached down to offer her his hand. Helping her to her feet, he laced his fingers through hers. Oblivious to the two wide-eyed witnesses hidden in the branches above, they ran laughing toward the lake.

Together, they cannonballed into the shallow water, kicking up splashes that caught the sun like diamonds. They swam, they frolicked, and they disappeared for a moment into deeper water until they looked up and saw us.

The sun betrayed us, slicing through the branches and lighting us up like a pair of deer caught in headlights. Irma Jean, submerged to her shoulders, let out a sharp, instinctive scream. Her arms moved quickly, wrapping across her body, as if covering what we couldn't even see. The shame rushed in anyway.

It was hard to tell whether Major was angry or amused. He wore a sheepish grin, but his voice told another story.

"Chris! Stefan! Get y'all asses down outta that tree and bring us our clothes! What the hell y'all doin' up there? Spyin' on us?"

We scrambled down. Before I could say anything, Stefan blurted out,

"Uh, we were hiding from the bears!"

They both gave him a look. The kind that said, *Really?* Then, surprisingly, they laughed.

We cautiously approached the edge of the lake and laid their clothes gently on the bank, careful not to look directly at either of them.

Still facing the water, we slowly backed away, Stefan a few steps behind me, as if retreating from royalty. The brush swallowed us back into our hiding spot beneath the tree that had served as our grandstand.

But what came next caught us off guard. Irma Jean and Major emerged from the water and got dressed right there, as if we weren't even present. She moved without a word, sliding into her yellow sundress with a grace that felt deliberate. Even if she never once looked my way, she had to know I was watching.

When I finally tore my eyes from her, I saw Major walking straight toward me, shirt half buttoned and jeans riding low on his hips. I was frozen, so caught up in the moment I hadn't even realized Stefan was gone.

"Chris, you know I like you. But if anybody hears about this, I'll hurt you. Understand?"

I nodded slowly.

Then, in a moment I didn't expect, he winked and gave a crooked smile. I turned toward Irma Jean. She met my eyes, raised her index finger to her lips, and made a soft shhh.

Just like Stefan had done earlier.

I nodded again. And smiled.

The next six summers flew by. In the blink of an eye, it was 1984.

Major had long since stopped being just the strong kid at the end of the cul-de-sac. By the time he left for Lorman, Mississippi, on a full athletic scholarship to play for the Alcorn State Braves, he had become a kind of local legend, someone the little boys still called Hercules.

After graduation, Major moved to Atlanta and eventually became part owner of a small chain of athletic training facilities. We saw little of him, but in the Mill Quarter, his name still carried weight.

Stefan and I stayed close through high school. He also ended up in Atlanta, attending Clark College, where he planned to major in English and minor in creative writing.

My parents died during my senior year in a head-on collision with a tractor-trailer on State Highway 129 between Fitzgerald and Ocilla. They were in Pops's prized Impala. Just like that, they were gone.

One minute, they were getting groceries. The next, I was standing in the living room with a state trooper who could not look me in the eye. I did not cry. Not right then. Instead, I stared at the wall and thought about the sound the screen door made when Pops came home from work.

I had just turned eighteen. My two sisters and I received a generous insurance settlement. They could not wait to leave Wilcox County, and honestly, I could not blame them. They combined their settlement money and bought a home in Ormond Beach, Florida.

At eighteen, seventy-five thousand dollars seemed like all the money in the world to me. I did not have a job. I delayed college. And like many folks in the group of houses that made up the Mill Quarter, I stayed right where I was, in a rental.

Many of our families had been in those houses for generations. Some worked steady jobs in Fitzgerald or made the long haul to the base in Warner Robins. Others picked up work when they could. Seasonal jobs. Fieldwork. Whatever paid.

We did not own the land, but we made homes. We kept food on the table. And we always, always held each other up. It was not easy, but it was ours.

Irma Jean had taken the job at the Jefferson Assembly Plant in Detroit, but after a round of layoffs, she found herself back in the Mill Quarter six years later. She blinked when she saw me, like she did not expect I would still be around, not after the settlement.

By then, Stefan's mother remained in her house, but all the other kids I had grown up with had moved on. Two of the five homes in the cul-de-sac were empty now. The porch swings were still. The laughter was gone.

I guess I had become what Pops would have called a lazy ass, or what my mother might have more kindly referred to as a ne'er-do-well. Truthfully, I did not mind. I had grown comfortable with the rhythm of doing nothing.

I had not had many actual experiences with women, but I had gotten good at lying about them. It became my specialty. Tall tales about my supposed conquests. The quiet truth was simpler. I got through high school without ever really dating anyone. I had a prom date. That was about it.

Irma Jean and I talked often and had dinner together regularly. She worked at the garment factory in Fitzgerald but was usually home by four. She was a decent cook, and I enjoyed her company more than I liked to admit.

The weather had shifted, cooler air to match the shorter days, and the holiday season was creeping in. I felt a flicker of excitement knowing Stefan would be home for Thanksgiving break. He said he would be in by midday on Wednesday.

That Tuesday evening, Irma Jean offered to cook dinner at my place. Over the stove, she mentioned that her family from Detroit would drive down for Christmas. They would be staying through the New Year. The car they were bringing would be hers, but she would have to drive them back to Michigan once the holidays ended.

She made a full meal. Cubed steak, yellow rice, green beans, and those cheap, soft dinner rolls they always served at church on Big Meeting Sunday. We sat together, ate quickly, then lingered at the table, talking the way we always did. Easy. Familiar.

Afterward, we moved to the kitchen to clean up. I watched her as she worked, the way her hips shifted when she reached for a dish, the way her shoulders moved as she scrubbed a pan. My mind wandered. It always did with her.

No matter how many fantasies I had carried since high school, they always circled back to that day at the Blackfish Hole, when Stefan and I saw her with Major. That image never really left me. Even now, watching her move around my kitchen, I felt it again. Like memory had teeth. Like it could still bite.

The kitchen grew quiet except for the water running over the dishes. I could hear my own breathing, heavy in the pause between us. Something in the room changed, some small permission that had not been there before.

With that memory burning behind my eyes, I stepped toward her. I slid my hands around her waist. I leaned in and kissed the back of her neck. To my surprise, she did not pull away. Instead, she turned to face me, and we started kissing.

My hands moved without restriction. She even guided me. Then she paused and softly took my hand and led me to the bedroom.

Only the glow from a small lamp lit the room. She lowered me to the bed, stepped back, and slowly slipped out of her form-fitting, mesh-knit flare dress. When it hit the floor, she stepped out of it and tossed it onto the chair.

There she stood, naked. I had to be dreaming. Her body had changed little from what I remembered that day by the lake. If anything, time had only made her more beautiful.

Then, oddly, but somehow perfectly, she stretched. I did not know if she was loosening her muscles for what might come next or simply letting me see her more fully.

This was only my second sexual experience. And the first, I was not really a participant. I did not choose it or ask for it. I did not even know what it was until it was over.

But this. My hand around her stretched waist, my chin on her shoulder, her breath on my neck. It was not just a fantasy fulfilled. It felt like something sacred. The stretch lasted only seconds, but to me it felt like forever.

In that span of time, I traced every curve of her body with my eyes, slowly, reverently.

In the dim light, I noticed the faint shadow of regrowth and uneven coloring under her arms. But below the waist, no razor touched her. My breath quickened. My nerves rose. And then she came toward me, unhurried, unblinking, leaned down, and met my waiting body.

After helping me undress, she climbed into bed beside me. We spent the night together, though we barely slept. It felt like I was making up for a lifetime of inexperience in just a few brief hours. No thoughts of consequences. No worries about the future.

Just us. Just this moment. It was magic. And for once, time stood still.

When morning came, she kissed me softly, then slipped out into the crisp fall air. She headed to work. I stayed home, stuck in the memory. Her imprint remained, not just on the sheets, but in some place inside me where loneliness used to live. The taste of her kiss lingered on my lips and neck, and I let it stay there, savoring it for as long as I could before the day demanded my attention.

Stefan arrived later that afternoon. And while I was quietly thrilled with how my night had gone, I was not in a rush to tell my best friend that I had finally fulfilled the fantasy we had shared, and that it had been with her.

His mother had invited her sisters from Florida for the holiday, and we both knew his time was already spoken for. Still, for old times' sake, we made plans to hit the lake that Saturday and do a little fishing. I did not mind spending Thanksgiving alone.

My day was filled with football and leftovers, cubed steak, yellow rice, and quiet reflection. By the weekend, we were back on the banks of the lake at the Blackfish Hole, rods in hand, laughter in the air.

Stefan set his rod aside, pulled his knees to his chest, and wrapped his arms around them.

"Hey man," he said, squinting toward the patch of grass across the lake, "you remember when we watched Irma Jean and Major over there?"

"How long ago was that?"

I laughed and pretended I had to dig through the back of my memory.

"Oh yeah, man, I'd forgotten all about that!" I said, grinning.

"What I remember is you left me and ran home!"

We both cracked up.

Still smiling, eyes fixed on the silver ripples dancing across the lake, Stefan said,

"That's a beautiful memory. That's a beautiful piece. A sweet piece. And she's a grown woman now. Trust me."

His words hit like a curveball I was not ready for. I paused, trying to process what he meant, then responded carefully.

"Yeah… I know."

Stefan continued,

"We couldn't take our eyes off her."

Then I threw a curveball of my own.

"Truth is, that's the only one I've ever really seen."

He squinted. "Only what? You still a virgin, Chris?"

"I didn't say that." I smirked, but my voice was soft.

"I just… I don't get around like you, I guess. And the ones I've touched… it was always in the dark."

"Chris," he repeated, more serious now, "are you still a virgin?"

I stared at the lake.

"Man... I remember every inch of her. I ain't gonna lie. I love how hairy she is."

Then I caught myself.

"I mean, was."

Stefan let out a laugh and shook his head.

"Trust me, I remember. You didn't shut up about that all year. Lucky for you, you stayed in the Mill Quarter. Girls in Atlanta? They shave. You'll do better staying here in the country, son."

He laughed again, then exhaled and picked up his rod, preparing to recast.

"You know... speaking of..."

He paused.

"She still got a whole lot of bushes coverin' that flower garden."

I chuckled, thinking he was teeing up one of his tall tales. That was Stefan, always spinning something.

I gave him a playful side eye.

"Alright, man, let's just fish."

But then he paused again. His face twisted slightly, just enough to make me uneasy.

"Nah... for real, Bruh."

Another pause.

"I was in that last night."

I froze.

My stomach dropped, and the laughter drained from my face like water from a busted pipe.

I turned and looked at him, almost angry and almost hurt. He kept talking.

"That's why I couldn't come to your crib," Stefan said.

"She just showed up. It was Wednesday. You know my mom was at the prayer meeting with her sisters. I had the house to myself, so I let her in... and it just happened. I didn't even have a rubber. But I didn't say no."

I fixed my face, stone still, pretending not to hang on every word. My jaw tightened anyway. He kept going.

"We're gonna be in our twenties soon. Life's about to get serious.

But right now? Pussy is here. And if they're giving it up, we need to get all we can, while we can."

"You're letting it pass you by. That's not a smart move, money man."

I hated when he talked like that. Like the world was a locker room and every woman a scoreboard. But I nodded, pretending to agree. My excitement had drained away completely.

I had let my inexperience and hope trick me into thinking that one night meant something to her. That I meant something. But hearing what happened the very next night, it all felt cheap. Like I had been nothing more than a moment to pass.

Sunday came. Stefan left for Atlanta. He said the campus was closing for most of December, but he wouldn't be back until Christmas week.

"We'll make the drive up," he told me. "Spend New Year's Eve in the city."

I agreed.

Whatever Irma Jean and I had, it vanished. We went back to being just neighbors. Cordial.

A month passed. When Stefan came home, I was genuinely excited about the trip to Atlanta. But underneath that excitement was a nervous energy that kept pressing at me. I had not spoken to Irma Jean about anything more than the weather or the mail. No more late night dinners. No more electricity.

So when I heard a knock at the door that afternoon, I was surprised to see her standing there. Yes, it was her. I let her in, and we exchanged the usual pleasantries. Nothing deep. Just light conversation. Still, being near her stirred something in me. It always did.

Something about her presence quieted me, even when I did not realize I needed calming. She made the world feel less empty.

Even now, after everything, she still moved through my emotions like smoke. Soft. Lingering. Impossible to hold. And the sting was still there too.

I rushed the moment and told her Stefan was on the way, and that we were heading to Atlanta. She smiled softly, but her eyes held something back.

"I don't want to mess up your weekend," she said.

"I know y'all got plans and all. I just wanted to talk to you about... us. You know, when you get a chance. It can wait until you come back."

Her words caught me off guard. *Us*?

Something shifted in my chest, quick and sharp, but I held it in.

"Us?" I repeated, gently taking her hand, my mouth pulling into a crooked smile.

"Yeah," she whispered. "Us."

Then she glanced toward the door, as if she did not want to stay too long.

"Like I said, I don't want to mess up your weekend. Enjoy your trip. Happy New Year."

She leaned in and kissed me on the forehead. Soft. Maternal. Final. And just like that, she was gone.

"Be safe going to Detroit," I said.

"I saw the Jeep in the yard. Congratulations. It's a nice car."

"Yes," she said, smiling. "It's a blessing. Good thing I know how to drive a stick."

She laughed lightly, but the air between us was still thick.

That was when I heard footsteps on the porch. Stefan's voice came through the door, as usual.

"Comin' in."

He knocked once as he stepped inside, catching both of us mid stare.

"Hey, girl," he said casually, walking over to give her a hug.

Then, turning to me with a smirk, he said,

"Son, we'd better hit the road." He winked.

I froze for half a second. Then I did the only thing I could think of. I reached out and shook her hand. She took it. Squeezed lightly. Said nothing.

Then she walked out the door.

A few minutes later, Stefan and I hit the road to Atlanta.

The New Year's Eve festivities were lively, full of music, drinks, women, and city lights. For Stefan, the night was fun. For me, it was noise. I was ready to go home. Back to the Mill Quarter. Back to quiet mornings and slow days. And most of all, back to finishing the us conversation with Irma Jean.

Much to my disappointment, Irma Jean spent all of January in Detroit. She had taken a leave from the garment factory and picked up a thirty-day contract through a temp agency, working on a construction project.

When she returned, she seemed happy to see me. But our conversations stayed surface level, like nothing had ever happened between us. I could not help but wonder if something had changed in Detroit.

Valentine's Day was coming up. And even though we had spoken a few times, that December conversation had never finished. I had no plan. No path. But for a moment, I let myself believe she might be the beginning of one.

That afternoon, I was out in the yard when I saw her Jeep roll past. I crossed the cul-de-sac toward her house.

"Need help with the bags?" I asked.

"Hey, Chris. Sure, thank you."

She opened the rear door. "I just ran over to Fitzgerald. Picked up a few things from Piggly Wiggly."

"I'm kind of in the mood to cook tonight. You got plans?"

"Not really," I said.

"Irma," I said, then stopped.

"Yes?" she replied, smiling but not slowing down.

"Back in December, you said you wanted to talk. About us."

She kept moving.

"Now it's mid-February," I said. "And we still haven't."

She did not look at me.

"Was I imagining that?"

"Oh, that," she said lightly. Too lightly. "I wasn't sure what I was feeling back then. I probably should not have said anything."

"Feeling what?" I asked. "About me?"

She shook her head. "No, honey. Not about you."

"Then what?"

"I'm confused," I said. "And honestly, I'm a little worried."

Her voice sharpened. Tired.

"Well, worry is one thing you don't have to do now."

She stopped. Looked at me fully.

"I left the baby in Detroit."

The words did not land right away. When they did, they stayed.

We used to laugh like nothing could touch us. Loud. Wild. Like thunder without a storm behind it.

Love does not arrive that way. Love comes quietly. Then it breaks everything open.

I smiled, like I understood.

Inside, something went still.

Not anger.

Just empty.

Chapter Five

Silent Crown

- The Runway Fades
- Loneliness Named
- Finally, The Promised Land

The Runway Fades

The Albany Mall was not much. Two long hallways, a Belk on one end, a JCPenney on the other. But Mama used to say it was her runway. Back when she was the fine girl of Westover High, Class of '78, boys would post up by Chick-fil-A just to watch her strut through the food court.

Back at Westover, she was not just fine. She could sing. Pep rallies, church programs, talent nights. If Mama had a mic, boys who never went to choir rehearsal suddenly found religion. They honked car horns outside our house in dented Chevys, swearing they would marry her one day. Girls whispered when she passed, pretending not to be jealous.

That was over forty years ago.

Now, at sixty-two, she walked three steps ahead of me, tugging at the scarf wrapped tight around her head. Fluorescent lights hummed above us, bright enough to expose everything, but nobody looked her way.

The man flipping through belts at Belk did not notice. Teenagers clustered near GameStop, faces lit blue from their phones, never looked up. Even the women, the kind who once sized her up in silence, let her pass without a glance.

She noticed. Not out loud. I saw it in the way her eyes lingered at the Bath & Body Works window, then darted away quickly, like she had caught herself staring at a stranger.

Mama had five kids, and I was the last. The one she never saw coming. By 2001, she was forty-one, her oldest children already grown and gone, the house quieting.

She had four kids before she turned thirty and thought her childbearing days were long behind her. When her cycle stopped, she figured it was menopause. The final curtain.

I remember her lamenting how she thought she was done with all that. Diapers, teething, carrying another human on her hip. Then the test came back positive.

By that time, Daddy was already halfway out the door. Two years younger than Mama, he married at eighteen, had four kids before thirty, and used to say he never had time to live.

He did not leave for another woman. Not exactly. He left for air. For space. For whatever freedom looked like to a man pushing forty. Mama gave him the divorce angrily but without begging. She found out she was pregnant with me a month later.

So while my siblings were starting college or working jobs, Mama was back in the maternity ward, delivering one last child her body had not planned for. She laughed about it sometimes, calling me her menopause baby, but there was always a bitterness under the smile. Like my birth was both a miracle and a reminder of everything she had lost.

Most days, it was just the two of us. Me, twenty and bald by choice. Mama, covering what time had taken. Alopecia had thinned her crown and stripped her pride. For her, hair was everything. Without it, she felt invisible.

I knew differently. I had it too. Instead of hiding, I shaved my head clean, slipped hoops big enough to brush my shoulders through my ears, and decided I would be seen on my own terms.

Men still looked. Women still whispered. But Mama could not see that as power. To her, beauty was hair. And hair was the one thing she could not get back.

She slowed in front of Victoria's Secret, eyes catching on a mannequin dressed in pink lace. For a second, her lips parted, like she was remembering something. Then they pressed tight.

"They don't make clothes for women my age," she said, half under her breath.

I wanted to tell her they did. That beauty did not have an expiration date. That she was still wearing a crown, even if now it was silent and hidden beneath a scarf. But she was already moving again, shoulders squared, disappearing into the crowd like another ghost in the hallway.

We did not stay long. Mama never does. A few bags in her hand. Lotion, socks, a scarf she probably would not wear. By the time we reached the car, the late-afternoon sun had turned the windshield into a mirror. She slid in slowly, like her bones remembered every step she had taken.

In the driver's seat, she pulled down the visor and checked her reflection. Her fingers went to the knot of her scarf, tugged it, smoothed it flat. For a moment she hesitated, like she might pull the whole thing off. But she did not. She sighed and let the visor snap shut.

"Funny," she said, almost to herself.

"I used to walk in that mall and heads would turn. Now I walk through and it is like I ain't even there."

I wanted to argue, but her words hung heavier than I expected. She was not asking for comfort. She was not fishing for compliments. She was just saying it out loud. Naming what I had already seen in her eyes back at Bath & Body Works.

I glanced at her hands on the steering wheel. The same hands that used to clap rhythms on the kitchen counter when gospel music played on Sunday mornings. The same hands that could hush a room with a single gesture.

You are still here, I wanted to tell her.

Still seen. Still crowned.

But the words stuck. I rolled down the window, let the hot Albany air rush in, and we drove home in silence.

She was not always invisible. I know because she told me so.

Back when the house stayed loud and the radio was locked on WJIZ, one hundred thousand watts of soul power, Doc Suttles ran Sunday mornings like church on the air. Mostly contemporary gospel, until he would slide a blast from the past into the set.

"All right, saints and ain'ts. Little quartet for your mama's kitchen. The Sensational Nightingales with 'On Jordan's Stormy Banks I Stand.' My mama called it 'I'm Bound for the Promised Land.'"

Bacon popped. My oldest brothers cut figure eights through the kitchen. Mama, baby on her hip, sang the refrain under her breath.

"I am bound for the promised land."

The notes sat warm and round in her chest, the way people sing when the song knows them back.

Doc rolled on to newer music, but that quartet detour always felt like a steadying hand. And in Mama's voice I could hear it, the echo of a woman who once wore her crown out loud.

The way she told it, you would think everything worth noticing about her vanished with her hair and her high-school-skinny body. That old Nightingales hymn was her safe place. The sound of a house that felt whole.

But I saw her differently.

She still had curves most women would kill for. A sway in her hips, even when she did not mean to. A softness that looked like strength, like every child she carried was still a part of her. Jill Scott in the flesh. Octavia Spencer fine.

Mama did not see that. She measured herself against the girl she used to be, not the woman she was now. And no matter what I thought, no matter how often I wanted to tell her men still noticed, it would not have mattered. The only gaze she trusted was the one that followed her down the halls of Westover all those years ago.

I leaned in the doorway, watching her fold a T-shirt with the same precision she used when I was a kid. This time she paused, holding the shirt like it had spoken back to her.

"Sometimes I look at these clothes," she said, not looking up, "and I remember when I wore a size smaller. I still feel the same inside, but the mirror don't lie."

She folded the shirt tight and dropped it on the stack.

I wanted to tell her the mirror was wrong. That it never captured the whole of her. The curve of her laugh. The weight of her presence. The way people still noticed even when she did not.

But I stayed quiet.

Silence had become our language.

Loneliness Named

That night, Mama sat in her usual spot on the sofa, a throw blanket pulled over her legs. The TV played softly, some game show she was not really watching. She kept the sound low, like noise was only there to keep her from hearing the silence.

On the end table sat her wig stand, a faceless head with curls pinned neatly in place. Mama had taken the wig off the moment we walked in, set it there like a crown at rest. The scarf was gone now too, her head smooth and bare in the lamplight.

She rubbed her scalp, not exactly ashamed, but carefully. Always carefully.

I watched from the hallway, arms crossed, wondering if this was what the rest of her years would look like. Quiet evenings. Folded laundry. A television talking into the room for her. She had never remarried, never even brought a man around since Daddy left.

"Mama," I said finally, stepping closer.

"You ever think about dating again?"

She gave an inaudible sound that did not reach her eyes.

"Girl, ain't nobody checking for me at this age."

She adjusted the blanket and turned her gaze back to the screen.

"Besides, I've got all I need."

But I did not believe her. Not with the way she sometimes lingered at Victoria's Secret windows. Not with the way she sighed in the car when she thought I was not listening.

She turned the TV down so low it was almost a hum. The wig stand sat on the end table like an offering, curls pinned neat, waiting for a head that did not always feel like hers. For a long moment we just listened to the house breathe.

"Come here," she said suddenly, patting the cushion beside her.

"Sit."

I crossed over and sat close enough to read the small things. The tiny scar on her thumb from when she burned herself on the stove years ago. The freckle on her collarbone that my father used to joke about.

Up close, she looked younger somehow. Not because the mirror agreed, but because the lines around her mouth softened when she was not trying to be brave.

"Are you ever lonely?" I asked, because the question had been rolling around in my chest since the mall.

She laughed again.

"Lonely, yes. Miserable or desperate, no. I've learned how to be by myself. That doesn't mean I like it. And I know there are younger men who claim they want a nurturing woman, but what they're really after is someone to mother them. I've raised my children. I'm not interested in raising another grown man."

There was a pause, a careful one, like a glass being set down. Then she reached across and took my hand, rough and warm.

"Women like me can start over, don't you think?" she asked, the question more to herself than to me.

"Sometimes someone just shows up. After the paths cross, you think maybe that's it. Maybe he looks at me the way they used to. But by the time you get the nerve, it's too late. People have already decided what you are and moved on."

"What if it's not too late?" I said, because I wanted to believe it for her and for me and for every woman who had been taught to count the years by who looked at her.

"What if somebody shows up and they like your whole self. Crown and all. Whether it's loud or quiet."

She cupped my hand against her cheek for a second and closed her eyes. For the first time since the mall, something in her loosened. Not a smile exactly, but the hint of one.

She whispered, "If somebody came." She paused and gave a devious look that suddenly became serious again.

"I don't know if I could show them everything. I don't know if I could take off my armor."

"You'd be surprised," I said.

"I wouldn't be the only person surprised."

She opened her eyes and looked at me as if she were weighing a decision. Then she nodded once, small and private.

A week later, a man from the neighborhood came walking door to door, slipping flyers into mailboxes and stopping to speak to anyone out front. He was inviting homeowners to a community town hall. Nothing dramatic. Just his way of saying people still mattered enough to be asked.

He paused at Mama's gate. Slow but sure, his voice was steady when he called out a greeting. She noticed his voice. Steady. Unhurried. Carrying a weight most men tried to rush past. At first, she mistook it for simple politeness. But the possibility between them lingered, unnamed and almost fragile, like a trace of sunlight catching her scarf that evening.

He did not stay long at the gate. He handed her a flyer, explained the town hall, and thanked her for listening. His voice carried the same steadiness as before. Clear. Unhurried. Not the kind of man who filled silence just to be heard. Then he moved on, house to house, the way people used to when neighborhoods were still neighbors.

Mama lingered a second too long at the door before closing it, the flyer still in her hand. She turned and caught me watching from the sofa and let out a laugh that was more nervous than she meant it to be.

"Girl," she said, fanning the flyer as if it were a wedding invitation,
"I just met the man I'm going to marry."

She smiled wide, tongue in cheek, her eyes daring me to play along. But beneath the humor, I caught the small spark she could not hide. That glimmer of wanting to be chosen again.

The meeting was held a week later in the fellowship hall of the neighborhood church. Folding chairs lined in neat rows, with a table of store-bought cookies and lemonade near the back. Nothing fancy.

When Mama walked in, she had taken care. Hair styled just so beneath her wig. A touch of perfume that trailed lightly behind her. A pressed blouse. She did not overdress, but she carried herself like a woman who still knew how to be seen.

He was at the front, shaking hands as folks arrived. When Mama reached him, he greeted her the same way he did everyone else. A pleasant handshake. A steady smile. A warm, "Glad you could make it." No more. No less.

She nodded, returned the smile, and took her seat. Nothing on her face gave her away. But I sat beside her, close enough to feel the small drop in her shoulders. The tiny exhale of air she let out as she crossed her legs and adjusted her purse.

She was not crushed or heartbroken. Just a little disappointed. The way you are when you have hoped for more and life offers you the ordinary.

Mama accepted it, smoothed her skirt, leaned over, and whispered,
"Well, that's that."

But I knew better. Because when the meeting ended and we walked back to the car, she still carried the faint trace of his cologne on her hand. And though she did not say it, she noticed.

We were halfway down the steps when I heard his voice behind us.

"Ma'am, you dropped something."

Mama turned, and there he was holding her pen. The cheap ballpoint she kept tucked in her purse for notes and shopping lists. She laughed, a little embarrassed, and reached for it. Their fingers brushed. Nothing more than an accident. But I saw her eyes lift to meet his.

"Thank you," she said, steady but softer than usual.

"You take good notes," he replied, smiling and nodding toward the small pad peeking out of her purse.

"Wish more folks did that. Makes it easier to hold us accountable."

It was not a compliment on her blouse, her hair, or her perfume. Nothing flirtatious. But something in his respectful and deliberate tone made her pause before she slipped the pen back where it belonged.

The ride home was quiet. Mama looked out the window. Not smiling or frowning. Just thinking.

When we pulled into the driveway, she gathered her bag, straightened her shoulders, and said, almost to herself,

"He notices things."

Later that night, after the town hall, I found Mama in the den. The TV was off. The wig was back on its stand. The house carried that stillness that settles after a long day. She was sitting in her chair with a photo album open across her lap, fingers tracing a glossy page.

It was not a posed portrait. Not the kind you send in Christmas cards. It was from one of the few vacations they ever took as a family. The six of them crowded onto a beach, water splashing, everybody laughing at something unseen behind the lens. Daddy had one of my brothers on his shoulders. Mama was caught mid laugh, hair pulled back, her hand reaching toward the camera as if to wave it away.

She had kept the picture visible on the bookshelf all these years, tucked behind glass in a cheap frame. She always said it was because it showed them together. But I realized then it was more than that. It was proof of when life felt whole. Husband. Children. Future. All lined up in front of her like waves rolling steadily.

I watched her lips press into a line as she studied Daddy's face. They had met back at Westover when she was a senior and he was just a year behind. People said he was the kind who would make a good husband. Churchgoing. Hardworking. Pleasant. Few girlfriends. No drama. A man whose head was on straight before his shoulders had even filled out.

He used to joke that his life felt unfinished. One girlfriend for a summer, and then Mama. The second. The last. Married at eighteen. Four children by thirty.

He said sometimes he felt like he had missed the part where he got to live. And eventually, he walked away, chasing that empty space.

Mama closed the album gently, slid it back onto the shelf, and sat there for a while with her hands folded in her lap. I could almost see the thought forming. That for the first time in over forty years, she was allowing herself to wonder if another man could belong in her story.

Finally, The Promised Land

The sun was high that Saturday, bright enough to warm the hood of Mama's Camry as she stood in the driveway with a sponge in her hand. Gray Nike sweatsuit, cap to match, and her newest pair of running shoes. She was not a runner, never had been, but she loved the way good shoes made her feel like she could go somewhere if she wanted.

The brim of her cap shaded her face, hiding more than just the sun. Folks in the neighborhood probably already knew, but Mama was not ready to let anyone see her bare crown. Not yet.

She dipped the sponge in the bucket, suds dripping down her arm, and scrubbed in slow, practiced circles. Music drifted from the kitchen window. Frankie Beverly, smooth and steady, filled the air like summer.

That was when he came walking by. Not in a hurry, just his usual pace, carrying himself with the ease of someone who did not need to rush. He lifted a hand in greeting.

"Good morning," he called.

Mama looked up, the brim of her cap catching the sun.

"Morning," she answered, wringing the sponge in her hand.

"You keep that car shining," he said, nodding toward the Camry.

"Looks better than mine most days."

She laughed, surprised at how easily it came.

"Keeps me busy," she said, but I could tell the compliment landed.

Not on the car. On the care.

He did not linger. Just lifted his hand again and kept walking. Mama watched him go, sponge forgotten in her hand, until the music shifted into another song.

Later inside, she slid off the cap and dropped the sneakers by the door.

"Girl," she said with a grin she tried to pass off as a joke, "he caught me out there washing a car like I'm twenty."

But I noticed the way she folded her sweatsuit carefully before putting it away that night, like it had become something more than laundry.

Mama doubted herself more than anyone else ever could. I saw it in the way she pulled at her cap. The way she downplayed her own laugh. What she did not see, maybe could not see, was that people noticed her anyway. Not with pity. Not with surprise. Just noticed.

That was the part she never believed. Mama was the only one who thought she had disappeared.

What started with a wave and a few words turned into something else, slow but steady. They ran into each other at the grocery store, at the gas station, and once at the post office when the line stretched clear to the door.

Each time it was simple conversation. Weather. Neighbors. The Braves. The price of eggs. But there was an ease in it, a comfort that stretched beyond small talk. Soon it was not just chance meetings.

He would call to ask if she wanted to ride with him to the farmer's market, or if she felt like catching a movie at the discount theater. Sometimes they went out for coffee. Sometimes just for a walk. Always casual. Never labeled.

Mama would laugh and say, "We're just keeping each other company."

And he would nod, hands in his pockets, as if to agree. But their hands had a way of finding each other in the dark of a movie, or across the table when the conversation turned soft.

Not every time. Not enough to make it official. Just enough to remind them both of what closeness felt like.

They had both been married young. Both carried stories of spouses who walked away. His wife had fallen in love with someone else. Hers had fallen out of love with the life they built. They talked about it once or twice, not with bitterness, but with the quiet understanding of people who had lived through loss and learned not to let it define them.

And that was the thing about them. They could talk about anything. Politics. Faith. The way the neighborhood had changed since the nineties. Even the aches that came with age.

The one subject they danced around most was the one that pressed in every time their laughter died down and silence settled.

Once outside her front door, their faces drifted close, the distance narrowing until only a breath remained. She felt his hand brush hers, his eyes steady on her mouth.

Then she stepped back, laughing too quickly, saying something about the late hour. He smiled, not offended. Not disappointed. Just patient.

It happened again a week later in his car, music low on the radio. Her head tilted toward him without her permission, his hand brushing the back of hers on the console. Again, no kiss. Just a pause. A smile. A safe retreat.

They did not call it dating. They did not call it love. But they both knew they had stumbled into something they had not expected. A friendship that leaned dangerously close to more.

One Friday evening they went to the discount theater, the kind that smelled faintly of popcorn and carpet cleaner, where the tickets were ten dollars and the seats squeaked if you leaned too far back. It was not about the movie. Neither of them remembered the title afterward. It was about the space carved out between them in the dark.

Halfway through, his hand brushed hers on the armrest. Neither of them moved it. The screen flickered light across their faces, and she noticed every detail. The steady rise of his chest. The warmth from his shoulder. The faint scent of cologne mixed with detergent and fabric softener.

When the credits rolled and the lights came up, neither of them rushed to leave. They lingered in their seats while the crowd shuffled past. Then he turned toward her, slow and deliberate, and for a moment it felt like the room had gone quiet again.

She thought this was it. The moment she would let someone cross the line she had guarded since Daddy left.

But he smiled softly and leaned back.

"Good movie," he said.

She laughed too quickly and grabbed her purse.

"Forgettable," she said, cheeks burning all the way to the parking lot.

He walked her to her car, hands in his pockets, not pushing. Not rushing. When she slid into the driver's seat, he leaned down just enough to meet her eyes.

"Drive safe," he said.

No kiss. No confession. Just a pause that lingered even after she pulled away.

Later that night, she caught her reflection in the hallway mirror. For a long moment, she stared at her face beneath the wig, her hand lifting almost on its own toward the seam where it met her forehead.

She did not take it off. Not yet. But for the first time, she wondered what it would mean if she did.

The truth between them

The night after the movie, they sat on Mama's porch with two glasses of sweet tea sweating on the table between them. The air was heavy. Locusts droned. The kind of Georgia night that made conversation slow and easy.

She was telling a story about her grandbabies when his laugh cut short. He coughed once. Cleared his throat.

"You alright?" she asked.

"Yeah," he said. "Just tired."

But when his hand slipped setting the glass down, ice rattling louder than it should have, he did not laugh it off. He looked at her, something shifting behind his eyes. Pride giving way to truth.

"I haven't told many people yet," he said.
"A couple of months ago, the doctors found something. ALS. The rapid kind."

The words sat heavy between them.

"That's why I pulled back at the theater," he said quietly.
"I didn't want to start something I might not be able to finish."

She reached across the table and covered his hand.

"Then let me at least finish this part with you," she said.

He did not pull away.

Crown uncovered

Days later, she stood in the kitchen long after the house had gone quiet. Cap on the counter. Wig on its stand. Her crown bare in the dim light.

For years she had told herself loneliness was safer than disappointment. Now she asked a different question.

Am I willing to hurt again just to feel alive?

When the moment came, it was unplanned. No ceremony. No music. Just the truth.

She removed the wig and set it aside.

"This is me," she said.

He did not flinch.

"I like you like this," he said.

Finally

When he kissed her, it was not rushed. Not hungry. It was deliberate. A kiss that said I see you.

When they parted, he whispered, "Finally."

The Promised Land

The sky was sharp blue the morning they gathered at the cemetery. Mama stood close to the casket, her crown bare beneath the sun.

When silence opened a space, she stepped forward.

"I am bound for the promised land," she sang.

Her voice rose steady and clear, not in grief alone, but in gratitude.

Love, however brief, had been worth the road.

She pressed her palm to the casket once and stepped back.

Her crown gleamed in the light.

Chapter Six

Notches

The altar mark

"Are you really going up there?"

I said it in an exaggerated whisper, like I could make the moment smaller if I kept my voice small. We sat side by side on the hard, high-backed pew, our knees touching, our hands clasped so tight my fingers tingled.

She did not answer me with words. She answered with a look that said she did not have a choice.

We were the same age. Fifteen. Old enough to know what shame felt like, and young enough to believe it could kill you.

She was my best friend.

I loosened my grip and she leaned forward, stood up, and stepped past the two teenagers between us. The aisle felt like a long hallway with no doors. Her kitten heels clicked against the loose wooden boards, each step loud in the stillness. The only other sound was the steady whir of two overworked window units at the back of the building, struggling against a summer heat that refused to leave.

Tears fell before she reached the altar. Not dramatic tears, not pretty tears. The kind that come when the body gives up trying to hold itself together.

Then the pastor's voice cut through the room.

"Hurry up," he barked. "We know what you been up to. Ain't no need to be slow now. Come on."

Her steps quickened, not because she wanted to move faster, but because humiliation will make you obey. She reached the front and stood before the altar, thin and unsteady, like the air itself was too heavy for her chest.

Across from her stood the man everybody called "Pastor," the man folks said had a gift, the man whose voice could make the saints shout and the sinners tremble.

He leaned forward like he was examining something spoiled.

His reading glasses were scratched. His stare was not.

The sweat in his black suit had turned into a smell, sharp and sour, trapped in fabric that had seen too many Sundays and not enough dry cleaning. He moved closer, close enough that she could not look anywhere else without looking like she was running.

Then he raised his voice so the whole room could participate.

"First Corinthians six and eighteen," he declared. "It commands us to flee fornication."

He lifted a finger like he was pointing at a crime scene.

"For every sin that a man doeth is without the body," he shouted, "but he that committeth fornication sinneth against his own body."

He paused and scanned the crowd, collecting agreement like offerings.

"That ain't me talking," he said. "That's the Book."

A few amens floated back, thin and nervous.

He turned his head and snapped his fingers toward his assistant.

"Johnny, get me Hebrews six, verse six."

Johnny stood quickly, eager to please, Bible already open like a weapon in trained hands. His voice trembled as he read.

"If they shall fall away, to renew them again unto repentance, seeing they crucify to themselves the Son of God afresh, and put him to an open shame."

The pastor repeated the words slowly, savoring them.

"That ain't Bruh Johnny talking," he said. "That's still the Book. Open shame. That's what I heard him say."

Then he lifted his chin and aimed for the finishing blow.

"And the Apostle Paul wrote in Romans chapter fourteen, verse twelve. So then every one of us shall give an account of himself to God."

He struck the pulpit with the heel of his hand.

"Somebody in this church ought to say Amen!"

"Amen! Amen!"

The amens grew louder, like the room needed noise to hide what it was doing.

I sat frozen in the pew, my stomach tight, my throat hot. I was upset that my friend had been singled out, that the whole service had been built like a trap and she was the offering.

But even at fifteen, I knew something else.

They were misusing scripture.

I had read it. I knew what those verses meant. I knew what they did not mean. I knew what mercy sounded like, and this was not it.

Still, what I knew did not matter.

The pastor leaned closer until she flinched, then he spoke in a low command meant to sound like authority.

"Give an account of yourself."

Her voice shook as she confessed. She told the congregation she had sex for the first time with a boy two years older. She did not say it like a story. She said it like a sentence.

The baby growing inside her had made the secret public.

The boy was not there that night, even though his family came to church faithfully. Even though his mother shouted louder than most. Even though his father sat on the deacon's bench like righteousness had a reserved seat.

But none of that was mentioned.

Only her body. Only her shame.

"You need to apologize to the congregation," the pastor said, loud enough to make sure she understood who owned the moment. "For bringing shame upon this church."

She looked down, shoulders caving inward, and I watched her shrink right in front of everybody.

My own virginity sat on me like a badge I had not asked for. A label that felt safe and heavy at the same time.

And one question kept circling the corners of my mind, sharp as a hook.

Was it worth it?

Dreams interrupted

We had heard the sermons our whole lives.

Sex outside of marriage was preached like a ritual. Like a devil waited on the other side of the altar. Like one mistake could stain you so deeply the whole church would smell it.

And like every little girl, I carried my own small dream.

A rich, handsome husband. Two daughters. One son. A house with curtains I picked myself. A life that looked clean from the outside.

Then she got pregnant. Then she disappeared.

"Middle Tennessee," the women whispered, as if geography could wash shame away. In our church, that is how sin traveled. Quietly. Quickly. Out of sight.

As if removing the girl could redeem the room.

I finished high school without her. The halls felt longer. The lunch table felt quieter. I fed the emptiness with homework, equations, margin notes, anything that kept my mind from circling back to that pew where she used to sit.

My father called education "good seasoning," but not the meal.

A woman's work, in his mind, was marriage. Keeping a home. Having children. He admired nurses because they were useful and respected, but not too ambitious. Not too loud.

So when the scholarship came, I accepted it like it was mine.

Vanderbilt. Biology. Pre-nursing. I told myself it was my plan. Sometimes, I still wonder if it was his.

Abi

College opened like a door I had been pressing against for years.

The scholarship demanded everything. Long nights of study. Mornings packed with lectures. Weekends hunched over lab notes. There was no time for parties and I did not care. No alcohol. No cigarettes. No sex.

My virginity made me an outlier, but it also made me curious.

Attention came easily enough. My beauty was unpolished but obvious. My name stayed on the Dean's List. People noticed.

Still, I kept myself hidden behind books and excuses.

Until Abi. Abilio Alexandre. Afro-Brazilian. A tennis star with a 3.85 GPA and a smile that carried sunlight.

He taught my P.E. tennis class as a graduate assistant. I had no skill for the game. I stumbled onto the court and he laughed, not to embarrass me, but to make me breathe again.

He was patient. Kind. Brilliant.

In so many ways, we were opposites. He came from a Catholic family, but carried faith like a quiet rhythm. More spiritual than religious. He respected my beliefs even when he did not share them.

That respect disarmed me. And I fell harder than I meant to.

Like a teenager, his name began to live in the blank spaces between my notes. His voice echoed in my quiet hours. After years of sermons that made desire sound like a curse, he felt like grace.

The promise made

We never went all the way.

But our bodies learned each other in fragments. Kisses that lingered too long. Hands that hovered just shy of permission. Desire stopped being a stranger. It took shape. It took rhythm. It took weight.

And I carried that weight home after every night with him.

Nursing school gave me the language for anatomy, but it did not give me language for longing. I learned that alone, in the quiet of my room, with substitutes I kept carefully hidden away.

Each ritual left me wanting more than release.

I wanted connection. Flesh and soul together. Not shadowed by shame.

Abi never pressed me. His patience stayed steady, but I could feel the waiting in him. Like a bow pulled taut, ready to let loose. He did not need to say it. I saw it in his eyes when goodbyes stretched too long.

I wanted to give him what the church taught me to fear. Not out of pressure. Not out of rebellion. Out of choice. For once, I wanted to say yes for me. So I made a promise.

When the gowns were folded. When the tassels turned. When the applause faded and the diplomas found their frames. Graduation night would be the night I crossed that threshold.

The night that never came

June 13, 1992.

The date glowed in my mind like prophecy.

My graduation at ten. His at noon. Lunch with family at two-thirty. Dinner with friends at six. And at ten that night, the Hilton Garden Inn.

A room we had chosen. A promise waiting its hour.

I did not call him the night before. He was busy gathering relatives, and I wanted the moment untouched. Like opening a gift without shaking the box first.

I went to bed smiling at the ceiling, rehearsing every detail, already feeling his arms around me.

The morning was perfect, all cap and gown and applause like thunder, tassel turned and diploma in hand.

I changed quickly, heart racing, and crossed campus to watch his ceremony. I found an aisle seat with a perfect view of the stage.

Then the dean of religious studies stepped forward.

His voice carried the hush of something that did not belong in a celebration.

"Please join us in a moment of silence," he said softly, "as we honor and posthumously present a degree to one of today's graduates."

The word did not land right at first.

Posthumously.

It hung in the air, waiting for my mind to catch up.

When it did, the air left my body.

A single car crash.

A celebration gone wrong.

Abi was gone.

I stood up like I could outrun reality, but there was nowhere to go. My family did not know. His family did not know. We belonged to each other in secret.

So my grief had to stay that way too. Silent, invisible and unclaimed. The night we had planned for years vanished in one sentence. The room stayed empty. The promise never reached its hour.

Success and silence

I buried myself in books, classes and exams. Long nights under fluorescent lights, chasing grades the way other women chased rings. Graduate school came with certifications, then promotions.

Titles stacked on top of each other until my résumé looked full, almost overflowing.

But the title that mattered most never came.

Not wife.

Not fiancée.

Not even girlfriend.

Just one title clung to me through the years, louder than all the others.

Virgin.

My friends married, divorced, remarried. They cradled babies, wore rings, swapped stories of honeymoons and heartbreaks. I sent congratulatory cards. I sat through baby showers. I smiled at the right times and swallowed the sting.

I still believed scripture, but my understanding shifted. The old sermons no longer sounded absolute. I did not want sin. I did not want rebellion.

I wanted experience.

I wanted touch.

I wanted to stop living like my body was a courtroom and my desire was on trial.

I told myself I was holding out for the right one.

But the years turned that promise into a burden.

I had success.

I had respect.

But when the lights dimmed and the room grew quiet, silence always had the last word.

Reclaiming a first

By forty-five, I had waited long enough.

Patience had turned into a prison. Standards had turned into chains.

I did not want forever anymore.

I wanted a first.

There were men. Plenty of them. Willing and eager. But I did not want chance. I wanted choice.

So I built the moment myself.

Online profiles became a catalogue of possibilities. I scrolled past faces the way I once flipped through scriptures, learning an unfamiliar language.

DDF.

NSA.

ONS.

SWT.

FWB.

LTR.

Friends with benefits I understood. The rest I learned like clues, piecing together a gospel I had never been taught. Abbreviations that read like coded prayers, each promising something or warning me away.

I filtered carefully.

Not forever.

Not love.

Just safe.

A few short messages became layered conversations. Careful at first, then bolder. Then came photos. Then video calls.

He was handsome. Seven years younger. French Haitian. Confident in a way that felt practiced. He carried himself like the world had been saying yes to him for a long time.

He even bragged, casually, about being uncircumcised, like it was proof of something rare.

"Good hygiene," he said, almost arrogantly. "Never any complaints."

I smiled at the screen, not out of giddiness, but like someone reclaiming what had been denied.

It was not innocence I wanted back.

Not even hope.

It was control.

So we booked a room at the Hilton Garden Inn and Suites.

The same chain I once imagined for Abi.

This time, the date was mine to choose.

The night was mine to claim.

The crosswalk

I took the day off and prepared as if it were my wedding.

Hair styled.

Nails done.

An outfit chosen to feel less like armor and more like an invitation.

At forty-five, I was finally stepping into a chapter I had written for myself.

I parked across the street from the Hilton Garden Inn, a silly frugal reflex from a woman who could certainly afford better. My overnight bag swung at my side as I stepped onto the sidewalk, my smile blooming with the thought of finally saying goodbye to that old title.

Virgin.

Just one crosswalk away.

The city pulsed around me. Horns blared. Bass thumped from a passing car. Footsteps pressed in every direction.

But I barely heard it.

In my head, I was rehearsing how to greet him.

Warm.

Confident.

Maybe even sexy.

I stepped forward and my foot sank.

My heel caught in a broken metal grate at the edge of the street. One second I was floating. The next I was kneeling, twisted, tugging to free myself without tearing the dress I had chosen so carefully.

The moment stretched.

Tires screeched.

Brakes screamed.

A woman shouted something sharp and urgent, but the words blurred under the roar of panic.

I looked up.

Headlights.

Chrome.

A grille like a wall.

The blunt face of a church bus bearing down.

The irony almost made me laugh.

Of course it would be a church bus.

My body froze, but my mind kept running through everything. Childhood sermons. Promises delayed. Years of saying not tonight. Years of waiting for a moment like this.

One step forward.

One step back.

The headlights swallowed everything.

Then nothing.

Chapter Seven

Minority Interest

Behind the closed bedroom door, the only light came from the blue digits on the clock, 5:29 a.m. The smell of fresh coffee and the soft shuffle of feet in the other room pulled me from sleep. Six months into my vegetarian lifestyle, the rich aroma of coffee was one of the last remaining comforts that reminded me of a real country breakfast.

Still curled in the fetal position, I tried to straighten myself and wondered if I was dreaming. From the other room, a voice sang along with Stevie Wonder's "That Girl" playing softly on the radio. It sounded familiar, but different.

As my senses returned, I remembered. Baby Boy was home for spring break from his first year at SUNY Brockport. I was still a little tipsy, with only scattered memories from the night before, but I vaguely recalled seeing him. Wondering why he had chosen the living room couch instead of his bedroom, I remembered smiling when I saw him curled up, completely cocooned in my old comforter. It reminded me of when he was a little boy.

He had not forgotten that his mommy had sworn off eating anything with a face. His new way of nourishing himself had turned him vegan long before I could follow. I had not made it there yet. So he must have figured coffee would be the perfect morning surprise, especially after the month I had endured. Between treatment, fatigue, and the strange new sensitivity to smells, he probably thought it might lift my spirits. I had little appetite, but I accepted what he made with gratitude.

I was excited to see him and quietly flattered that he had arranged his own ride from the airport. Always thoughtful. That was one of the few lessons he never needed to be taught.

He had not traveled alone either. In recent video chats, he introduced me to a new friend. Some kid who looked like Adam Levine, someone he clearly adored.

I did not fully understand the nature of their bond, but he was fond of him. Given Baby Boy's deep appreciation for his own culture, I was a little surprised. Still, I had always trusted his judgment in choosing friends.

Sitting up slowly, yawning and stretching, listening to the steady rhythm of my breathing, I thought I was past this stage. This heaviness. I reached under my nylon head wrap to scratch a sudden itch and murmured to myself, "This is a great day. Every day is a great day. Get up. Let's make it a great day."

Instead of a smooth scalp, my fingers met the cross stitched fibers of my lace front wig, the one I never slept in. The mattress felt wrong too, firmer than mine. The blanket clinging to me was unfamiliar. Not a comforter. Something rougher and heavier.

I had made it through six cycles of treatment, but I was still a long way from feeling like myself. Each day brought some new ache, some unfamiliar shift in my body. Today did not match any of my yesterdays.

As I shifted upright, I realized I was wrapped in an unfamiliar covering. The dim lighting could explain some of it, but not the scent. That I knew immediately.

CoCo perfume lingered the way it always did, long after it touched skin or fabric. One of my favorites back when I used to sneak samples from the cosmetics counter at work. But the CoCo was different this morning because it was not alone.

Beneath it was something else. Something distinctly masculine.

The treatments had sharpened my senses, especially my sense of smell. I only worked four days a month now, but I could still out sniff anyone on the floor. I had once been the best fragrance matchmaker in the city.

That was when I recognized it. Versace Dreamer.

Baby Boy had hypersensitive skin. He was a naturalist to his core. Caribbean locs crowned his head and a coarse beard softened his youthful face. He never sprayed anything chemically manufactured on his skin.

I did not understand it, but my body did.

I lowered the covering and my breathing shallowed. Sixteen days out from cycle six, even the soft brush of fabric against my chest made me wince. My nipples had been tender for months, but this was different. This was a quiet, sharp ache.

Bare breasts. Where was my nightshirt?

I had practically lived in it for six months. It had grown so worn that on his last visit Baby Boy laughed and said, "This started out as a cotton tee, but now it's basically lingerie."

I wore it the night the sisters gathered and prayed over me, speaking affirmations into my body. That shirt was my security blanket. I never went to bed without it.

I sat there, dizzy, disoriented, head pounding. Maybe I had gotten up too fast.

"Lie back, close your eyes and start again." I told myself.

There was no job waiting for me today. Just over two weeks had passed since my final round of treatment for chronic lymphocytic leukemia. If anyone had earned a pause, it was me.

Still in disbelief, I turned onto my side. A dull ache pulsed low in my body, different from the treatment pain. I drew my knees up and it sharpened. It did not fade. It spread.

By then Stevie had faded out, replaced by Kool and the Gang's "Too Hot." I hummed along and reached for the lamp.

Extending my arm sent a sharper jolt through me. When the light came on, clarity did not follow.

What I had mistaken for a comforter was a double sized beach towel. I was lying on another one too. A matching set. Then I noticed shadows moving beneath the door and heard voices.

Two of them.

One was Baby Boy. The other belonged to his friend.

If this disease did one thing well, it forced intimacy with your body. But this soreness felt older than illness. Like echoes from somewhere I had not visited in a long time.

Maybe it was age. Maybe it was memory. Maybe it was nothing.

But I felt clammy. Moist in a way that unsettled me.

I slipped the wig off and wrapped the towel around myself. Walking to the door was harder than I expected. A throbbing ache traced a private internal path upward.

Thankfully, I already had a late morning appointment with my oncologist. I would mention it then.

"Hey, Baby Boy. Welcome home, sweet man."

"Asubuhi njema, mpenzi wangu."

"I'm just going to assume that means good morning."

"You're right. Swahili."

As we separated from the hug, he studied me.

"You okay, Queen?"

"I'm good," I said too quickly.

He held my gaze a second longer than usual.

The circumstances that first brought me to my oncologist had been the worst of my life. Chronic lymphocytic leukemia had rearranged everything. But over the months, he had become one of the steadier presences in it. Direct. Calm. Never theatrical. Never evasive. I trusted him.

That morning, the waiting room felt colder than usual. Or maybe I did.

The appointment began the way they always did. Vitals. Weight. Routine questions about fatigue, appetite, nausea. He listened. He nodded. He documented.

Then he mentioned that a fellow would join us.

She entered quietly. Young, composed, observant in a way that felt more analytical than warm. When she began the exam, something shifted. Her touch was not rushed. It was precise. Intentional. She asked me to describe the pelvic pain again. Location. Duration. Intensity.

I answered.

She examined me longer than I expected.

The room grew quieter.

My oncologist eventually stepped out to review labs. The fellow remained. Her expression had changed. Not alarmed. Not panicked. Focused.

Hours later, she returned alone.

That was when I knew something had tilted.

"Are you sexually active?" she asked carefully.

I shook my head.

"In the last twenty four hours? Any intercourse? Any sleep aids?"

"No."

She drew a careful breath.

"Your exam showed trauma consistent with forceful penetration. Vaginal and anal."

She paused.

"Your bloodwork came back positive for Rohypnol."

The word settled slowly.

"This points to drug facilitated sexual assault."

The room felt smaller.

Detectives from the Special Victims Unit arrived quietly and methodically. Each question pressed against skin. What I had eaten. Who I had seen. What I remembered. What I did not.

Later, I texted the safest thing I could.

The appointment did not go as planned. I'm okay. Just not up for company.

His response came instantly.

No worries, Queen. Soul Vegetarian is already ordered.

When I got home, lavender candles glowed warm and thoughtful.

Then the doorbell rang.

Baby Boy opened it and in walked a tall, lean Italian carrying food like he belonged there.

Versace Dreamer cut through the room.

"Queen, this is my friend," Baby Boy said. "The one from FaceTime."

The hug lasted a bit too long.

"Nice to meet you," he said gently.

"For the second time."

My smile stayed in place, but something inside me stalled.

"For the second time?"

He tilted his head, almost playful. "You don't remember?"

The room felt warmer. Or maybe that was me.

"I was awake last night," he continued casually. "You came out to the kitchen. Grabbed a drink from the fridge. We talked for a minute."

Talked.

My stomach tightened.

"You took a shower after that," he added. "A long one."

Baby Boy shifted in his seat, laughing lightly. "Man, she does love her showers."

I searched my memory. Restaurant. Wine. Laughter. A ride home. Then nothing. Just blank space where hours should have been.

"I must've been more tired than I thought," I said carefully.

He smiled again, calm and assured.

"It happens."

Versace Dreamer wrapped around me again. Thick and familiar.

Too familiar.

I glanced at Baby Boy. He avoided my eyes.

The candles flickered.

Something in the room felt rehearsed.

And then Baby Boy stood.

"Okay," he said, clapping his hands once like he needed courage.

"I didn't bring him here just to surprise you."

Baby Boy crossed the small space between us and took my hand. His grip was steady, but there was something in it I could not quite name. Resolve. Or fear.

"Queen," he began softly, "I love you. You've always told me to live in truth. To stop hiding who I am."

He reached for the Italian's hand.

Their fingers fit together easily. Naturally.

"I wanted you to meet him properly," he continued. "Not just through FaceTime. Not just in passing."

My chest tightened, but I nodded.

"This is not just my friend," he said.

He looked at him, then back at me.

"We're engaged."

Silence filled the room in a way that felt heavier than the lavender and the spices.

I swallowed.

Engaged.

I had prepared myself for this possibility for years. For this truth. For this declaration. I had told myself I would respond with grace when the day came.

So I smiled.

I stood and pulled them both into an embrace that lasted long enough to convince everyone in the room, including myself.

"I'm happy for you," I said. And I meant it. I did.

We sat back down. Containers opened. Steam rose. Conversation attempted normalcy.

The fiancé leaned back in his chair, relaxed, almost amused.

"And if you ever need help sleeping," he said casually, "I've got benzols. They'll knock you out cold."

Help sleeping.

My pulse thudded in my ears.

"In the last twenty four hours? Any sleep aids?"

The fellow's voice replayed in my head with clinical calm.

Any sleep aids?

I felt the fork grow heavy in my hand.

Rohypnol.

Knock you out cold?

The room tilted almost just enough to unsettle me.

He was still smiling.

Still calm.

Still wearing Versace Dreamer.

The word landed strangely.

Benzols.

My fork paused midair.

I looked at him.

He held my gaze just a fraction too long.

Versace Dreamer lingered between us.

The same scent.

The same weight.

I chewed slowly.

I smiled again.

Because survival is not always loud.

Sometimes it is quiet.

Sometimes it is simply staying seated at the table.

Chapter Eight

Iambic Pentameter

- The Invitation
- Off Meter
- Called to Account

The Invitation

"Man, they ought to call this March Sadness. My bracket ain't even close, Bruh!"

I smiled as Lester held the door open, as always. On the way in, and again on the way out, palm outstretched, hoping for change. I'd lift my mail as proof I wasn't carrying cash. Still, he tried. Our Monday, Wednesday, and Friday ritual.

I nodded and pulled away from the Piedmont Avenue Post Office, coasting through stop signs and taking two quick lefts toward Ansley. The glove compartment buzzed. My phone was locked away for peace of mind, difficult to reach while driving, and of course I caught every green light until the Ansley Shopping Center.

Trying to knock out a few errands, I parked outside Ansley Wine Merchants to grab a bottle of red to go with the steaks I planned to grill later. I unlocked the glove box and pulled out my phone. There was no surprise waiting for me. Her text sat at the top of the screen, followed by a ping on Messenger and then another on Instagram. I sighed, slipped the phone into my pocket, and stepped inside.

The associates knew me. So did much of Midtown. I lived out in DeKalb, but I kept work and life in separate lanes. That's why I bought a house near I-285 and Memorial Drive. Easy to slip in and out of the city when I needed to.

I walked the aisles, scanning bottles. My jacket buzzed again, her name lit the screen. I smashed the side button like killing the alert might erase her from my life. Then I spotted a Château Montelena. Thirty bucks more than planned, but worth it.

At the counter, cardholder in hand, I froze. Her voice—clear and unmistakable—cut through the room.

"You want me to get that for you?"

My chest dropped. She stepped around, hips brushing mine, sharp and deliberate, like punctuation. Then she leaned in, slid her Centurion card across the counter. The cashier swiped without hesitation. Her smile carried the weight of a secret. Her tone was low.

"Honey, would you gift that bottle for me?" she asked, nodding toward me with a glance that sealed it.

"I want to keep his hands free so he can return my texts." The cashier smirked, slid the bottle into a silver gift bag, and tied it with a triple ribbon. A wink her way, a handoff my way. I forced a thank-you.

We left arm in arm. In the lot, my eyes kept scanning shadows.

"Why so paranoid?" she whispered. "This isn't our first trip to the land of steal-away ecstasy."

Always lyrics, never silence. She wasn't wrong, we'd been here too many times. She was fire and temptation, but I met her heat with dread. I hated her framing of our quick encounters, like souvenirs from a cheap vacation.

To the world, she was a powerhouse. Three booming nightspots and a confidence that filled every room. To me, she was predictable, commanding, and inescapable. I admired it even as I loathed it. She didn't lure me with sweetness. It was sheer force.

I wish I could say I fought it, but I didn't. I followed her into the backseat with my pants already around my ankles. This time was no different. Reclined in the back of her Lexus, she pulled me in like a magnet. Her moans filled the air as we moved through the same choreography, familiar, mechanical, and empty.

Minutes later, clothes straightened and goodbye sealed with a limp handshake, I stepped out. Her SUV was tucked behind the Kroger-Publix loading docks, our usual stage. I walked back to my car numb, carrying nothing but the echo of what had just happened.

She was beautiful, forty-three going on twenty-eight, her ginger locs swinging with the kind of confidence that turned heads and kept them there. To everyone else, she was a show. To me, just another round. My second encounter that day. The first hadn't even looked at me. At least this one had a name. I sat there, wondering when names had stopped meaning something.

Sex wasn't a desire anymore. No closeness or craving, just routine. Like brushing my teeth or checking the locks at night. A function that left me colder each time.

At the front of the shopping center, I reached my car and realized I'd left the wine in her back seat. Another thing I'd managed to forget, like peace, purpose, and prayer. My life used to move in rhythm, steady as a choir that knew the song by heart. Now it was noise, off-key and off-balance.

Tonight, I would need help to make it through. Spirits became liquid peace for a soul running on empty, a poor stand-in for the faith I once believed in.

Reentering the wine shop, the cashier greeted me with a smile and a snide question.

"Back already?"

I chuckled, trying to sound casual.

"The menu's changed. Now I need some cognac. Hennessy Black. No gift wrap this time."

She ducked below the counter, the rustle of brown bags filling the pause. My eyes drifted to a fishbowl by the register, stuffed with business cards like confessions tossed into a wishing well.

The fishbowl was full of forgettable white and black cards, the kind you'd never notice twice. But one, boldly inked on thick stock, seemed to glow under the halogen light. I slipped it out quickly and quietly before she popped back up with the bag.

Back at the car, I tossed the Hennessy onto the passenger seat and joined the crawl of traffic pushing east. The stop-and-go rhythm was maddening, the kind that makes drivers talk to themselves, hum old soul songs, or scroll their lives away at red lights.

I tapped the wheel, restless, until my hand brushed the edge of the card. I pulled it out. The handwriting was bold, looping, almost theatrical. Like it wanted to be read aloud.

It listed an address I recognized. The Prado, a historic strip near where I'd just been. Below the address, a time, 9:50 p.m. and one phrase. ***Iambic Pentameter.***

I wasn't sure what *Iambic Pentameter* meant in this context, but I had a guess. On the way, I ducked into a CVS for a fresh pack of latex. Old habits die hard, preacher's kid or not.

I kept a garment bag in the trunk. A clean shirt, pressed slacks, toiletries. A relic of discipline I could never quite shake. My lifetime LA Fitness pass gave me a place to rinse off the afternoon sins and re-emerge polished.

The anticipation stretched every minute. By 9:45, I pulled up in front of the address on the card. Lawn lights glowed against the mailbox. Make no mistake, I was in the right place.

I filled my jacket pockets like a soldier stocking his gear. The contents of the CVS bag, my phone, Biotene, five crisp hundred-dollar bills, my ID, and the card.

Just as I raised my hand to press the bell, the door swung open. A well-dressed couple stood there, composed, stylish, self-assured. From their accents and appearance, I guessed Puerto Rican, maybe mid-forties.

The man spoke first, his voice steady and precise.

"What is your favorite poetic rhythm?"

"Iambic Pentameter," I answered without hesitation.

They asked for my membership card. I handed over the one I'd taken. The woman accepted it with a knowing nod and motioned me inside. He stayed at the door as she led me forward.

The modest home gave way to a staircase I hadn't expected. At the bottom, the space opened wide and felt cavernous, humming with heat. Hardwood floors stretched out beneath Indonesian batik art draped across the walls. Candles flickered like fireflies in every corner.

Sculptures stood like sentinels. Clear glass containers held a top-shelf assortment of latex, not the cheap kind you find at a gas station. This selection was intentional and indulgent.

Maybe twenty people filled the room. They sprawled across rugs, mattresses, and lounges. Some were clothed, most were not. The air throbbed with lavender, jasmine, and something feral, musk and sweat laced with memory. In a side room, an open shower glistened under soft light, with robes and towels neatly hung and waiting.

A moan rose above the murmurs. I knew that sound. Her. Again.

She saw me and didn't stop. Two muscular men flanked her. Her body arched between them. If anything, she leaned into it more.

Before I could think my way out, my clothes were gone and I was in it, surrounded by sweat, motion, and bodies I didn't recognize. Just strangers. No names. No words. Only heat, skin, and the hollow promise of whatever it was I kept chasing.

I didn't stop or care. I just let it happen. It wasn't new. It wasn't anything at all. Later, still hollow, I left.

Off Meter

The steaks had long been forgotten, but hunger lingered. The Ansley Shopping Center came to the rescue again, Kroger this time.

A bag of Wavy Lays and a bottle of green tea. Just enough to quiet the emptiness for a few minutes. As I pushed through the automatic doors, I caught sight of a shadow leaning against my car. The face was hidden in the low light, but something about the posture pulled at me. Familiar and unmistakable.

The closer I walked, the more the outline sharpened into someone I knew.

"Lester!" I called out.

He straightened and smiled wide.

"What are you doing on this stretch of Piedmont?"

"Man, I work the street," he said.

"Saw your car. Thought I'd help you out."

I laughed.

"Help me with the note? I don't need help with the door."

We both chuckled, the kind of shared laugh that comes from routine and recognition.

"Well, a man like you, keeping the hours you do, don't need to be out here without help," he said. "I got you covered."

He tugged gently on the locked handle, testing it like he meant it.

Another post-orgasmic low settled over me. Lester, like my red-haired companion earlier, had a way of appearing when I needed someone to talk to, even when I did not know I needed it. I hit the unlock button and motioned for him to climb in.

"Where to, my friend?" I asked.

"Home, James!" he replied in a gruff voice, then laughed again and clapped his hands together.

I smiled, but something in the way he said it stayed with me. As if, just for a moment, he was letting himself imagine that someone was taking him somewhere he actually belonged.

By home, he meant the Pine Street homeless shelter.

The mile and a half felt longer than usual. We talked, real talking. I had never heard more than a handful of words from him before, but tonight he had a vocabulary I did not expect. He spoke in full thoughts. Stories. Half-formed reflections that sounded like they had been waiting for an audience.

When I mentioned it, he slipped back into his old banter and mumbled something about being bipolar. He said it kept him from ever landing anywhere steady, from holding on to anything too long.

We pulled up to the curb. I leaned over to open the door, but he paused. He reached into his jacket and pulled something out.

A Ruger SR22.

I jumped.

"Don't worry," he said quickly. "It ain't loaded. I can't afford no bullets."

My chest tightened anyway.

"Found it in the dumpster behind the store," he added, like he was talking about a pair of shoes. "With everyone at the shelter as crazy as me, I figured I better make sure nobody else get their hands on it."

He smiled, half joking, and for a moment the joke landed like a prayer.

"See you around," he said, setting the pistol carefully on the seat before closing the door.

I picked it up, confirmed it was empty.

Lester handing me a gun without asking for money felt like something I did not yet know how to read. I slid it under the passenger seat and told myself *I'd take it to the buyback next week.*

Called To Account

The thought did not linger. I pulled onto Courtland, swung left onto Ralph McGill, and waited at the light at Piedmont. That was when a figure stepped out of the dark and came toward my car.

She was curvy, with a blonde wig tilted just enough to suggest a long day. Yoga pants clung like a second skin, and a Raiders jacket hung short on her frame. Still, something about her held me there.

Maybe it was the sway in her step. Maybe it was the way she looked straight at me, as if she already knew I would say yes. And I would have. Emptiness has a way of disguising itself as connection.

We locked eyes without blinking. Then came her voice, thick with a Gullah cadence, low and practiced, carrying both story and warning. She leaned in just close enough to be heard.

"My car's at the BP on Piedmont and Ponce. I ran out of gas. I just need a couple of dollars to get back to the east side."

She looked different from the usual faces out here. Maybe too different. But I did not question it. Not then. We both knew what the exchange meant.

The door handle clicked before I could stop myself. She slipped into the passenger seat like she had done it a hundred times before, like she knew I would not stop her even if I wanted to. She gave directions easily, confidently, guiding us toward the far edge of the Highland Apartments parking lot where the lights thinned and shadows gathered.

I had been here before. I knew the steps, the script, the geography.

She watched every movement I made. When I reached inside my jacket pocket, she stiffened.

"Just the cover and the cabbage, dear. I won't hurt you, I promise," I said, trying to sound calm, trying to sound like I belonged in that moment more than I did.

I pulled out a condom pack and a crisp bill.

She smirked.

"Oh, a C note. Big spender. What you expecting?"

"It's Saturday night," I said, forcing a smile. "I'll take the special."

She laughed, low and knowing, then softly sang the first bars of *Another Saturday Night*.

I felt myself relax. I fumbled with my belt.

Then the singing stopped.

I looked up.

She was holding a gun. Bigger than Lester's. In her other hand was a badge.

One second she had been speaking with that slow Gullah cadence. The next it was gone, clean and sudden, and her voice snapped into command.

"Keep your hands where I can see them. You move, you bleed."

Her teeth clenched, and the warning carried like a siren.

"Do not make me shoot you."

Blue lights flooded the lot. Doors flew open. Hands yanked me out of the car, while cuffs were biting into my wrists. The words came next, the familiar script about rights and silence, but it sounded less like law and more like a funeral being read aloud.

"Do you have any drugs or weapons on you or in the vehicle? Is there anything that can hurt me?"

"No sir," I said. "I was just giving the lady a ride."

"Sure you were," one of them muttered, flipping through my wallet.

I sat in the back of the cruiser for what felt like forever. Then he came back, holding the Ruger.

Lester's gun.

I had forgotten all about it.

"We'll be adding a weapons charge to the solicitation," he said.

Then came the line that gutted me.

"Well, Pastor," he sneered, "I guess you'll need someone else to deliver your sermon later this morning. I saw your wife's ordination last week. Good thing you promoted her to co-pastor. Maybe she's available."

Chapter Nine

Sarcophagus

Blythe offered a small smile and a giggle that almost sounded sincere.

"Carwyn, I meant nothing by it. It was just a question. I hope you're not offended."

I could not bring myself to look at her. No one had ever mistaken me for athletic.

Still, I was a boy, no matter how often my body tried to argue otherwise.

My voice barely rose above a whisper.

"Please call me Wyn. Only my mother called me Carwyn, and she died five years ago."

I said it the way people recite facts for a school project. Quick. Clean. Practiced.

What I did not say was that her absence still lived in that house. It sat in corners. It lingered in doorways. It moved through rooms like a draft that never left.

"They declared her legally dead right after we moved into her dream home."

I traced a square in the air, illustrating the size of the house we had just moved into when they made it official. It always struck me as strange. Moving into the place she wanted most, only for her to vanish inside it. As if the walls had claimed her.

My voice came out sharper than I intended.

"I was twelve. And somehow, in those short years, I had already filed her away. Not my present. Not my future. Just history. So please do not remind me of her. Thank you."

Some things hurt less when you keep them buried. But secrets do not stay quiet. They rattle when someone speaks the wrong name out loud.

I paused, then added with more force than I meant to show.

"And by the way, the answer to both of your questions is no. No, I'm not offended. And no, I'm not gay."

Blythe blinked, then softened her mouth into something like understanding. Or maybe she was only pretending. With Blythe it was hard to tell.

I knew why people made assumptions about me. My quiet nature. My standoffish distance. The softness I could not scrub out of my mannerisms.

I was not overweight. Not even chubby. But I had no real muscle either.

What I did have was my mother's pale Irish skin, a crown of bright red hair, and hips that sat too wide on my frame. Wide enough to make jeans fit wrong. Wide enough to make people look twice.

To make matters worse, my chest had started to bud, just enough to resemble a girl on the edge of puberty. I felt like a specimen behind glass. Somewhere between their stares and their whispers, my body stopped belonging to me. It became something other people named, other people explained, other people laughed about.

Blythe was the only person I considered a friend. At least she had the decency to ask me directly instead of whispering behind my back like everyone else.

She clicked her tongue, winked, and tugged my cheek in the way she always did, as if my face were a little brother's face and not a classmate's.

"Okay then, Wyn," she said, light as air. "Thanks for the interview."

Her iPad slipped into its case with a soft snap.

I smiled because it was expected, and lifted my hand in a small wave as she walked off to rejoin her friends. It was the closest thing I had to friendship. A smile, a wink, and a tug at the cheek. A reminder that some people chose curiosity over cruelty. At least for now.

Neither Blythe nor I attended a traditional school. We were part of a homeschool co-op that filled our calendars with evening and weekend activities, all designed to keep us properly socialized.

For most of the others, it worked. They collected friends like arcade tickets.

I collected stares.

Tonight's activity was cosmic bowling, one of those group outings meant to convince our parents we were normal teenagers with normal lives. Neon lanes. Loud laughter. Teenagers throwing gutter balls and pretending they were not watching each other.

I usually had to be dragged into going. Crowds made me nervous. Not because of the noise, but because the more eyes there were, the more likely someone would notice what I tried hardest to hide.

Still, I survived another night. One ill-timed, unwelcome peer interview included.

Relief washed over me when the scoring marquee confirmed our three-lane rental had hit its time limit. We all bagged or re-racked our balls and drifted toward the food center for shakes and appetizers.

As the group of eleven homeschoolers claimed a table, I slipped away toward the exit.

Blythe caught up with me near the doors and extended an invitation. She said it lightly, like she did not care either way, but

I saw a flicker of something behind her eyes. Maybe pity. Maybe loyalty. With Blythe, it was always hard to name.

"They don't like me," I mumbled, still walking.

"And they don't want me around."

She started to say something, then stopped herself. She did not chase me beyond the threshold.

I kept moving toward the parking lot, assuming my father was already waiting, even though he had not responded to my text. Since my mother's disappearance, and the eventual legal declaration of her death, it had been just the two of us.

To those who knew us well, her disappearance was devastating. Most described it as mind-boggling, given how few details ever surfaced. The police asked questions, but their visits stopped abruptly.

Father said it was because there were no leads. I believed him, but sometimes I wondered if they had found an answer and decided not to share it with me.

Father did his best to create normalcy. He hired an Irish au pair named Alannah. She was young, well-educated, and entirely focused on my care and academic instruction. Tall and pale, with inky black hair, she reminded me of Miss Landers from the black-and-white reruns of Leave It to Beaver.

Alannah carried herself with a discipline that made even silence feel like instruction. She spoke carefully, but kindly, as if every sentence had already been proofread in her head.

Father believed that hiring Alannah as my hands-on teacher might help balance out my teenage awkwardness. To me, it felt less like he was balancing me and more like he was building a team to manage me, as if I were a problem to solve rather than a son to raise.

My awkwardness, especially around women, ran deep, likely a residual effect of my Klinefelter's Syndrome diagnosis.

As a baby, I did not sit up unassisted until I was over a year old, and I did not walk until I was two. Father chalked it up to my being a late bloomer. But my mother was more concerned. Against his wishes, she took me to a pediatric diagnostician.

I still remember her face that day. Eyes set. Jaw clenched. As if she already knew what the tests would say. Father called it an overreaction. She called it love. That was when they confirmed the double-X chromosome abnormality.

Because Klinefelter's often came with psychological complications, a family friend who was also a psychologist encouraged my mother to learn everything she could about the syndrome. Now fully informed, she became determined to make me as independent as possible.

Father took the opposite approach. He became overprotective, hovering, smothering.

Like tonight, showing up at the game center without texting me first.

He hovered the way some people stand too close to a painting, so near you cannot see the art anymore, only the cracks in the canvas.

He was nothing like me. Handsome and chiseled, with a stubbly beard and a commanding presence, Father was a forty-three-year-old Welshman who had once made a name for himself as an international rugby star. His career ended early, derailed not by injury but by whispers. The investigation into my mother's disappearance followed him everywhere, like a referee no one could shake off the field.

I loved him, truly. But I always dreaded our so-called quality time. It was never just dinner or a movie. It was a sermon, a life lesson, a forced closeness that felt more like performance than connection. Sometimes when he preached about strength or resilience, I wondered if he was reminding me or convincing himself.

Tonight's ride home lecture was the usual mix of outdated advice and disconnected optimism. A well-meaning monologue about loving myself for who I am. It sounded noble enough, but coming from him it felt less like advice and more like an order.

He urged me not to seek acceptance from others, and then, without irony, singled out my homeschool co-op friends as people I should not try to impress.

A devout atheist, Father had a habit of using oddly spiritual language, as if trying to comfort me with a faith he refused to claim.

"You should stand out from others," he said. "That's the reason for your creation, and also the reason you're purposely different."

His words never matched his beliefs. He used the language of faith like a man wearing clothes that did not fit, familiar in outline, uncomfortable in practice. The seams always showed.

To say I was created implied the existence of a creator, and I knew he did not believe in one. But Father meant well.

So, as always, I listened. Then I offered polite responses to make sure he felt heard.

As we pulled into the driveway, I hesitated before opening the van door. This was usually the part in our talks when he would take a deep breath, sigh, rest his hand on my shoulder or knee, give it a small shake, and say something like this.

"You mean more to me than anyone or anything on earth. And there's nothing you can't talk to me about. Nothing."

I could repeat it word for word. He said it so often it felt memorized. Sometimes I wondered if he practiced it in the mirror before delivering it to me, just to make sure it landed right.

And the truth was, I believed him. He had always been present. Active. Protective.

When I stepped through the back door and into the kitchen, I was surprised to see Alannah at the counter, busily chopping mint leaves for one of her signature Mediterranean salads.

Equally surprised, she greeted me with a high-pitched, "Well hello there. I didn't expect to see you tonight. It's Friday. I thought it was cosmic bowling night."

"It is," I replied. "And it was. I called it a night after ten frames and skipped the after-party."

As I rounded the corner toward the utility room to put away my bowling bag, something caught my eye.

Two wine glasses sat on the counter. Beads of condensation ran down their sides, as if they had only just been poured.

For a moment, I wondered if she had company, if Father had already been home. The thought passed quickly, but not before it left a mark.

"Expecting company?" I asked casually.

She did not answer right away.

I asked again, more pointed. "New boyfriend?"

That got her attention. She smirked but did not look up. She just kept chopping.

"Not that it's any of your business," she said, not bothering to hide the edge in her voice, "but your father asked me to make dinner tonight. Somewhere along his travels, he's developed a taste for Middle Eastern food."

"My assignments as an au pair have exposed me to international cuisine on par with an executive chef, thank you very much. Now, is that enough information for you?"

Her knife struck the cutting board harder than before. Each chop sounded sharper than the last.

I returned the smirk and headed upstairs.

My room was my personal paradise. Spacious enough to include a lounge area with a large-screen TV, it offered the escape I needed after nights like this.

It was not just a room. It was the only place where my body did not feel like a costume someone forced me to wear. In here, I could decide who I was, even if it lasted only until I stepped outside again.

My workstation housed a computer table with dual 27-inch monitors, visually divided by a beautifully hand-thrown ceramic vase. A queen-size bed anchored the space, guarded by a generously sized walk-in closet with custom shoe racks and plenty of room to disappear for a while.

My favorite room in the house, my castle, was the bathroom.

It connected my bedroom to the guest room where Alannah slept, but I always considered it mine. I spent far more time there than she ever did.

The shared space featured a full-sized, stand-alone shower with dual heads, an antique clawfoot tub, and two luxury bidet toilets with elongated seats.

But my favorite feature, the crown jewel afforded by my father's success, was the walled spherical mirror.

Mounted in a recessed arch, the concave glass gave off a reflection that felt larger than life. Perfectly contoured. Almost imagined. Sometimes when I leaned close, the glass curved my reflection into something unfamiliar, my cheekbones sharper, my eyes older, a face I swore was not mine.

Once or twice, I thought I saw another figure beside me, gone as quickly as it appeared. I never knew if it was memory, imagination, or something the mirror wanted me to believe.

Every day, before and after showering, I stood before that mirror as if it were a judge. Posing and adjusting. Waiting for a verdict only I could hear.

It was the one space I credited my mother for. She left behind only one thing I could truly call mine. Sometimes I wondered if she chose it for me on purpose, as if she knew the reflection would matter more to me than anything she could have left in a will.

Thinking of her sent me spiraling into a familiar daydream.

Even though an entire team of physicians had assured my family that Klinefelter's was not hereditary, I had always believed otherwise. I blamed her. She spent so much time trying to make me functional and independent, disguising it as love, when it often felt like guilt.

Her hands had always been gentle, but behind every touch I imagined an apology she never spoke aloud.

I hated my hair. My pale skin. My curvaceous hips. The way my body blurred lines I never asked to blur. I hated what it meant, what it suggested, what it threatened to confirm before I ever had a chance to decide.

The mirror told me things I already knew. Every day. In a silence I could not escape.

The dreams I had of one day making love to Blythe, or to any of the girls in the co-op, were just that.

Dreams.

My father's booming voice shattered the thought, echoing up the stairwell like a command.

"Wyn, would you like to join us for dinner? Alannah made an amazing Fattoush salad."

"No, I ate at the game center. I'm fine," I called back.

I waited until I heard his footsteps retreat down the stairs before undressing and stepping into the shower.

Like my mother, I was an immaculate germaphobe. I always took extra care to leave the bathroom tidy, out of respect for Alannah, and maybe out of respect for the illusion of order the house demanded.

Afterward, I did not bother with a nightshirt. I reclined across my bed, wrapped in a damp towel. At some point, I drifted off. The towel loosened as sleep pulled me under, and for a moment I thought I felt the mirror's curved gaze still watching, holding me in its warped reflection even with my eyes closed.

Hours later, the sound of running water and soft humming startled me awake.

Alannah's voice was unmistakably melodic. Light as a lullaby. A sound you could trust without question.

That made what I saw next even harder to believe.

Half-asleep and curious, I crept toward the cracked door of our shared bathroom. Steam curled through the opening. The shower doors were clouded, but my vision and my imagination did the rest.

Through the fog, I saw her. Her bare form, from the waist up, tilted back beneath the water as she massaged shampoo into her hair. A soft moan escaped her lips.

For a heartbeat, I let myself imagine what it might feel like to be wanted like that. To be chosen. I almost believed the scene belonged to me, as if the house was offering me a private fantasy as a mercy.

Then she lowered her hands and looked down.

I did too.

A shadow rose along the bottom edge of the glass.

It did not belong to me.

It belonged to him.

My father.

He kissed her torso, then stood and pressed his lips to hers with fervor and familiarity. I froze, captivated, confused, and horrified as their bodies moved together in the clouded glass.

For one suspended second, his eyes locked on mine through the fog.

No shock.

No shame.

Just recognition.

As if he had been expecting me all along.

In all the commotion, I had not noticed that the towel that had once been wrapped around my waist was now crumpled at my feet, as if the house itself had stripped me bare.

I turned to run, caught my foot in the towel, and stumbled. My head smacked hard against the corner of my computer table, and everything went black.

I came to moments later, a sturdy pair of hands gently cupping my face.

"Wyn, son. Are you okay?"

Aside from the throbbing in my skull and the flood of shame, I was fine.

Morning came.

What surprised me most was that neither my father nor Alannah mentioned what happened. Not the fall. Not the other thing.

The silence was worse than any lecture. By breakfast, it was as if the night had been erased, scrubbed clean like steam wiped from the mirror. But the image clung to me anyway, permanent and raw.

Even school days with Alannah resumed their usual rhythm, as if nothing had changed.

Until the next scheduled night of cosmic bowling.

By then, my father's face had started showing up everywhere. On billboards. In magazine spreads. Smiling from full-page ads.

He was becoming the kind of person Madison Avenue loved. Sleek. Confident. Untouchable.

The ads looked like neat, polished promises.

The house felt like a stage where the illusion of family came undone quietly, one seam at a time.

That night he told us he would be out late. A scheduled dinner with an executive from a well-known suit maker.

Alannah said she would drive me. She did not look at me when she said it, as if there were an agreement between adults that I had been excluded from.

I clung to the idea of time away like a life raft.

For me, the night could not end fast enough. When we got home, I fell into my ritual. I took a shower, then wiped down the bathroom until it was spotless.

Exhausted and wanting only the small mercy of sleep, I slid into my nightshirt and collapsed onto the bed.

The house settled around me with its usual noises. The hum of the fridge. The click of a distant door. The low sigh of the vents. I tried to let them lull me, but they always led back to the same ache.

Around midnight, the urge to pee pulled me out of sleep.

I moved through the dark with practiced confidence, a boy who knew the house's geography by memory. My feet found the rug. My hand reached for the door.

I stopped.

Alannah's voice came from the bathroom, bright and animated, the sound oddly domestic in the dead hour.

Then the words cut through me, clean and precise.

"Seriously, I've never seen anything like it. Not on someone his age. It's the size of an infant's. I've seen bigger pee-pees on the babies I've nursed."

A man's voice cut in over the speaker, softer and nasal, carrying the lazy amusement of someone entertained.

"Yeah, he was spying on me in the shower a few weeks ago. The little perv knocked himself out trying to run. I actually felt bad for his father. He looked embarrassed, seeing that microscopic organ. It was pitiful."

Their laughter followed. Bright and careless. It landed on me like acid. Each syllable etched itself deeper into my skin.

All the things I had swallowed, the shame, the humiliation, the cold little betrayals of other people's curiosity, rose up as if they were a tide.

Fury flared behind my ribs, hot enough to make my hands tremble.

I crossed the short span of carpet to my workstation and wrapped my fingers around the ceramic vase.

It had always been pretty, an artisan piece Father liked enough to show guests. I used it as decoration, as a divider, as something to keep my desk from looking too empty.

Now it felt cold. Solid. Unexpectedly heavy.

Her mocking voice replayed in my head. It was not only this night. It was every stare. Every whisper. Every pitying half-smile.

The thought of being the punchline forever lit something in me that did not want to laugh back.

I walked toward the bathroom slowly.

Each step was measured, as if I needed to prove I meant it. My breath was shallow. My heart hammered so loudly I half expected the house to hear it and answer.

The door was unlocked.

I pushed it open.

Alannah looked up.

Her eyes widened.

Her body was bare, perched on the elongated seat of the bidet.

She gasped.

I did not.

I raised the vase.

For a moment I thought I might lower it, that maybe I would wake up and everything would dissolve into steam and humiliation.

But her laughter replayed in my head, sharper than ever.

My arm did not listen to doubt.

I brought it down.

The sound was more hollow than I expected. A grunt. A stifled cry. Then silence.

I struck again.

And again.

When it was over, the room was still.

She lay motionless on the floor, nude, bloodied, unrecognizable.

Her body was still warm, which should have horrified me.

Instead, I noted it like a fact in a textbook.

And I felt nothing.

I reached for a towel, tilted my head from side to side, and let my eyes trace the shape of her body one last time. I do not know why I did it. Maybe it was remorse. Maybe it was reverence. Maybe it was simply the mind trying to make a moment mean something when meaning had already rotted away.

I rolled the towel and placed it beneath her head, either to slow the bleeding or to make it seem like I cared.

Then I lay beside her.

And slept.

I woke to the now-familiar sound of my father's voice, deep and steady, oddly comforting.

"Wyn, son. Are you okay?"

I blinked up at him, unsure of what part was real.

When he spoke again, it was not the tone of a man discovering a crime.

It was the tone of a man arriving right on schedule.

He did not ask what happened.

He did not even look surprised.

He only said, "Give me your nightshirt, and use my shower to clean yourself up."

I did not ask why.

I did not speak at all.

I did what he said and stood under the water for what felt like hours, the longest shower I had ever taken.

The steam made it hard to breathe, but I did not want to leave.

When I finally returned to my room, everything was gone.

The bathroom had been cleaned.

There was no blood, no ceramic, no Alannah.

And in the corner, where the suit garment bag had once held promotional materials from his latest endorsement, it now bulged with something uneven and heavy. The bag sagged in the middle, swollen as if it were breathing.

My father grunted as he lifted it and hoisted it over his shoulder as though it weighed no more than a duffle of laundry.

He did not look at me.

And I did not ask where he was going.

"Wyn," he called. "Get your head in the game and come with me."

I followed him down the stairs, through the garage, and into the utility house. He took the back steps two at a time, moving faster than I expected.

Once inside, he pointed to the fuse box and whispered, "Open it."

I did.

Just below the row of switches, a lever waited.

I looked at him.

He nodded.

I pulled it.

A scraping sound echoed beneath us, followed by a sliver of light seeping up from the floorboards.

The house itself was opening its mouth.

Setting the garment bag down, he slid the metal rack where I kept my bowling gear. Underneath was a thick rubber mat. Breathing heavily, he rolled the mat away.

A trapdoor came into view, perfectly flush, its seams so tight they nearly disappeared into the wooden floor. The hinges groaned as it opened, like a throat clearing itself.

The opening smelled of damp earth and something older, as if the house had been waiting years to exhale this secret.

Together, we opened it.

Without being asked, I helped him drag the garment bag down the narrow staircase.

The air below was thick. Earthy. Untouched.

He peeled back a heavy burlap square, revealing another bag beneath it, discolored and decaying.

The canvas looked ancient, but undisturbed.

Same size.

Same shape.

Dust clung to it like ash.

A sweet, faint smell hit me, clinging at the back of my throat.

Lavender.

My mother's perfume.

Or maybe just my imagination punishing me.

My father nodded again, and I understood.

We strained to fit the newer bag beside the old one. There was barely enough space. I dropped to my knees to catch my breath while he stood above me, panting.

When our eyes met, his breath steadied, as if this was the moment he had been waiting for, the one rehearsal finally performed with an audience.

"Son," he said softly, "let's go upstairs and get some sleep. We've got to be at the store first thing tomorrow for the lime."

Kneeling in the dust beside him, I understood how our family handled secrets. We stored them.

They were layered.

Left to rot quietly in the dark.

We buried the night in silence, dust, and lime, and neither of us said a word about what we had just done.

Chapter Ten

Irrelevant and Immaterial

Outside, the summer heat pressed down on northwest Atlanta. The street beyond the window was still—somewhere between Bankhead and Howell Mill—where faded murals clung to old storefronts and weeds split the sidewalks. Inside, silence.

"In biblical times, they would've stoned you," he said, fingers clamping her chin, forcing her to meet his eyes. "I'm saving your soul."

"If you just walk out now, I promise I won't tell! Please—just let me go. Please!"

Her voice trembled, then sank as he released her. Pain shot through her shoulders—her arms yanked tight behind her, locked in a stress position soldiers used to break prisoners. Her bare knees dug into the hardwood, a thin throw pillow offering little relief.

She trembled from withdrawal, breath hitching between soft, panicked sobs.

Across the room, he sat motionless, sipping from a plastic water bottle just beyond her reach.

Behind him, a warped window framed the cracked sidewalk and a flickering streetlight.

A Waffle House sign glowed across the intersection. Atlanta kept moving, even if time in this room had stopped. Near her feet, a silver bracelet had slipped loose—scratched and dented, but engraved. She mouthed the name etched there over and over, her whisper almost inaudible.

Through the haze she murmured, "Why you doin' this to me? You said you wanted a date. You said you loved me."

"I picked you up off the streets. You're a whore. A junkie whore."

His voice dropped lower as he closed the distance, his hand snapping up to seize her jaw. She screamed—one last burst. The bedroom door exploded inward. Men in body armor flooded the space, shields raised, voices colliding in a storm of commands.

"Get down!"

"Police!"

"Step away from her!"

The man froze, the water bottle clenched in his fist.

"Drop it!" an officer barked.

"I ain't got no gun!"

"I said drop it!"

Before the command could echo, a second officer fired. The TASER probes punched into his side. His body locked rigid, then toppled to the floor in a violent shudder as the current tore through him.

The instant the shocks ended, four officers swarmed. They rolled him over, cuffed his wrists, bound his legs, their movements swift and practiced. Two dragged him toward the door. The others rushed to the bed, slicing through nylon ropes that had carved deep red grooves into her arms and ankles.

"Easy now," one murmured.

"We've got an ambulance on the way."

He pressed his radio. "Need a bus and CSI to four-zero-four Vine Street, West Midtown. Repeat—bus and CSI to 404 Vine."

She stayed still. No tears.

Her whisper broke the silence: "Are you going to arrest me?"

"Not yet," the officer said, his voice softening though the cadence stayed abrupt.

He worked the last knot free.

"What's your name?"

"I'm Bethani—Bethani Christian."

He paused, repeating it with a trace of disbelief.

"Bethani Christian?"

"Like the nonprofit?"

A faint smile tugged at her lips.

"Yes. Except I spell mine with an 'I.' My mother was an artist."

He gave a single nod, then shifted back into protocol.

"Alright, Bethani Christian. For now, I need to detain you—for your protection. I'll put you in cuffs, and we'll finish this at the precinct on Northside Drive."

As he guided her onto the porch, Bethani glanced back. Her captor—now awake—was being shoved into a patrol car. The officer noticed her stare. His tone went flat.

"You're lucky. Two other bodies turned up in houses just like this one. Same setup. Same torture."

With fear and exhaustion colliding, the queasy churn in her stomach surged. She bent over the porch railing and vomited the little she'd eaten in hours. The officer stepped aside, muttered a curse under his breath, and kept his eyes fixed on the street.

Minutes later, she sat in the back of a cruiser, riding in silence toward the precinct on Northside Drive. At a metal desk inside, cuffs finally removed, she faced a plainclothes officer—"the lady cop," as the others had called her with a smirk that sounded more like mockery than respect.

The questioning began. By the third unanswered question, the officer's tone had shifted. Less patient now, her words terse, edged with irritation.

Bethani's high still clung to her. Her thoughts were scattered and her vision blurred.

She caught fragments of the woman's voice, broken like static.

"You're lucky"... "could've been worse."

Then one phrase cut through. An anonymous caller from the neighborhood watch had reported a figure slipping into the boarded-up house. That was how they found her.

Bethani had been using for years but only working the streets for six months. She'd heard the rumors—the two white men, the random attacks, but the bodies that were never official. Some believed them. Some didn't. She hadn't cared. Until now.

The officer refreshed her laptop, fingers tapping impatiently against the keys.

"Your name?" she asked again.

This time, Bethani didn't hesitate.

"Jennifer Richards."

Out of the corner of her eye, she saw the officer who had cut her free, standing with his arms crossed.

"Well," he said with a smirk. "What'd you do with Bethani?"

Her jaw tightened.

"My name is Jennifer. Jennifer Richards."

The lady cop didn't flinch. Her eyes narrowed slightly.

"ID."

Bethani reached into her jacket with shaking fingers and handed over her state-issued card. The officer scanned it, then turned the screen toward her partner.

"Looks like you were right, sir," she said dryly.

"We're speaking to Bethani Christian."

The desk officer exhaled sharply, the sound pointed, deliberate. Bethani didn't react.

She stared at the table and whispered, "Is he going to prison?"

"That's not my call," the officer said.

"But I'm confident he'll face charges—for the murders of your colleagues, and for your attempted murder."

Two hours later, the detective leaned back.

"Is there someone we can call to pick you up? Or would you prefer a ride?"

Bethani gave a tired half-smile.

"I'd appreciate a lift... but a taxi voucher would be better. I don't want to step out of a squad car—or an Uber driven by someone I know. You understand, right?"

The officer didn't answer. She left the desk, then returned minutes later with a signed voucher for Atlanta-Lenox Taxi.

Bethani's ride ended at a refurbished house on the edge of the gentrified strip of West Midtown—just off Joseph E. Boone Boulevard. It was only a short drive from the boarded-up house where she'd nearly died. Too short.

When she stepped out, the driver gave her a look—snide, judgmental.

"I'm sorry," she murmured. "I don't have any cash."

"Figures," he muttered, shifting into gear. "Streetwalkers used to carry cash."

He sped off before she could answer. Her high was gone now, completely. Stomach cramps and tremors hit hard, the kind that usually sent her chasing her next fix. She climbed the steps slowly, every joint aching.

The porch was spotless, freshly painted. Too clean for the body that dragged itself across it.

She rang the bell. Inside, the sound of small feet—two pairs—followed by excited chants of Mommy. The sound tugged a fragile smile across her face.

A strong, familiar voice broke through the chants—her brother's.

"Okay, guys, hold on just a minute. I'm sure it's Mommy."

She could hear the smile in his voice, lighthearted, almost laughing.

There was a pause as he checked the peephole, then the welcome sounds of deadbolts and chain sliding open.

"Beth, come on in," Simeon said, swinging the door wide. "I almost called, but then I remembered—your phone's probably in somebody else's pocket or a pawnshop."

His tone softened when he looked down. The twins had wrapped themselves around their mother's thin legs, holding tight. His voice trembled, and his eyes became wet. It was always like that with them. King Solomon and Queen Esther—six years old—clung without hesitation, their love loud and immediate.

"Mommy loves you. You know that, right?" she whispered.

They nodded. She bent low, kissing each forehead.

"Give me your nose," she said, the familiar game flickering light across her face.

Their giggles filled the room as their noses bumped hers. The sweetness was almost too much to bear. Simeon let it linger before stepping in.

"Why don't you let them stay with me again tonight? Just for a while. Until you get it together."

Her spine stiffened.

"Simeon, you've been great. For a little brother, you're amazing—to me and to them. But I'm their mother. I'm just... having a minor setback, is all."

She heard the weakness in her voice and hated it. Simeon didn't argue. He turned to the kids, smoothing the moment.

"Alright, munchkins, upstairs. You're staying the night—and so is your mom."

Bethani's jaw tightened. He said it as if he were granting permission. She caught the look on his face—half-concern, half-judgment—and her stomach clenched. It was the same look he'd worn when she got caught sneaking out as a teenager.

The worst part? She knew he was right. And that truth made her want to cry.

An hour later, she felt Simeon's gentle hand on her shoulder.

"The twins have had their baths and are tucked in. You're not sleeping on the couch. The guest bed's ready."

She blinked, still groggy.

"So... no lecture tonight, baby brother?"

"Of course not. You know me better than that," he said, quiet smile on his lips.

She sat up slowly.

"I just need to run out for a minute. Get some air. It's been a long day."

Simeon's face stayed calm, but his voice carried weight.

"Yeah. You can tell me all about it after some rest. But you're not going anywhere tonight." He paused in the doorway, voice low but firm.

"You can't keep doing this to the babies. They deserve their mother. Not this."

The words echoed long after he fell asleep. Bethani waited, listening to his steady breathing. Then, with practiced silence, she unzipped his backpack. Her fingers slid out his corporate credit card and three of the five crisp twenties tucked in the phone case. The guilt was familiar, but so was the need. She crept to the front door, every step measured.

Her hand touched the lock—

"Mommy, where ya goin'?"

Two small voices floated from the top of the stairs, sleepy but perfectly in sync. She froze.

"Shhh," she whispered up at them. "You'll wake your uncle. Mommy's just stepping out for some cigarettes. Go back to bed. I'll see you in the morning."

The twins lingered a moment, then disappeared into the bedroom.

For Simeon, the next few hours passed like any other—until a sudden storm of sounds dragged him from sleep. The twins thundering down the stairs, the phone beeping and knocks at the door with the doorbell chiming in between.

Shaking off his grogginess, Simeon called out, steady and composed, "Hey, you two grab a seat. I'll fix your breakfast in a minute."

He scanned the room.

"Where's your mother?"

They shrugged.

At the door stood a tall man, shoulders squared, badge clipped to his belt. His presence filled the frame before he even spoke.

"Good morning," he said, voice firm, carrying weight. "Detective Chase Harris. Atlanta Homicide. I need to speak with Simeon Christian."

"I'm Simeon," he answered, the word catching in his throat. "Homicide?"

The detective's gaze flicked past him, noting the twins in the hallway. His tone dropped an octave, still steady but commanding.

"Mr. Christian, is there somewhere private we can talk?"

Simeon nodded quickly. "Of course. Come in, officer."

Kneeling to the twins, he kept his voice light. "Hey, guys, head upstairs for a bit. Everything's fine. I'll be up in a minute."

Extending his hand, Simeon gestured to the chair.

"Have a seat, officer."

As the children's footsteps faded upstairs, Harris began to speak. Simeon cut in.

"Let me guess—you're here about Bethani."

The air in the room shifted, heavy. The detective nodded.

"A female body was found near the auto junkyard on Vine Street this morning. She had a credit card with your name on it. We couldn't confirm the identity. The body's at the morgue."

Simeon didn't answer. His chest rose, then fell. The ticking wall clock was louder than the words. Louder than everything. He blinked—not in disbelief, but as if refusing to let himself feel.

"Did you... see her?" he asked, voice low, steady.

Harris shook his head.

"No. The scene was cleared before I arrived. We'll confirm through dental records. The details... are rough."

Simeon's eyes wandered past him—juice cups half-filled on the counter, the folded blanket on the couch where Bethani had slept.

"She was here," he whispered.

"Last night. She tucked the twins in. Kissed them good-night."

The detective stayed silent, letting the words stand as Simeon pulled back the curtain. The morning haze was lifting, the sun-light was ordinary and cruel. The world looked the same—and that made it worse.

Turning back, he asked, "What happens now?"

"We'll need you to come to the morgue," Harris said.

"For confirmation. If you're able."

Simeon nodded once, then glanced up the stairs.

"I'll need to find someone for the twins."

Cartoons murmured faintly from the second floor. That sound—so normal—made his chest ache. He climbed the steps slowly, not knowing what to say but certain of one truth: they couldn't lose their mother and their childhood on the same day.

When he returned, Harris had pulled a tablet from his bag. He tapped a few times, then turned it toward him.

"I have some images. The credit card led us here, but we need you to confirm. If this is Bethani, we'll still require a morgue ID—at least we can stop calling her Jane Doe."

Simeon took a breath, steadying himself. His hand hovered over the tablet for a moment before he finally looked. Three photos stared back at him. He forced his eyes to meet the first, but he couldn't bring himself to linger.

A glimpse was enough. His stomach clenched, his throat burned. He looked away. A quiet nod.

"Yes, sir... that's my sister. That's Bethani."

He barely glanced again. Once was enough.

The detective gave a respectful pause.

"I do have a few questions, Mr. Christian—but they can wait. I'll meet you later this afternoon to finalize the identification, if that works for you. For now, I imagine you'll want to be with your kids."

"Yes," Simeon replied, choosing not to correct the officer's mistaken assumption about the twins.

He worked to make the twins' transition into full-time life at his three-bedroom townhouse as smooth as possible. Still, the two months that followed were anything but easy. The homicide investigation crawled forward, uncovering few leads.

Detectives offered polite check-ins, but to Simeon, their lack of urgency felt like indifference. Most of his energy was consumed by parenting Sol and Essie—the names the twins insisted on after asking him to stop calling them "munchkins."

They grieved in their own way, and he did his best to be both uncle and mother, protector and provider. The only person who poured energy back into him—who kept him steady—was his life partner, Eldred Steward.

Neither Simeon nor Eldred was prone to public displays of affection or curated social media posts. Still, their relationship wasn't exactly a secret. They simply chose to live in separate homes—Simeon in a modest neighborhood of West Midtown still finding its footing after waves of reconstruction, and Eldred in a spacious five-bedroom house in Kennesaw.

Whenever someone asked why they weren't married, their response was always the same—

"We're exactly where we want to be."

Those who knew them well understood the *fuller* truth. Both men came from deep South Georgia roots—families where phrases like *love the sinner, hate the sin* or *Adam and Eve, not Adam and Steve* echoed in Sunday sermons and family gatherings.

They had weathered enough judgment from preachers, politicians, and well-meaning biblical literalists to know the cost of living their truth out loud. They loved their families deeply, but the illusion that their relationship was "normal"—by traditional definitions—remained a difficult pill for their relatives to swallow.

The permanent seal of marriage, with its public acknowledgment, was a reality their families simply weren't prepared to embrace.

As Sol and Essie settled into life without their mother, Simeon and Eldred began to find their rhythm as fathers. Together, they navigated pediatric appointments, school enrollment, errands, and endless reruns of kids' programming. Saturday afternoons at Chuck E. Cheese became a treasured ritual.

The idea of becoming a permanent family unit grew louder in their minds—especially on afternoons like this, as the four of them piled into the new Acura RDX.

Essie, unprompted, blurted out, "I hope we can stay like this forever. I love both my daddies."

"Me too," Sol added, fumbling with his booster seat until Simeon leaned in to help.

Simeon glanced at Eldred, who met his eyes with a quiet smile. No words were needed. Both men understood what came next.

Four months later, they held a small ceremony with close friends. The family moved into Eldred's home in Kennesaw, nestled in a neighborhood where families like theirs weren't an anomaly.

Simeon valued the strong schools and the sense of belonging. Sol and Essie, resilient as ever, thrived in the warmth and stability of their new life.

Bethani's murder was eventually classified as a cold case. For Simeon, that label only hardened his resolve. Cold case. Cold comfort. He would make sure the children's future was secure.

With Georgia's recent adoption law changes, he and Eldred believed they were the clear and rightful choice.

Simeon was already the twins' temporary guardian, and their marriage certificate made official what was already true in spirit: they were a family.

The twins' biological father, known only as "Gipp," had long since vanished—leaving nothing behind but pain and the shadow of his role in Bethani's descent into addiction. He had never been a presence in their lives. Neither man expected any obstacles.

The following weeks were intense. They endured medical exams, financial reviews, background checks, parenting classes, home studies, safety inspections. It was exhausting, but every step felt hopeful—forward-looking.

Six months after Bethani's death, the last meeting with the judge and attorney felt like a formality. There was just one step left—a final attempt to contact any remaining legal guardian or biological parent. A box to check. Nothing more.

Or so they thought.

The illusion of certainty shattered with a single voicemail—its tone urgent, its message unsettling. The investigator working with their attorney requested that they report to her office immediately.

As director of human resources at the State University in Kennesaw, Eldred cleared the rest of his afternoon without hesitation. Simeon, hands trembling as he returned the call, arranged for the twins to stay with their trusted neighbor.

They drove in silence. The twenty-seven miles from Kennesaw to Symphony Towers stretched on like a sentence with no punctuation. Traffic moved, but time felt suspended. Neither man spoke more than a few terse phrases, each lost in thought. The air between them was thick with questions they didn't dare ask aloud.

Something wasn't right. And both of them knew it.

At the parking deck, they found a spot at street level and rushed inside. Without a word, their hands locked. That anchor being their only exchange of strength—as they hurried toward the elevators.

Ms. Simmons—former APD detective turned lead investigator—was waiting near the lobby. Her face gave nothing away.

Simeon, barely holding himself together, whispered through clenched teeth,

"Just tell us."

She didn't blink. "There's no easy way to say this. Pastor and Mrs. Felton Givens are upstairs in the conference room."

Simeon stopped cold. "Pastor?" he spat, the word as sharp as profanity.

Eldred blinked. "Wait—who is Felton Givens?"

Simeon turned slowly, eyes wide with disbelief.

"Gipp."

Eldred's voice dropped. "The twins' father?"

"Yes," Simeon and Ms. Simmons said together.

The elevator dinged. They stepped inside, the silence was heavier than before. Simeon stared at the polished metal walls, fighting the wave of nausea that rose in his throat, metallic on his tongue.

He hadn't seen Gipp since Bethani's pregnancy. And now... this. When the doors slid open, there he was.

Gipp.

Clean-cut and sharply dressed. Charm clung to him like cologne. No longer the ghost who'd left his sister wrecked and addicted.

His pudgy midsection pressed against the buttons of his shirt, proof that discipline still slipped his grasp. Yet, somehow, he looked—dangerously—like a man who knew he could still be found attractive.

And somehow, that made it worse.

Gipp stood smoothly, extending his hand as though they were old friends at a reunion.

"Simeon, you look well—as you always have."

Even his voice was different now—drawn-out vowels, dramatic pauses, the practiced swell and dip of a man performing holiness rather than living it. Simeon felt his stomach twist. The man sounded practiced, not changed.

"I'll get right to the point," Gipp said, charm coating every syllable.

"I know I'm the last person you expected to see, but I need you to know—my life is different now. I'm sorry about your sister."

"Her name is Bethani," Simeon corrected, his tone flat as stone.

But Gipp pressed on, unfazed.

"I'm not making the same choices I made when we were together. I've given my life to Christ. This is my wife, Kacey. We're doing the work of ministry now. I really appreciate you taking care of my babies, but... it's time for them to be with their daddy."

Simeon studied him—the expensive suit straining at the midsection, the well-oiled delivery, the way he wrapped himself in a title he hadn't earned. Pastor. As if a new word could bury the old man.

Despite the disbelief tightening Simeon's jaw and the flash of anger in Eldred's eyes, Gipp kept going, his tone righteous and smooth.

"You can go on and live your life. Your life—with all due respect—isn't the kind I want my babies witnessing. The Word preaches against it. And so do I."

Eldred snapped.

"I don't give a damn what you preach against. You've got a lot of fuckin' nerve walking in here judging anybody's lifestyle. I don't know a damn thing about you—but everything I've heard says you're a loser. And now what? A married loser in a suit with a congregation full of folks too blind to see the truth?"

Gipp acted as if Eldred hadn't spoken, his focus sliding back to Simeon with a patronizing calm.

"Again, Simeon—no disrespect. I love you, as God commands. But I can't approve of this lifestyle. My twins living in Atlanta is bad enough."

He paused, lowering his voice to a grave whisper.

"Their mama is dead... and now this? They've just been through too much—seen too much. Like I said, you can live your life, and how you live it is between you and God."

"Essie and Sol are my life. They are our lives," Simeon angrily responded, his grip tightening around Eldred's hand.

Eldred pulled in a breath, his words sharp as glass.

"So you think you can just come in from nowhere, flip our world upside down, and call yourself a preacher? Bitch, please. Take that self-righteous storm and let it rain on somebody else's damn parade."

Gipp stayed calm—but too calm. His voice was low, almost tender, like he was trying on a softness he didn't own.

"I came as soon as I heard."

Eldred cut toward their attorney. "Can he even do this?"

The attorney, who had been silent until now, answered evenly. "Unfortunately, yes. Within the first year of the adoption process, biological parents retain the legal right to challenge the proceedings."

Eldred's eyes narrowed.

"And how exactly did you find out about Bethani?"

Kacey glanced at Gipp, her hesitation obvious.

"We, um... saw something online. A story about a woman near the junkyard. It didn't list a name at first, but... we just had a feeling."

Gipp jumped in quickly.

"Then one of my cousins down in Macon called, said it might've been your sister. That's when we knew."

Simeon crossed his arms, jaw set.

"That was six months ago. And you waited until now to care?"

Kacey's smile was tight, practiced, her tone almost scripted.

"We've been preparing. This isn't something we take lightly. We wanted to come... correct."

"Spiritually, financially..." Gipp added, nodding with rehearsed gravitas.

"The Lord moves in His time, in His own powerful way."

Eldred muttered under his breath, just loud enough for Simeon to hear.

"Let me guess—Bible verses by day, OnlyFans by night."

Simeon didn't laugh. His glare cut into Gipp, sharp and unblinking, a silent warning that his patience was already paper thin.

Ms. Simmons spoke carefully, her words steady but restrained.

"Because the twins' DNA was collected during the initial investigation, we were able to confirm Mr. Givens' paternity."

"The legitimation process is complete, and he has formally challenged the adoption. The paperwork has already been filed with the court. I'm sorry."

The weeks that followed blurred into interviews, home visits, and endless evaluations of the Givens' fitness as parents. Simeon and Eldred did their best to explain it all to Sol and Essie, but the children grew more anxious as the court date loomed.

On the day of the hearing, the courtroom felt colder than usual.

The judge—a woman known for her conservative leanings—listened without expression. Her questions were polite, but her pauses, her tone, even the way she emphasized certain words made Simeon uneasy. He could feel which way the wind was blowing before she ever spoke her ruling.

"I have read the statements from both parties and their counsel. I have considered the investigations and weighed the evidence. Both Queen Esther and King Solomon are blessed to have two families who love them and want the best for them.

But I must decide not on sentiment, but on what I believe is in the best interest of the children—not only today, but as they grow into productive members of society.

That decision is this: they belong with their biological father, who has proven to be stable, and who has committed to raising them in the nurture and admonition of the Creator."

She looked directly at Simeon, her eyes narrowing just slightly.

"Mr. Christian, I commend you for the safety and stability you have provided since their mother's passing. But after all they've endured, I believe a home with both a mother and a father is the most appropriate environment."

The words landed like a blow. Simeon's chest tightened, Eldred's breath caught, and both men gasped as the final words fell.

Across the aisle, Sol and Essie shifted uneasily in their seats between a court-appointed aide. Essie clutched her brother's hand so tightly his knuckles turned white. Sol's lips moved soundlessly at first, then found a whisper.

"No... no... we don't want to go."

Their protest was small but raw, enough to draw glances from the gallery. Eldred's eyes brimmed as Simeon leaned forward instinctively, as if he could shield them from the words already spoken.

"Full custody of the minor children, Queen Esther Christian and King Solomon Christian, is hereby granted to Mr. Felton and Mrs. Kacey Givens. An immediate transfer of residence is ordered. That is my ruling."

The gavel struck once, sharp and final, echoing through the courtroom like a sentence neither child nor guardian could escape. Sol let out a broken wail. Essie buried her face in her brother's arm. The sound of their cries carried across the chamber, filling the silence the gavel left behind.

The judge banged her gavel, stacked her papers, and swept from the bench as though the matter were settled. Devastated,

Simeon and Eldred chose not to contest the ruling publicly. When the verdict was delivered, they requested time alone with Sol and Essie, who had been moved to a separate room.

The children were devastated, their lives shattered. Wails tore through the quiet office, rising into screams. Their small bodies flailed in defiance—kicking, twisting, striking out at the social workers who reached for them.

"We don't want to go!" they cried, voices raw, fists balled tight against the inevitable.

Simeon and Eldred rushed in, pulling them close, wrapping themselves around the children like a shield. Through tears, they whispered the only comfort they had left.

"You're going to be okay. We love you. We'll keep fighting."

Simeon turned, his face wet but his voice steady, directing his words at Gipp and Kacey.

"We'll pursue every legal option available. This isn't over."

But the couple dismissed him coolly. Kacey smoothed the hem of her dress as if brushing away dust.

"The children need time to adjust," she said. "No further visitation—for now."

The cruelty of it was plain, though masked behind a smile.

As expected, everyone was emotional when they left the courthouse. Simeon's hands shook as he carried the children's small suitcases. He had packed just enough essentials to last the week, clinging to the hope that they'd be back home before long.

They stood silent as Gipp loaded the bags into the back of the dark blue minivan. The automatic sliding door opened with a mechanical hum. Sol and Essie, tear-streaked and clinging to one another, lifted their small hands in weak waves.

Simeon knelt, kissing each of them on the forehead.

"We love you. We always will," he whispered, swallowing the ache in his throat.

Eldred stood beside him, jaw clenched so tightly it trembled. Together, they stepped back as the door slid shut.

From the passenger seat, Kacey swiveled, faking a sugary smile for the children.

"Don't be sad. Everything's going to be alright."

Without warning, she pulled a phone from her designer handbag. As the van eased forward, she raised it high, angling the shot to frame the twins.

"Say hello to all our friends," she chirped, her voice unnervingly bright.

"These are our sweet babies—Queen and King!"

She beamed into the camera as if this were a homecoming instead of a court-ordered separation. The twins didn't move. Their faces were blank, their eyes hollowed by shock.

From the curb, Eldred's eyes narrowed.

"What the hell was that?" he muttered.

Simeon didn't answer. His gaze was locked on the license plate, burning the numbers into memory as the van disappeared into traffic.

Inside, Kacey kept nudging the twins, tilting the phone until she got the shot she wanted.

"Tell everybody your names."

They hesitated.

"More to come," she whispered with a conspiratorial wink, then slid the phone back into her purse.

By the time the newly assembled family reached their home in Milledgeville, the twins were quiet, too quiet. They ate dinner without a word, heads bowed over their plates.

Afterward, Kacey clapped her hands as though announcing a party game.

"Alright, bath time! Let's get you all cleaned up."

"Don't we need our clothes from the suitcase?"

Essie asked, her voice small.

"Oh no, sweetie. I bought you brand-new things. We're going to have so much fun tonight. You get to help me and Daddy make a movie! Save your pajamas from the suitcase for tomorrow."

The twins exchanged a hesitant and uneasy glance. They didn't enjoy bathing together, a boundary Simeon and Eldred had always honored. Still with no choice, they obeyed.

The twins quietly walked into the bathroom. The sound of running water and their hesitant voices carried faintly down the hallway. When they emerged, damp and shivering in their towels, Kacey was waiting, her tone bright and coaxing.

"Come on, babies," she chirped.

"There's something special I want to show you."

She guided them down the hall to a room she cheerily called *the studio.* They paused in the doorway. Inside, the space was transformed.

Two cameras sat mounted on tripods, red lights blinking like watchful eyes. Laptops glowed blue on a folding table, their screens alive with streaming software. Four harsh studio lights flooded the room so brightly they washed the walls white.

At the center sat a low wooden bench—painted with cartoon faces. Dora. Elmo. Paw Patrol. The kind of images meant to comfort children, twisted here into something staged.

Essie's voice trembled.

"Is this where we're gonna make the movie?"

Gipp turned from the equipment, smiling as though he'd been waiting for the question. His preacher's polish was still there, but thinner now—just enough to show the hunger behind it.

"Yes," he said softly. "Right here."

He stepped forward, hands outstretched, reaching for their towels.

He stepped forward, hands outstretched.

"Let me help you," he said gently.

The twins instinctively stepped back.

Kacey's voice floated in from behind them, still bright, still falsely sweet.

"Don't be shy. Mommy and Daddy are just teaching you something special."

Sol's fingers tightened around his sister's hand.

The studio lights hummed.

One of the cameras adjusted with a soft mechanical click.

Gipp crouched so he was eye level with them.

"Everything we do," he said softly, "is for *His* glory."

The red recording light blinked steadily.

Outside, the neighborhood was quiet. Lawns trimmed. Porch lights warm. A picture of ordinary.

Inside, the door to the studio clicked shut.

And the cameras kept rolling.

Chapter Eleven

Transgresión

The church wasn't small by any measure. Thousands filled the sanctuary each weekend, rows of polished seats stretching beneath screens the size of billboards. In the mornings, the English service carried the hum of suburbia — young families, professionals, polished voices.

But the evening service, the one Camila attended with Jonathan, moved to a different rhythm. Spanish choruses swelled from the choir, hands lifted high, a sea of voices rolling together in praise. On some Sundays, the music turned contemporary, the choir lifting arrangements of Kirk Franklin or Yolanda Adams, Texas voices reimagined in worship.

It was a church that spoke two languages but claimed one heart, a place where heritage and faith braided together beneath the Dallas skyline. Behind the sanctuary, tucked away from the noise of the crowd, Pastor David's office held its own stillness.

The walls lined with books, a framed verse over his shoulder, the leather-bound Bible resting on his desk. It was here that Camila sat, her fingers tangled in her hair, thick waves that seemed alive even in the quiet.

"Pastor David," she began, her voice low, almost swallowed by the room. "I need to tell you something. But it can't leave here."

David leaned forward, not as counselor but as shepherd. "Camila, whatever it is, the Lord already knows. My role is to help you carry it."

She inhaled sharply, bracing herself against an unseen wind. "I betrayed Jonathan."

The words sat between them, heavy, unholy.

David kept his face still, trained. Years of counseling had taught him how to listen without rushing to fill the silence, without showing what churned inside.

But even as he kept his counselor's mask steady, he couldn't stop Jonathan's face from coming to mind — the man's easy laugh, his steady way on the court, the kind of husband who didn't seem like the type to ever see this coming.

They weren't best friends, but they knew each other — from the courts, from the fields, from the way men bond over shared sweat and scoreboards. Jonathan was steady, competitive but fair, a man you could trust to call a foul on himself.

And here was his wife, unraveling in the quiet of his office, admitting she had trespassed against him with someone who didn't even matter.

David's chest tightened. He was a pastor first, yes, but in that moment, he also felt like a teammate hearing the ref had cheated the game. He breathed deeply, pressing the thought down, forcing himself to stay with Camila's trembling words.

Her voice wavered, but once the words began, they tumbled faster.

"It wasn't love," she said, shaking her head, eyes fixed on the floor.

"It wasn't even temptation, not really. Just... a moment. A stranger. Someone whose name I barely remember. It was over before it began, and it meant nothing."

She pressed her palms together, as if she could wring the memory out of her hands.

"But I can't live with it. Every time Jonathan smiles at me, every time he thanks me for something simple — dinner, laundry, just being his wife — I feel it burning in my chest. He thinks I'm faithful. He thinks I'm worthy of him. And I—" her breath caught, her shoulders folding in—.

"I betrayed him with a man who didn't even matter."

David nodded slowly, his face steady, the way he'd been trained. Neutral. Listening. He made small notes in his mind, the HR part of him cataloging her words.

not love... no attachment... shame outweighs desire.

It was the pattern of a confession that wasn't about passion, but about emptiness, about crossing a line just to see what was on the other side.

But inside, Jonathan's face lingered — the steady man, the fair competitor, the kind of husband who didn't deserve this weight. David felt it press against his ribs, heavy as her words. Still, he held his silence, letting hers fill the room.

David leaned back slightly, giving her space to breathe. His voice came measured, softened by years of guiding broken hearts without rushing them to answers.

"Camila," he said, "you've carried this alone, and it's eating at you. I can hear it in your words. But understand this — confession isn't just about exposing sin. It's about releasing its grip. God's grace doesn't minimize what you've done, but it does meet you in the place you are right now."

Her eyes lifted.

"You say it meant nothing," he continued, "but your spirit knows it meant something, because it wounded the bond between you and Jonathan — and between you and the Lord. That's why it burns every time he smiles. It's not because Jonathan is blind. It's because the Spirit inside you refuses to let this stay hidden."

He let the words settle, not pressing further.

"You came here because you want freedom. And freedom always begins with truth. You've taken that step. The question now is — what do you want healing to look like?"

Camila let out a jagged laugh, more broken than amused, and wiped at her eyes with the back of her hand.

"Healing?" she echoed.

"How do you heal something you've destroyed? Jonathan... he's a good man. Too good. And if he knew."

Her voice cracked. "—If he knew, there'd be nothing left to heal. He wouldn't look at me, Pastor David. He wouldn't forgive me. I see it already. Every time I think of telling him, I see the look in his eyes, and it kills me before the words even leave my mouth."

Her hands gripped the arms of the chair as if she were holding on against a storm.

"You talk about grace, but Jonathan is not God. He's a man, and men don't come back from this. Not when the betrayal is with... with no one. With a man who meant nothing."

Tears rolled freely now, streaking the face people often mistook for Brazilian — beautiful even in anguish, but undone.

David exhaled slowly, his chest heavy with the weight of two truths: the pastoral call to guide her toward repentance, and the unspoken knowledge that, one day, Jonathan's trust — his friend's trust — would lie shattered at his feet.

Camila leaned forward, her voice dropping low but urgent.

"Please," she whispered, "you can't tell him. Not ever. This... this has to stay between us."

David felt the air shift, the line she was drawing in the carpet between them. As a pastor, he'd heard confessions bound in confidence before. But this was different. This was Jonathan.

"Camila—"

"No," she cut in, shaking her head, her hair falling wild around her face.

"I came here because I trust you. Because you're not just *a pastor*, you're Pastor David. You know us. You know him. If you told him—if you even hinted—" she clenched her hands, "—I'd lose everything. He'd walk. He'd never forgive me."

David sat forward now, folding his hands, his voice firm but steady.

"Camila, listen to me. I believe with all my heart that Jonathan deserves to know. Marriage can't heal if truth stays buried. But it is not my place to speak that truth for you."

Confidentiality was sacred in pastoral counseling. Unless a life was in danger or a crime involved, what was spoken in that office stayed there. David knew the rules. What he hadn't known was how personal obedience would feel.

"If this were criminal — if someone's life or safety were in danger — I'd be bound to act. But this... this is yours to carry into the light."

Her lips parted, eyes wide, brimming again.

He went on, softer now.

"As much as I want to protect Jonathan, my role isn't to take your confession and use it against you. My role is to guide you toward repentance and toward honesty. That path belongs to you. And only you can decide when — or if — you'll take it."

Camila pressed her hands to her face, shaking her head.

"You don't understand... if I tell him, I lose him."

David's chest ached at her words. He understood more than she knew. Because in silence, he realized, he was already losing Jonathan himself.

A man who trusted the world to be fair. And in that moment, David knew that his silence, however pastoral, was already a betrayal of that trust.

He bowed his head, his voice low, inviting Camila to do the same.

"Lord," he prayed, steady but heavy, "You see what no one else sees. You know the burdens we carry, the sins we hide, the fears that keep us silent. Tonight, we place them in Your hands. Give Camila the courage to walk in truth, the strength to face what honesty requires, and the assurance that Your grace does not run dry. Heal what is broken and guide her steps into the light."

Camila whispered a fragile *amen,* her tears falling into the silence that followed.

David opened his eyes, but not without weight. He had prayed for her — but the words still hung unspoken for Jonathan, waiting in the shadows between them.

By the time the checks were paid and the group drifted off into the night, only David and Jonathan remained, leaning against their cars under the wash of the parking lot lights. The restaurant's neon sign hummed faintly behind them, a backdrop to their quiet.

Jonathan stretched, folding his arms across his chest. "You ever feel like you're standing right where you're supposed to be?" he asked.

David tilted his head, waiting.

Jonathan smiled, not with the broad grin from inside, but with a softer one. "Work's solid. The degree paid off. I'm not chasing anymore. I've got Camila at home. I mean... she stuck with me through every late night, every class, every exam. Most women would've walked. But she stayed. She believed in me when I had little to give."

He exhaled, his breath curling in the cool Dallas night.

"Man, sometimes I think God gave me more than I ever deserved. I don't say it enough, but she's the reason I made it through. I look at her and I know I'm in the right place, with the right person."

David swallowed, the words catching in his throat. He wanted to speak, to affirm, but the truth pressed so heavily he could barely breathe. Jonathan's gratitude was pure, unguarded, and David felt every syllable like a stone sinking deeper into his chest.

For a moment, neither man spoke. The silence wasn't awkward — it was weighty and full. Jonathan glanced up at the stars, then clapped David lightly on the shoulder.

"You're good people, Pastor David. I'm glad our paths crossed."

David managed a smile, though inside the secret screamed louder than ever. The parking lot emptied around them, but in his heart, he knew the truth was crowding every corner.

Jonathan shifted his weight, keys jangling in his hand.

"You ever notice how some guys are always chasing the next thing? Next job, next woman, next rush. I don't want that life. I want roots. I want Camila, kids, the whole thing. That's enough for me."

David nodded, his throat tight. "That's a rare kind of wisdom, Jonathan."

Jonathan grinned, easy and unguarded.

"Maybe. Or maybe I just know when I've already got the prize."

He slid into his car, waving as the engine turned over. David stood watching the taillights fade, the weight of Jonathan's words pressing harder than the Texas night.

The months slipped by in a rhythm that felt almost ordinary. Sunday services, league games, dinners with friends. Jonathan and Camila glided through it all with the glow of a couple admired by everyone who saw them. To the church, they were a picture of blessing. To the guys on the team, they were the couple that made marriage look effortless.

But to David, every laugh, every touch, every whispered compliment was another weight added to the scales. He had prayed for release, for clarity, for some way out of the burden. Yet nothing came. Jonathan grew only more devoted, more vocal in his gratitude.

And Camila smiled, hosted, played her part with practiced ease. If the guilt still gnawed at her, she hid it well. Sometimes, in fleeting glances across the sanctuary, David thought he caught the shadow of it. But she never spoke to him again about that night. She left him to carry it alone.

By the time a year had passed since her confession, David's silence had become its own kind of trespass.

It followed him into sermons, into sleep, into every shared moment with Jonathan. He had kept his word, but the cost kept rising.

One evening after another easy game and another round of laughter spilling into the night, David knew he could not keep carrying what was not his.

Jonathan had to know.

The sun was sinking low, throwing long shadows across the tennis courts. Their arms were slick with sweat, the final set hard fought but clean. Jonathan lunged, returned the ball with a crisp backhand, and when it thudded inside the line, he threw both arms up like a champion.

"Perfect match!" Jonathan shouted, laughing, chest heaving. He twirled his racket like a trophy. "Six love, six love, six love. A perfect match, Pastor David!"

Something inside David snapped.

His racket clattered to the ground.

"There is no such thing as a perfect match!" David shouted, voice echoing against the chain link fence. "I am sick of hearing about it. Sick of hearing about your perfect marriage, your perfect wife, your perfect life."

Jonathan froze. His laughter died mid breath. Confusion flickered across his face, then hardened into offense.

"What are you talking about?" he asked, voice sharper now.

David stepped forward, chest rising and falling like he had run a sprint. His eyes stung.

"Camila," he said.

Jonathan blinked. "What about her?"

David's voice broke, not as a pastor, but as a man unraveling.

"She came to me. A year ago. She confessed. She cheated on you, Jonathan. It was not love. It was not someone she cared about. But it happened. She told me and I have carried it. And God help me, I cannot keep it in anymore."

The words fell heavy between them.

Jonathan stared, as if the air itself had changed shape.

For a moment he did not speak. Then his jaw tightened.

"What did you just say?" His voice went low, dangerous.

David swallowed. "Camila came to me and confessed."

Jonathan snatched up his racket and slammed it against the asphalt. The crack rang out across the empty courts.

"Do not play with me, David. Do not you dare play with me."

"I am not," David said, voice raw. "I wish to God I was."

Jonathan slammed the racket again. The frame splintered.

"You are telling me my wife cheated on me? And you knew? You have known for a year?"

David's throat burned. "Yes. She begged me not to tell you. I wanted her to tell you herself. I pressed her. She would not. And I could not hold it any longer."

Jonathan's breath came hard. He looked away, then back, eyes wild.

"Say it plain," he said. "Say the words. Tell me it is true."

David's voice dropped to a whisper. "She betrayed you. It happened."

Jonathan's racket slipped from his hand and hit the ground with a hollow clatter.

He did not crumble. He did not cry. Fury took his place like armor.

Not how could she, but how dare she.

How dare Camila stain what he had built with discipline, with loyalty, with sweat. How dare she invite a nameless man into what Jonathan had guarded like sacred ground.

He walked off the court without another word.

By the time Jonathan walked through the door that Saturday evening, his decision had already hardened into something cold.

Camila was in the kitchen preparing dishes for the church social the next day, humming softly, moving with purpose. She looked up, smiled.

"Hey, baby. You hungry?"

"Yes," he said.

She turned back to the counter. "I can heat something up."

"No," he said.

She glanced over her shoulder. "Everything okay?"

"Yes," he answered, and his tone made the word feel like a wall.

Later, he stretched out on the couch in his man cave and let sleep take him there. He did not announce it. He did not make a scene.

Camila barely noticed. She was busy arranging platters, distracted by tomorrow's event, mistaking his silence for tiredness.

On Sunday, Jonathan did not go to church. Camila assumed he wanted to avoid the after service social. She carried on, smiling with friends, accepting compliments, never realizing her husband's anger had already built a wall she could not see.

By Monday morning, Jonathan was gone to Houston for a week long company sponsored hackathon. He left early with a brief kiss on the cheek that felt routine.

The calls that week came only because Camila dialed. Each night his voice reached her from a hotel room, polite but hollow. He answered questions about his day, about the competition, about the team. He did not ask about hers.

No warmth. No playful laughter. No intimacy. Just the cold efficiency of a man who had shut a door and locked it from the inside.

When he returned, Camila met him at the door with genuine relief. She kissed him, asked about his flight, about the hackathon, about the hotel food.

He answered with clipped details, just enough to keep her talking. She carried the conversation like a woman watering dry ground, smiling, trying again and again to coax him into the easy rhythm they had always shared.

She was so glad to have him home that she barely noticed how little he gave in return. She filled the space with chatter until she ran out of breath, pausing and waiting for him to take the thread.

Jonathan looked at her then, really looked at her. Anger was still there, sharp and burning, but something else rose to the surface and drained the heat from his face.

Disappointment.

It hit her like a change in weather.

Camila's smile faltered. "What?" she whispered.

Jonathan did not answer. He stood, turned, and walked out of the room without a word.

The silence he left behind spoke louder than any accusation.

Monday morning, Camila dialed Jonathan's office. She wanted to surprise him, maybe invite him to lunch, maybe smooth whatever wrinkle had passed between them. The receptionist's voice caught her off guard.

"Mr. Reyes did not report to work today."

Camila frowned, thanked her politely, and hung up. She told herself not to overthink it. Maybe he was working remote. Maybe he needed a day.

That evening, Jonathan walked through the door with a warmth she had not seen in weeks. His smile was easy. His kiss lingered. Camila's heart soared. Whatever cloud had shadowed him seemed to have lifted.

They went to their favorite restaurant. They laughed like before. Back home, they curled up on the couch with sports murmuring in the background. Camila pressed against him, and for the first time in days, he held her close.

"I am going to shower," Jonathan said, glancing at her with a look she knew by heart.

Camila followed.

In the hours that followed, they gave all of themselves. It felt like a reunion, raw and consuming, a return to the marriage she had been trying to rescue with smiles and patience.

Afterward, Camila lay against him, convinced the storm had passed. The tenderness in his eyes soothed something in her that had been panicking for weeks.

"I did not want to ruin the moment," she whispered, "but are you okay? You did not go into the office today. I was worried something might be wrong. Health wise, I mean. You have been withdrawn."

Jonathan's hand brushed her hair. His voice was calm, almost gentle.

"I was not at a doctor, Camila. I was at ONDA Law."

The name hit her like ice.

Orsinger, Nelson, Downing and Anderson. High profile divorces. Power cases. The kind of firm people whispered about.

Jonathan's gaze did not waver.

"I started divorce proceedings," he said. "I will be moving into one of the corporate apartments in a few days."

Camila's body went cold. Her mind scrambled, disbelief wrapping around her like a choke.

Jonathan slid out of bed and walked out of the room without another word. A moment later she heard the man cave door close, then the quiet click of the lock.

Camila lay in the dark, staring at the ceiling, breath shallow, as if the room had lost oxygen.

The next day, Camila walked into the church lobby with her heels clicking against the polished floor. The receptionist smiled politely.

"Good morning."

"I need to see Pastor David," Camila said flatly, using his full name instead of the familiar Pastor David.

The receptionist hesitated. "He is in a meeting right now. If you would like, I can"

Camila heard David's voice drifting down the hall, steady and pastoral, as he escorted a couple from his office.

"God bless you both," he said warmly. "Keep leaning on each other."

Camila did not wait. She brushed past the desk, moved down the hallway, and stepped into his office, closing the door behind her.

When David returned, he stopped short in the doorway.

Camila sat in the chair opposite his desk, posture rigid, eyes burning.

"Camila," he said carefully, still holding the doorknob. "I saw you in the lobby."

"I did not come to wait," she replied. "I came to talk."

David set his Bible on the desk, slow and deliberate. The air felt thick.

"You told him," Camila said.

David's brow furrowed. "Told him what?"

"Jonathan," she snapped. "You told him about me."

David's face tightened. "No. I did not betray your confidence. Jonathan came to me while he was in Houston."

Camila blinked, thrown. "What?"

"He asked for counsel," David said. "He wanted a biblical perspective on divorce. We sat in his hotel room. He told me he had made up his mind."

Camila's voice sharpened. "And what did you tell him?"

David's eyes lowered. "I told him what Scripture says. That God hates divorce because it breaks covenant, but He permits it in cases of unfaithfulness. I also spoke about forgiveness and restoration. But Jonathan had already decided. He said when he returned to Dallas, he would file."

Camila's hands curled into fists.

"And you did not think I deserved to know?" she demanded. "You held his secret, but not mine?"

"Camila," David started.

"No," she cut him off, eyes blazing. "I came to you because you were supposed to guide me, protect me, help me find a way back. I trusted you. I begged you to keep my confession in confidence, and you did. But when Jonathan comes to you, suddenly you are the vault. Suddenly you guard his words like treasure."

David's voice cracked. "He asked me not to share. Just as you did."

Camila laughed, bitter and jagged. "The difference is when I bound you with silence, I still had a husband. When he bound you, I lost one."

The room went quiet except for her breathing.

Camila rose, eyes wet with anger.

"You were supposed to be God's man," she said. "But you trespassed too."

She walked out and slammed the door behind her.

David stood in the silence, feeling the words echo through him. Trespassed.

He wanted to argue. Wanted to defend himself with theology and procedure and the rules of pastoral care.

But the truth was he had been living inside compromise for a year.

Shortly after Camila stormed out, Jonathan appeared in David's doorway. His face was steady, unreadable.

"She came to see you," Jonathan said.

David nodded slowly, gesturing for him to sit.

"Jonathan," David began, "are you sure you want to do this? Divorce is final. There is counseling. There are paths toward healing."

Jonathan shook his head once. "My mind will not change."

David leaned forward, searching his friend's eyes. "Why? You are not even willing to try?"

Jonathan's voice stayed calm, but steel ran underneath it.

"Pastor, thank you for flying down to Houston when I asked. I will never forget that. But that was not the most important meeting I had that day."

David frowned. "Your project team?"

Jonathan shook his head.

"Lunch," he said. "I sat with three guys from my stand up team. They started joking about women, pushing me to share. I stayed quiet at first. But even though I was angry with Camila, I still praised her."

Jonathan's jaw tightened.

"I told them she is Latina," he continued, "though her look is so exotic people often think she is Brazilian."

David watched him carefully, feeling something cold gather in the room.

"One of them grinned," Jonathan said. "He said, yes. Our taste in women is quite similar. He said he was in the DFW area a little over a year ago and met an exotic woman like that. He said it was the first time he ever had anonymous sex. He laughed and said it was great."

Jonathan's eyes burned, his voice dropping into a final quiet.

"That is how I knew who it was with, Pastor," Jonathan said. "He was not anonymous at all."

David felt the room tilt, as if the air itself had shifted to make space for what could not be undone. He opened his mouth, but nothing came. There were no verses that could reverse a year. No counsel that could unbreak a covenant once it was exposed to the light.

Jonathan stepped back, not angry now, not loud. Just decided. His face held the quiet of a man who had finished grieving before anyone else realized there was a funeral.

"I used to think the worst part would be the act," he said. "But it is not the act."

He looked at David then, eyes steady.

"It is the way she let me praise her in public. The way she let me build a future on a lie. The way she let me call it perfect."

He exhaled once, controlled.

"You were right about one thing," he added. "There is no such thing as a perfect match."

Jonathan turned toward the hallway. His steps were measured, almost respectful, as if he were leaving a sanctuary.

At the door he paused, his hand on the frame.

"I wanted roots," he said without turning around. "I wanted children. I wanted a home where the truth lived with us."

His voice lowered.

"But truth does not live where it is hidden."

Then he walked out.

David remained standing in the quiet, staring at the Bible on his desk as if it had become heavier in his sight. He had carried Camila's confession like a sealed envelope, believing silence could hold it.

Now he understood what confession really was.

Not an ending.

A breach.

And once a line is crossed, the ground does not return to what it was.

Chapter Twelve

At First Sight

The front door swung open with a sharp thud.

Maria stepped inside and tossed her keys onto the brass tray on the mail table. The sound cracked through the foyer like a gavel. Gil lingered in the doorway, shoulders rounded, moving with the slow shuffle of a boy called to the principal's office. His eyes dropped at once.

Rose petals lay crushed across the hardwood. What had been arranged as welcome now looked like debris, flattened beneath the soles of her shoes.

She kept her back to him as she slid off her coat. It fell to the floor, revealing pink lace chosen with intention. The freckles across her chest and shoulders caught the low light, scattered and striking. He had always loved them.

The lace did not belong with the running shoes still on her feet.

Gil glanced toward the kitchen. A bottle of Moët leaned in its ice bucket. Condensation slid down the glass. The table was half set. A red and white cloth draped the counter.

Anniversary.

Seventeen years.

He had forgotten.

"Do you have any idea," Maria said without turning, "how humiliating it is to drive across town and pick up my husband from a police precinct."

She faced him now.

"Again."

Gil swallowed. His hands hovered near his pockets, unsure where to rest.

"We left Charlotte because of this. We moved here to start over. I fought for this house. For this neighborhood. For some dignity." Her voice sharpened. "And tonight, of all nights."

"I'm sorry," he began.

"Do not."

The word landed hard.

"Sorry does not erase exhaustion. It does not erase embarrassment. I am tired, Gil."

She stepped into the living room.

"Do you even remember what tonight was supposed to be?"

She did not wait for his answer. She gestured toward the petals at his feet.

"Seventeen years, and you could not give me one night."

"It won't happen again."

"It already has. Over and over."

She stepped closer.

"You promised me when we moved here. You promised you were finished with this. And tonight I am sitting in a precinct lobby staring at your name on a clipboard."

Her voice dropped.

"Do you think I deserve that?"

He said nothing.

"And the worst part," she continued, "is that you called me. You dragged me into it. Do you know what I looked like running into that building dressed like this?"

Her hand swept toward the front of the house.

"These neighbors do not even use curtains. Glass everywhere. Everything on display. And you still could not stop yourself."

"You just had to stand there watching until someone called the police."

The truth rooted him silent.

"You need help," Maria said. "Not apologies. Not promises. A psychologist. A program. Something real."

She held his eyes.

"Because I will not do this anymore."

The ice in the bucket hissed softly.

"If you refuse to get help, I will call this marriage what it already is."

Her voice did not rise.

"Over."

Silence filled the house.

Maria turned and walked down the hall. The bedroom door closed. Not a slam this time. A decision.

Gil remained in the foyer. He looked at the petals pressed into the wood like bruises. He reached down and brushed one with his fingertips, then pulled back.

He did not deserve to touch what she had laid down for him.

Seventeen years. No children. She had wanted them once. He had stalled. Excused. Delayed. Maybe he feared responsibility. Maybe he knew something in him would never be steady enough.

Maria believed in vows. In permanence. In him.

And he had given her precincts and promises.

He loved her. That part was true. He loved the freckles across her chest. The careful locs she tended with patience. The way she believed in things.

But he also loved the distance. The watching. The quiet thrill of seeing without being seen.

That first moment had branded him.

He had been thirteen, crouched near a chain link fence in late summer heat. A woman stepped into the yard next door, unaware, urgent. The sound of water striking dirt. Her head tilting back. The fact that she did not know she was seen.

It was not lust.

It was trespass.

The doorway into something hidden.

And once he crossed that threshold, he never quite stepped back.

Upstairs a drawer slid shut. Maria was still there. Present. Real.

He would have to answer her.

Therapy. Help. Change.

Standing among crushed petals and unopened champagne, he knew the part he could never confess.

He was not sure he wanted to be fixed.

He opened the bottle. The cork cracked through the silence. Foam spilled onto the cloth she had laid out with care.

Upstairs Maria heard it. She closed her eyes.

She came down slowly this time.

"You celebrate alone now?"

He set the glass down.

"You were not thinking," she said. "That is the story of us."

She poured herself a half glass and drank it without ceremony.

"You need help. I cannot carry this."

She left him with quiet.

Morning arrived pale and exposing.

A week later, Gil sat in a clinic waiting room off Peachtree. The carpet smelled faintly of disinfectant. The receptionist handed him a clipboard. He filled it out carefully.

Then he noticed the hallway.

Two open arches.

MEN.

WOMEN.

His pulse quickened.

No doors. No barriers. Just open thresholds.

For the first time, no one was watching him.

And that was the problem.

He stood between the signs, eyes shifting. The men's side was steps away. The women's side glowed with the same pull it always had. Not desire. Not even curiosity.

Trespass.

He moved toward the men's side.

His breath paused.

His body pivoted.

He angled toward the other opening.

Chapter Thirteen

Put Asunder

Journal Entry: Kahrl

October 12th, and our fifth anniversary is just days away. I never thought I'd mark this kind of milestone from a wheelchair. But here we are, still laughing, still surviving, still in love. I keep thinking about everything we've built and everything we've lost. Sometimes I wonder if my body will ever return. And then other times I just thank God I still have her...

"I remember living like this. I still can't believe it though. A Friday night in Buckhead, Del Frisco on Peachtree! This amazing European Bordeaux. Appetizers, steaks on the way, and now you're telling me to save room for the Lemon Deborge Cake? It's a good thing you like curvy women. Safe to say, I now fit the BBW description in every algorithm that matters."

She giggled, leaned in, and kissed him.

He gave her a quick wink and smiled.

She whispered, "Thank you, dear. You've made this girl's dreams come true. At least for a night."

Still grinning, she returned her full attention to her jumbo lump crab cake appetizer.

He reached across the table to brush her hand. "Jahni, you know I love you. You're more than worth the sacrifice."

"This means a lot, Kahrl. I just can't help wondering—how are we paying for all this? I'm tired of the struggle too, but we have to stay smart with the little money we have."

"Listen, girl! It's our anniversary."

It had been three years since Jahni had suggested they make it official with a quick trip to the courthouse. They followed it with a sleek Vinings apartment, back when money wasn't so tight. Now it all felt like a lifetime ago.

Kahrl continued, "We've got our struggles, but I don't want to hear about them tonight. Let's enjoy this dinner, alright?"

Jahni gave a soft laugh.

"Yeah, I got it. Not another word, I promise."

The server arrived just in time with the main course.

"Twelve-ounce filet mignon, medium, for the lady. And a sixteen-ounce New York strip, medium-rare, for you, sir."

"Thank you," they said together.

Kahrl leaned forward, eyes gleaming.

"Jahni, I was gonna wait until dessert, but I know how you worry. So here it is. I've got good news."

"Good news?" She raised an eyebrow, intrigued.

He smiled.

"Do you remember Peyton? My friend from *UGA*?"

"You mean the white guy on your cheer squad?"

Kahrl chuckled.

"Yeah. The white guy. We've stayed in touch since college. He reached out last month with something interesting."

"Interesting how?" she asked, sipping her drink.

"Well, Peyton's doing well. He mentioned an opportunity he thought I'd be perfect for."

"Wait. Is this with his dad's company? I remember his family being loaded."

He chuckled again. "Can I finish? And yes, he's a creative director now. He runs video campaigns for one of his dad's company's media branches."

Smiling, she caught herself. "Sorry. Go ahead."

"Anyway," he said, scooting closer, "he's connected to the Total Package Tour. Ever heard of it?"

She gave him a blank look.

"New Kids on the Block," he clarified with a tiny sigh.

Continuing his explanation, Kahrl let out a breathy laugh.

"The opening acts are Boyz II Men and Paula Abdul. It's a forty-six-city national tour running just under six months, with possible Canadian and European dates down the line. Anyway, they held open auditions here in Atlanta for dancers and..."

"And what?" Jahni asked, eyes wide with curiosity.

"And... you are now having dinner with the principal dancer and associate choreographer for Ms. Paula Abdul!" he said, beaming. "Hoisting and tossing those girls all these years finally paid off. I always knew it would."

He raised his glass. "Here's to dreams coming true."

Their glasses clinked, and Kahrl kept going.

"Rehearsals start next week. We were all given a per diem and allowance for travel and lodging. Since I'm local, tonight's dinner is courtesy of Ms. Abdul's tour budget."

He lifted his glass again, grinning. "Here's to no more broke days."

"I know that's right!" Jahni laughed.

"Speaking of broke days, how much does this gig actually pay?"

Kahrl leaned back, confidence radiating. "Three thousand dollars per performance. Plus, per diem. Plus, a wardrobe allowance."

Their celebration rolled on with another bottle of wine. As the restaurant's closing time crept up on them, Kahrl caught the server's eye and motioned for the check. The server approached, but before the presenter could land, Jahni reached across the table and took it, her fingers brushing his with a grin that lingered longer than it should have.

"Let me see that. Oh, my... $226? And that's *before* the tip? Good thing you're a celebrity now."

She handed the presenter back with a smirk. "All yours."

Kahrl scanned the bill line by line. "Wow, we really celebrated tonight. What kind of tip do you think I should leave?"

With an attitude that reflected Kahrl's earlier display of surliness, Jahni responded, "I think fifteen dollars will do."

Laughingly rolling his eyes, he slipped three crisp hundreds into the folder.

"No change."

Hand in hand, they strolled out, laughter still lingering as they reached the valet stand.

"Ticket, please."

Jahni shook her head, laughing.

"We didn't valet, remember? Parked at the church lot by Maggiano's."

"Guess we had one glass too many."

Arm in arm, they crossed the street toward the Nissan.

As they crossed the street, Kahrl's Nissan sat waiting in the thinning lot. Most of the cars that had been there earlier were gone. A few scattered vehicles remained, along with a lone man in a reflective safety vest, pacing slowly near the far end.

As they got closer, it was clear. A bright yellow wheel clamp was locked onto the front tire

Jahni spoke in frustration. "They booted your car? I can't believe it. You're parked in a legitimate, non-reserved space. What's up with that?"

They approached the car, and Kahrl removed the info card from the driver's side window.

General parking violation. Leaving the premises. Citation fee: $75.

"Seventy-five dollars!" he snapped. "Damn."

Kahrl fumbled for his phone, yanking it from his pocket so hard that the rest of his per diem cash fell to the pavement.

"Here," he said, handing her his phone and quickly stuffing the loose bills back into his pocket. "Just make the call for me."

Turning her back, Jahni dialed the number and began speaking with the parking enforcement agency. As she handled the logistics, Kahrl kneeled to inspect the wheel clamp. He could hear her wrapping up the conversation, finalizing payment and arranging for a roving agent to remove the boot.

Then came her scream.

A sharp, wind-like sound tore through the air, followed by a bone-jarring thud. Jahni's body collapsed a short distance away from him.

His heart pounding, Kahrl turned, only to freeze. A split second later, the air shattered again.

A white-hot bolt of pain tore through his side.

He staggered, reaching for something, anything to hold him upright. But his legs gave out beneath him. Then, darkness.

He came to with a faint voice cutting through the fog.

At first, it was just sound—no words, no shape.

Then something clearer, his name, repeated softly.

A hand brushed his arm.

The scent of antiseptic hung in the air.

He tried to move, but his body felt weighted and distant.

A bright light pressed against his closed eyes. And then, slowly, he remembered the dinner, the street... the pain.

"Kahrl, can you hear me?"

He opened his eyes, blinking until Jahni's silhouette came into focus. Her hair a halo of soft curls against the hospital light.

"Where am I?"

"Piedmont Hospital," she whispered. "They came out of nowhere. They were checking everything in the lot. One of them hit me. I went down hard, but I saw everything."

"You turned... and they shot you. In the back, near your side. They say I've got a concussion. You've been in surgery. But the doctors believe, with time and rehab, you'll come back to yourself."

The weight of it all settling over him, Kahrl exhaled.

"You need your rest, babe."

As his eyelids grew heavy, he murmured,

"Rehearsals... the tour... I need to call the casting agent."

Jahni touched his hand. "Shhh. Just rest, Kahrl. Don't think about anything else right now."

He asked again about the tour, but Jahni didn't answer right away. Her silence told him enough.

The days that followed moved slowly. The first twenty-one days blurred into one long stretch of pain, loneliness, and the kind of silence that says more than words ever could. Jahni spent as much time as she could with Kahrl, but her work schedule and just needing a break from the heavy atmosphere at the Spinal Cord Injury Center where doctors had moved him, gave them plenty of time apart.

Eventually, even the silence started speaking**. Not** with comfort, but with truths neither of them wanted to face. Voices that reminded them how much had changed, how unfair it all felt, and how far they were from the life they used to know. Day twenty-two brought the long-awaited meeting with the neurosurgeon. Jahni walked alongside the physical therapist as he wheeled Kahrl into the consultation room. The neurosurgeon joined them shortly after.

"You were in incredible shape before the injury, and internally you're healing well from the surgery," the doctor said.

"I believe you're ready to begin a daily regimen of physical therapy."

Obviously frustrated, Kahrl asked, "When am I gonna get my legs back? Can you tell me that?"

"Kahrl, we have to take things one day at a time. The bullet caused severe damage to your spinal cord. We were able to repair the internal organ damage, but from a neurological perspective, the prognosis and chance of regaining full use of your legs is very limited."

"Doc, may I speak to you alone?"

"No, I want to stay with you," Jahni interjected.

"Jahni! Please, just give us a moment. Thank you."

The doctor gave a slight nod to the therapist, who gently placed a hand on Jahni's shoulder and escorted her from the room, closing the door behind them.

Kahrl struggled to wheel himself closer to the doctor's table. "Doc, I need you to be honest with me. I can't make a living from this chair. Will I ever walk again? I'm a 27-year-old former cheerleader who dreamed of making it as a professional dancer."

"My body, my athleticism, has always been my way in. I'm married. My wife is young, beautiful, and highly sexual. From where I'm sitting, our lives are over."

"Well, Kahrl, even though this is my specialty, I won't pretend to understand exactly how you feel. I deal in scientific certainties. I'm not here to offer false hope. I would never say never, and there are extremely rare cases where this kind of neurological damage reverses itself, but they're just that, extremely rare."

"You still have a chance for a fulfilling life. It'll just be different. A new normal. It'll take time, but with your drive and discipline, I believe you'll rise to the challenge."

"Well, tell me this, Doc. During therapy this morning, I got excited."

"Excited?"

"Yes. My dick got hard. First time since the shooting. That's gotta mean something, right?"

Kahrl leaned in, his voice low but urgent. "Look, I know you're trained to be clinical, but I'm not built for this chair. This body's all I've ever had. My dick woke up. My legs will follow. I *need* to believe that."

The doctor kept his tone steady. "Kahrl, I deal in science, not miracles. Erections after spinal cord injuries happen for three reasons. Psychogenic—from arousal, reflexogenic reaction to touch, which sounds like your case. And spontaneous—usually triggered by a full bladder."

"It's not unusual, and it doesn't guarantee motor recovery. But I can say this, you *can* still have a fulfilling sex life. Things will change, but they don't have to end. Not for you. Not for Jahni."

That sliver of hope, however small, lit a fire in Kahrl.

With Jahni's support and a chip on his shoulder, he threw himself into therapy. Now labeled a paraplegic, he refused to let the word define him. The same discipline that carried him through years of gymnastics and cheerleading kicked in.

Every sit-up, every lift, every stretch—he attacked it all like he was training for a comeback, not adjusting to a new reality.

Peyton, the old college friend, became a lifeline. He helped secure housing, paid their bills when Kahrl couldn't, even covered the cost of modifying their SUV. Thanks to him, they'd moved into a new wheelchair-accessible apartment.

He still held on to the idea that this wasn't forever. And with anniversary number four around the corner, he and Jahni kept it small—just the two of them, and Peyton, who had become family in all but name.

Peyton arrived early with roses and wine. Jahni greeted him with a peck on the cheek and a rushed goodbye.

"I'm headed to get the steaks. I'll be back. Make yourself at home."

"Happy anniversary, sir," Peyton said with a soft smile, crouching beside Kahrl to kiss his cheek.

"I love you, man."

"I love you too," Kahrl said, his voice catching.

"You saved us. You saved me. It's deeper than friendship at this point. You're like my own soul walking beside me."

"Kahrl, come on. You don't owe me anything. That's what real friends do."

"No, man. You got us in this place, paid bills we had no way to cover. We couldn't have fixed the SUV without you. You kept us afloat when we were drowning. And now Jahni wants to go back and finish her degree, but she's stuck, working a job that barely covers gas, always worrying about me. We just... we can't keep living like this."

"Kahrl, you know I can help with that."

"Brother, I can't keep asking you for more," Kahrl replied, his voice firm but grateful.

"I've got to figure out how to support my family on my own. Disability checks barely cover groceries. But enough about the struggle. I'm glad you're here tonight. Wouldn't feel like a proper celebration without you."

When Jahni returned, she whipped together a hearty dinner, and the evening unfolded with laughter, college memories, and clinking glasses.

"Oh, wow! It's after midnight?" Peyton glanced at his phone. "I'm in no shape to drive. I guess I'll call a rideshare and come back tomorrow for the car."

"You'll do no such thing," Jahni cut in. "We've got towels. You can crash in the guest room."

She glanced toward the hallway. "I know you don't need the roll-in shower, but you'll be sharing the accessible bathroom with Kahrl—it's the only one that's decent for company. He already used it before dinner, so it's all yours."

"Thanks, Jahni," Peyton said, kissing her lightly on the cheek.

"I'll just take a quick rinse, catch a few hours of sleep, and slip out early. I'll leave you two lovebirds to finish your anniversary."

Peyton disappeared into the hallway and awoke later to his phone buzzing—3:33 a.m.

Still groggy, he got dressed and tiptoed down the hall, guided by the faint light spilling from the couple's cracked bedroom door. As he approached, he heard soft moaning. Curious and unsure, he leaned in, intending to say goodbye, but paused.

Jahni's breathy whimper drifted into the hallway. Surprised, Peyton froze, his eyes now unintentionally fixed on the intimate scene unfolding inside.

Peyton heard the sound first. Soft, rhythmic, unmistakably intimate.

He should have turned away.

Instead, he glanced toward the cracked door.

Jahni's body moved in slow arcs against the light. Kahrl's wheelchair sat locked beside the bed, angled with precision. What Peyton witnessed was not desperation. It was choreography. Adaptation. Love finding new pathways.

He stepped back immediately, heat rising to his face.

He had not expected beauty.

He had not expected strength.

He had not expected to feel like the one intruding on something sacred.

Breathless, they held each other, his arms around her, her head tilted back to rest against his shoulder. Then they both froze. Something in the air shifted. They looked towards the door. They weren't alone.

"Oh, my God! I'm so sorry. I was just trying to let you guys know I was leaving," Peyton stammered, backing away from the doorway.

A few seconds later, Jahni, now in her robe, joined him in the living room, still catching her breath but wearing a half-smile.

"Don't worry about it, Peyton. You're safe."

They both chuckled, easing the tension.

"So..." Peyton began, "where do we go from here?"

"Well, sir," Jahni replied with a sly grin, "I don't know about you, but I'm headed for a shower. You might as well stay the night. Keep your friend company. He loves to talk after sex. Me? I'm just good for the bed right now."

She called out on her way back to the bedroom. "Kahrl, go talk to your friend. I think we scared him."

Still nude, Kahrl wheeled himself into the living room. "You good, dude? You're standing there like you've seen a ghost. Give me a sec—I'm gonna freshen up real quick. Like she said, might as well crash here tonight."

He disappeared into the hallway bathroom. When Kahrl returned, the towel around his waist, Peyton still looked sheepish.

"Kahrl, I'm really—"

"Man, you're good. I told you that. I hope we didn't scar you for life. As you saw, we do things a little differently now. Gotta work with what we got."

Peyton gave a nervous laugh. "Well, me having never been with a woman, *everything* is done differently."

They both laughed, and Kahrl offered him a fist bump.

"You two aren't hiding," Peyton said carefully.

"Most people would. You aren't ashamed. That's powerful."

He hesitated.

"What if that's the business? Not sex. Not shock value. Education. Visibility. You showing couples that injury doesn't end intimacy."

Kahrl leaned back.

"You think people would pay to watch a paraplegic love his wife?"

"I think people would pay to believe it's still possible."

Over breakfast, he laid it out carefully. Jahni listened, quiet but not closed off. When he finished, she surprised them both.

"I'm in," she said. "If we're gonna do this, let's do it right. If we can show people that love and passion don't have to end with injury, then maybe it's worth it."

Her voice trembled slightly, but her eyes were steady.

And so, *Kahrl and Jahni's Dreamtime* was born. Not out of desperation, but out of defiance. A refusal to be invisible.

With Peyton's crew behind the camera, they launched the site with intention, paying attention to lighting, angles, scripts, and consent at every step. Their vulnerability became their value, and their connection became their currency.

They told their story publicly first. The more intimate content was offered through subscription, for those who wanted to go deeper. The raw, the intimate, the real, shared with care, not shame. Social media buzzed. Within a year, they had built a loyal following. Some watched to learn, others to hope, still others just to be moved by something real.

Combined monthly revenue now gave them room to breathe.

But more than money, what they built was proof. Love adapts. Desire survives. And dignity, if fiercely protected, can turn even pain into power.

Wedding anniversary number five found Jahni living her dream. She'd finally enrolled in the University of Georgia's satellite program in Atlanta. As they had done for the past two years, the couple celebrated their anniversary at home, sharing dinner with the one person who had helped them hold everything together, Peyton.

This year's highlight was the purchase of a plot of land where their custom-designed and build their fully accessible home. They had completed the plans, and the future they'd shaped together felt more real with each passing day.

After dinner, as the laughter settled into soft conversation and Peyton excused himself for the night, Jahni glanced across the room. She noticed Kahrl's bare feet resting on the elevated footplates of his motorized wheelchair.

"Oh, my goodness," she said with a chuckle. "All this traveling and celebrating, I'm behind on my pedicure duties. Those eagle talons need some attention."

She walked over, grabbed the manicure kit from the closet, and kneeled beside him. With loving ease, she lifted his left foot from the rest and began massaging it gently. Kahrl let out a soft moan, half-laughter, half-relief.

But something in his voice made her pause. She met his eyes, playful at first, then puzzled. She reached into the kit and pulled out the pointed nail file. She pressed it gently against the arch of his foot.

He flinched. Not a reflex. But a response. They froze.

Jahni looked up slowly.

Kahrl did not breathe.

The room went silent in a way that felt louder than the shooting ever had.

Journal Entry: Jahni, Epilogue

I always believed in Kahrl's healing—maybe not the kind that brings back nerve endings and movement, but the kind that lets a man rebuild his life with dignity. For a long time, that was enough. We adjusted. There was joy. And somehow, we made our own kind of magic in the cracks of the broken places.

But last night, something shifted.

He felt it.

I watched it land in his eyes—confusion first, then fear, then wonder. And just like that, the world opened up a little wider. We didn't cry right away. We just stared at each other, like two people standing at the edge of something sacred. A beginning disguised as a tiny flinch.

I don't know what comes next. Maybe it was a one-time nerve spark. Maybe it's the start of something bigger.

But whatever it is, I know this: we're not the same as we were. Not broken, not waiting. Just two people still choosing each other—still daring to believe that even the impossible has a right to knock on our door.

And sometimes, it does.

Chapter Fourteen

Leafless

Base coat

The swelling had gone down, but the bruise around his eye and nose still held its color, stubborn as memory. When Jacksyn's gloved thumb grazed too close to the bridge of his nose, he flinched and leaned his head back. A split lip completed the evidence of last night's activities.

With confident precision, she brushed foundation across the Corporal's face. Her kit spread across the portable counter like a medic's field tray: powders, sponges, a palette of concealment, each tool with a job and a clean place to return to.

Across the studio, Amelia adjusted her lighting rig. A low hum filled the room, the camera's idle sound a quiet counterpoint to everything neither woman asked.

"You're a few days shy of thirty," Jacksyn said.

"You'd think by now you'd be done proving your manhood in barroom brawls, Mr. Retired Corporal."

"Pretty sure our agreement only covers you making me look good," he replied, voice pleasant, measured, controlled.

"Or does the full-service package come with lectures now?"

She deepened her voice and gave him a mock salute. "Yes, Corporal."

Then, softer, as her brush moved under his eye: "Hold your chin up a little more, please. Concealer can handle the bruise. That nose is going to take real magic. Lucky for you, I'm a miracle worker."

He was one of her favorite clients. Handsome, well-built. Not quite six feet, but his body and his smile made up for it. The high-and-tight military cut showcased brushed-in waves and a premature patch of gray near his front hairline. She enjoyed pushing his buttons just to hear him speak.

That voice, rooted in Brooklyn, sanded smooth by years in a working-class neighborhood in Montreal, was hard to resist. A Canadian transplant to Atlanta, he carried dual citizenship and the quiet discipline of someone who had seen things and learned to bear them.

Pain catalogs itself quietly. Eye tender. Nose swollen. Lip split. Makeup is a field dressing with better storytelling. It doesn't heal. It edits.

With his chin still lifted, Jacksyn leaned back to admire her work. With a few additional strokes of her brush, she beamed.

"Voilà."

She peeled the paper kerchief from beneath his black hooded robe.

"Alright," she said, flashing a smirk. "Let's take the shine off that body."

He stood, let the robe slip from his shoulders, and tossed it onto the back of the empty director's chair.

"Full body today?" she asked, dusting powder across his chest.

"Yes. Full frontal." He kept his gaze where it belonged—up and away. "I suggested the red towel, but the promo team wants the Santa cap and those ridiculous socks only."

She laughed. "It's kind of hard to get in the Christmas mood in the middle of May. But Amelia's a magician behind the lens.

I'm sure she can convince them a red towel says holiday just fine."

Maintaining professionalism while kneeling in front of his nude body was always a challenge. Not because she couldn't keep her hands steady. Because she could, she had learned how.

"Oh, my—you've got a scar," she said, brushing a finger near the mostly healed laceration on his abdomen.

Without asking where it came from, she added, "I'll take care of that for you."

Inventory check: bruises, cuts, scars. Cover is not concealment. Wounds announce themselves even when the face looks perfect.

"Good work," he said softly, still not looking down.

"Looks like it never happened."

Amelia poked her head around the partition. "Everything's set up. You ready, Corporal?"

"I am."

He made eye contact with her as he walked by. The makeup artist winked; the photographer returned the gesture, an unspoken agreement that everything from his look to his attitude was spot-on. Then he disappeared behind the partition to the set.

He slowed his breathing the way he'd been trained. In through the nose. Out through the mouth. Longer out than in. Pain always receded once it was named and set aside.

He stepped into the lights leafless, but never unguarded. Nakedness was part of the act. What the crowd saw was skin and muscle. What they never saw was the discipline behind his eyes. Guarded was survival.

Aftercare

Thirty-seven miles later, the Corporal turned onto his quiet street off Windy Hill Road. Eager for ritual, he parked on the street and hurried up the driveway. Music pulsed from inside the house.

He rolled his eyes. Not today.

Detouring to the side entrance, he found the laundry-room door already cracked open.

"Well, well, well... if it isn't the supermodel himself."

Didi said it like a joke, but her eyes didn't laugh. She leaned against the dryer with a glass in hand. Even with smeared make-up and a sweatsuit that looked slept-in, she was striking. Statuesque and Afro-Cuban, she stood two inches taller than him. Her mother named her Deidre; her grandmother's love of German meant everyone called her Didi.

"Didi," he said, keeping his tone even, "just step aside. I need a shower."

"Why?" she asked, lifting her chin. "I can already smell her on you."

He inhaled, steadily.

Rules of engagement: de-escalate. Don't return fire. There are battles you win by refusing to swing.

"You're drunk," he said. "And I don't have time for this today. Alexa, music off."

The bass died mid-beat. Silence rushed in like cold air.

She let him pass, then dashed what remained of her cognac across his cheek.

He froze.

"I'll be in the shower," he muttered. "You should consider the same."

The annex spa was his sanctuary of acoustic panels, soft light, jars lined with military precision. He unscrewed the Noxzema, washed away the makeup, and watched the water take the story down the drain. He filled the freestanding tub and poured in vanilla-rose oil. Candles flickered. Vanessa Williams's "Constantly" floated in the background.

Steam rose slowly, softening the edges of the day. He let himself sink beneath the surface and counted his breathing the way he always did—longer out than in—until the ache dulled and his pulse slowed.

If he could make himself still enough, quiet enough, then nothing was exposed. He wasn't leafless.

He was simply clean.

Forty-five minutes later he woke in tepid water, climbed out, and wrapped himself in a sleeveless black robe. Concern tugged harder than avoidance. He walked down the hall, peeked into the bedroom—empty. Upstairs, he found her slumped in the massage chair, passed out.

From the weapons closet, he pulled an old army blanket, draped it over her shoulders, removed the bottle from her limp hand, and kissed her forehead before leaving.

He moved through the house carrying all of it at once, the caregiver, the protector, and the one quietly absorbing the damage. He had always treated vows like orders, and orders were what kept you alive. Until they didn't.

With the tension eased, he rolled out a mat for yoga, then streamed a few vintage episodes of *The Wire* until sleep came easily.

Tomorrow will bring another argument. Tonight, there was only stillness.

Three miles

Wednesday morning arrived in typical Southern fashion, the sun streaming through open windows, a soft spring breeze stirring the curtains. It pulled him from sleep just as he felt her presence hovering nearby.

"Good morning," she said, voice careful. "Did you sleep well?"

He covered his mouth with his hand, the gesture half yawn, half shield.

"You feel better now?"

She dodged with a smile that didn't reach her eyes.

"It's beautiful out. Wanna go for a quick run?"

Her fingers brushed his cheek, soft where they'd been sharp the day before. He kissed her palm.

"Didi, I'm sorry for yesterday. I should've called to check on you. A run sounds good."

Three miles was nothing to them. He had once been a sprinter, an Olympic hopeful. She'd dominated college middle-distance races. They moved in perfect rhythm, stride for stride, looping the path near Circle 75 and nodding to the other regulars. Within half an hour they were back where they started, sweaty but calm.

Their strides matched without effort, breath settling into the same rhythm. For a moment, they looked like the kind of couple people picture when they talk about forever. Moving together like that, it was easy to forget what didn't fit.

The drive home was silent, but not tense. Just still.

In their bathroom, he turned on both showerheads while she queued up the playlist. Her auburn waves tumbled down her back as she stepped in beside him.

"Hey now—that's why I turned on both showerheads," he joked, lathering his pouf.

She didn't move. Instead, she pressed her body against his back, teasing his earlobe with her tongue. Her hands slid slowly across his abs. He covered one with his own, guiding it lower. His body responded fast, grateful and familiar.

He still wanted her. That had never been the problem.

When he turned to face her, their mouths met in steam-heavy kisses—comfort and hunger braided together. He lifted her, her legs wrapping around him with the ease of a woman who knew exactly where she belonged. The water, the rhythm, the music—a symmetry that made life feel simple for a moment.

Afterward, he held her close, eyes locked on hers, as if holding the gaze could hold the marriage.

"I love you more than anyone or anything," he whispered.

She said nothing. She let her hands fall away and moved under the other showerhead, rinsing off, hair slicked back, with an unreadable expression.

The words landed between them and went nowhere. She kept rinsing her hair.

He stayed quiet, turned away, and resumed scrubbing. By the time she finished her routine—washed, dried her hair—he was already dressed. They crossed paths again in the hallway; she was wrapped in a towel, he in street clothes.

"Headed somewhere?" she asked.

"Not urgent," he said. "The team's got a new DJ. She sent some mixes. I want to review them before tonight's show. You need something?"

Her tone sharpened. "Do I need something? Is that a real question?"

"Didi—"

"Well, Colonel Sulaimon Harrison-King," she snapped, the full name like a slap. "Maybe the something I need is for my husband to actually be here with me!"

The temperature in the room shifted. He did what he always did, kept calm, careful not to fan the flames.

"So, you can be with me, be inside me, and then walk out like it's nothing?"

My silence is not weakness; it's the only armor I have left.

She flung the towel onto the couch. Naked now, voice rising.

"What is this, a scene from *Fatal Attraction*? Do I look deranged to you? A new DJ—that's your excuse? She must be really important."

He knelt in front of her, voice soft, hands open like surrender.

"If you want me to stay, I'll stay. You know how I make our money. Who we were then, who we are now. It's work. What we have at home... that's what matters."

She pressed a finger to his forehead.

"I hate you," she said, voice thin. "Just go."

"Didi—"

"Just go!"

He stood, gave her one last look, then walked out. The door clicked, and gently shut behind him, just before something shattered against it from the inside.

They could run three miles in perfect rhythm and still not find their way through a single conversation.

Backing his car out of the garage, he gave a short nod to the landscaper at the gate. The man was tall and athletic, shirt stretched across his shoulders as he tested the latch like it had personally offended him.

"You might want to tell your husband this thing's sticking again," he called out, still rattling it.

Didi appeared at the end of the driveway, drink already in hand. Sunlight caught the curve of her collarbone. She did not look at her husband first.

"He knows," she said evenly.

The landscaper let the gate fall shut, metal ringing once before settling.

"It's not the first time."

Her eyes lingered on him a second longer than necessary. Not smiling. Not apologizing either.

"If it bothers you that much, Diogo," she said, voice low, "you own half the street. Fix it."

He finally looked at her then. Slow. Assessing.

"I fix what's mine," he said.

The latch clicked.

House lights

The venue smelled of pine cleaner and fresh paint, the kind of detail Ellie always insisted on before a show. She strode across the stage, headset snug, laptop open, lights flickering into sequence.

"Corporal, meet Ellie," Jacksyn said with a grin. "I've told her all about you."

The passenger door of the rental truck swung open. A woman who looked like Jacksyn stepped out.

"Wow," he said. "Twins?"

Ellie laughed. "Not quite. I'm the knee baby. Dad wanted all boys, so he gave us sons' names—Elyot and Jacksyn. Mom got creative with the spelling."

He smiled. "I like that."

Ellie powered up her turntables, testing beats against the rigged lights.

"The lights are mine too," she added. "We run a full-service setup. Each entertainer pays the stage fee and keeps their tips."

"What's the door price?" he asked.

"Enough to pack the house," Ellie said. "Trust me, with me on the decks, you'll pull three grand easy."

Jacksyn chimed in, smoothing stray strands of hair into her bun. "And don't forget, security's ours too. It's all one show."

Stage prep smells like deployment prep. Same hum of cables, same inventory check. Except this time the weapon is me.

Later, at Taco Mac, Jacksyn leaned across the table.

"So, Corporal in the Canadian Army? Did your parents see that coming and name you Colonel?"

"Not exactly," he replied. "My mother was a fan of Colonel Abrams. Unique names aren't a problem for your family, either."

She smirked. "Is that really what you think I wanted to ask you?"

He met her eyes. "Ask."

"What's the story between you and Deidre?"

His smile thinned. "I wasn't aware you knew much about either of us."

"Relax. I'm curious."

He took a sip of water, then said it with a quiet certainty he rarely offered anyone.

"She's the love of my life. Always has been. Every other relationship was just a lesson on how to find her."

The words landed harder than he intended. Jacksyn laughed it off, but something in her chest tightened.

Back at the venue, Ellie's beats rolled through the speakers, sharp and pulsing. Jacksyn lingered near the side of the stage, brushes tucked away. The Corporal stepped into the lights, smile precise, muscles gleaming, body transformed into a symbol.

The crowd roared.

Jacksyn whispered, "House lights up. Guard down."

The shine stayed on the stage. He made sure of that.

Thirteen

The show wrapped close to midnight. Even with three other names on the flyer, it was clear who the crowd came for. He signed autographs, posed for photos, and slipped into street clothes with the practiced efficiency of someone who knew how to leave without lingering.

At the bar, as he lifted his bag from the stool, the strap slipped. The bag tipped, scattering its contents across the floor. A towel. A water bottle. A folded clip of cash.

"Damn," he muttered, crouching quickly to gather everything before eyes could settle too long.

He patted his pockets out of habit.

Empty.

The wallet was gone.

Thirty minutes later, headlights washed across his driveway. The garage door was already lifting. Didi sat naked on the stairs just inside, her head bowed, hair falling forward like a curtain pulled halfway closed.

"Didi," he said, moving toward her.

She looked up slowly. Her eyes were glassy, unfocused, her breath heavy with alcohol.

"Oh," she said. "You're home."

He knelt and lifted her chin, careful, gentle. "Let's get you inside."

Another set of headlights swept the drive, paused, then cut off. A car door closed somewhere behind him.

"Colonel," a voice called out. "You dropped this."

Jacksyn stood near the garage, his wallet in her hand, the porch light catching the edges of her face.

He turned sharply. "What are you doing here?"

"You left it at the bar. I checked the ID and figured I should bring it back."

"No," he said, too fast. He steadied himself. "Thank you. But we don't need help."

He took the wallet without looking at it. He lifted Didi into his arms and carried her inside, leaving Jacksyn standing alone in the driveway, the garage light still humming above her.

The house was dark. Silent in a way that felt arranged.

He set Didi gently on the sofa. Her hand brushed his arm as he straightened. She did not open her eyes.

He turned toward the foyer.

Something moved behind him.

The first blow landed hard against his cheek. Light burst white. He staggered, instinct lifting his arms too late. A second strike crushed into his shoulder. A third drove into his ribs and folded him inward.

He never heard footsteps. Never heard a voice.

Only close and breath.

A final impact struck the back of his head, precise and devastating.

The floor rushed up.

When he woke, the world was fluorescent and narrow. A nurse practitioner leaned close, her hands steady as she tied the final suture.

"Thirteen stitches," she said. "You're lucky."

She ran through the list without drama. Concussion. Bruised ribs. No fractures. Light activity only.

"You're in excellent shape," she added. "But don't test it."

Later, at reception, he paid without comment. The clerk glanced up as she handed him the paperwork.

"I didn't work last night," she said, smiling. "But my sister did. She said you were incredible. Fifty of those dollars were hers."

He returned the smile automatically.

Outside, the night air cut clean and sharp.

As he sat in the car, fragments began to align.

The silence in the house.

The timing of the second car.

The way the blows came from behind.

The precision.

The lack of panic.

And then the detail that would not leave him.

The smell.

Fresh-cut grass and earth.

The faint chemical bite of fertilizer.

Diogo's hands had smelled like that earlier in the week when they shook at the gate. Tall. Athletic. Smiling too easily. Talking about the latch that stuck.

He closed his eyes.

Didi had been waiting on the stairs.

The house had been empty on purpose.

He had been meant to walk inside alone.

The applause from the night before felt distant now, unreal. The stitches pulled when he smiled, so he stopped trying.

What followed celebration was always quiet.

This time, the quiet told the truth.

Range

The glass doors of Sharp Shooters whispered shut behind him. The air inside smelled like gun oil and cordite, clean in its own way. He signed in, loaded his bag onto the counter, and scanned the rental forms.

Inventory check: pistol, ammo, targets.

"Colonel?"

He turned. Jacksyn stood there, red carrying case slung over her shoulder, eyes alight with surprise.

"I'm the one who's surprised," he said. "Didn't know you were a shooter."

She grinned. "Another well-kept secret. Looks like our lanes are side by side. Want to double up? Loser buys lunch."

"I wouldn't do that to you," he said, smirking. "Marksman, you know."

"I've been shooting a while," she replied, snapping goggles into place. "You should've taken the time to get to know me."

The first shots cracked like thunder in a canyon. They fell into a rhythm: load, aim, fire, reload.

Targets don't talk back. Targets don't cry in showers. Targets just fall when you hit them.

When the smoke cleared, she had outscored him.

"Hubris doesn't suit you," she teased. "Take the loss."

He raised his hands. "Okay. You win."

Admitting defeat is easier when it's paper silhouettes. Harder when it's love.

At The Vortex, they sat by the window with burgers and salt-rimmed drinks. Conversation came easily, lighter than it should have been. He opened up more than expected, talking about Didi, about loving someone whose demons sometimes arrived with fists, about vows he still treated like orders.

Jacksyn listened. Said little. Her quiet felt like space, not pressure.

His phone buzzed. Didi's voice floated through the receiver—calm, casual, a rare moment of peace. She was meeting friends, wouldn't be home 'til late.

When he hung up, Jacksyn leaned back, eyes steady.

"So," she said, "free for a little longer?"

"Looks that way."

"Then let's call this a draw," she replied. "And see where the night goes."

Leafless

Jacksyn's condo smelled faintly of lavender and citrus cleaner, the kind of cozy she'd bragged about when showing him around. Six units total, only two occupied. Safe, she'd said, tapping the lock.

Now the lock clicked behind them, and the quiet felt heavy with choice.

He stood near the balcony door, watching twilight paint the city in streaks of orange and violet. Behind him, she moved through the kitchen, pulling down two glasses. Ice cracked. A bottle tipped.

"Help yourself to a nightcap," she called.

He shook his head with a faint smile. "It's barely eight."

"Then call it a preview," she shot back, voice lilting, playful, carrying the kind of invitation she rarely voiced outright.

The shower hissed alive down the hall. Her laughter followed, muffled by the walls.

"You okay out there?" she called.

"I'm good," he answered too quickly.

Too good. Too free. This isn't the man I'm supposed to be.

Steam curled into the hallway. He stripped without thinking, as if his body had been waiting for permission longer than his conscience could admit. One push and the plexiglass door slid wide.

Startled, she gasped, lather slick across her skin. "You're getting water on my floor, sir."

He stepped in without a word. Lifted her easily. She clung, thighs strong around his waist, back arching as his mouth found her neck.

His eyes remained closed.

Eyes shut means control. Eyes open means consequence.

He carried her out, still holding her, through the hall and into the kitchen. Steam trailed behind them like a confession. The balcony door banged against its frame. Cool night air rushed in, raising goosebumps on their skin.

She caught her breath against his ear as he pressed her back toward the railing.

"Wait—" she whispered, half fear, half thrill.

The rail was slick with humidity.

He knew that.

He tightened his grip anyway, jaw clenched, as if discipline could keep gravity from doing what it always does.

Choice is rarely loud. It is usually one small step too far.

A gasp cut through the night.

Not hers.

His eyes snapped open.

Two figures stood below by the pool, water dripping, moonlight shining off bare shoulders and wet skin.

Didi.

And Diogo.

Shock surged through him. Through her. Her grip faltered, her balance lost in a fraction of a second.

She fell.

Hair whipping, limbs flailing, body flipping in the air like a marionette cut loose.

The crack of concrete silenced everything.

"Jacksyn!" His scream tore out of him, unfiltered and useless.

Naked, unguarded, he bolted down the stairs and through the gate, dropped to his knees, cradling her head. Blood smeared across his hands and chest, warm and immediate.

"Stay with me," he pleaded, voice breaking. Her eyelids fluttered once, then stilled again.

He looked up.

Didi's face hovered between horror and something like recognition. Diogo stood just behind her, frozen, one hand half-raised as if he might step forward and didn't know if he was allowed.

Didi's voice shook. "Is she... is she okay?"

Leafless. No mask, no vow, no camouflage. Only truth, exposed in blood and concrete.

Aftermath

Blood doesn't blend the way makeup does. It spreads. It declares.

He pressed two fingers to her neck. Pulse—thin, present. He bent to her mouth. Breath—ragged, wet at the edges.

"Call 911!" he shouted toward the fence without looking up.

"I'm calling," Didi stammered, fumbling the phone.

The operator's voice crackled through the speaker.

"Nine-one-one, what's your emergency?"

He took the phone from her, voice steady by force.

"Adult female fell from a second-story balcony. Unconscious. She's breathing. Pulse present. Possible head trauma."

"Keep her still," the operator instructed. "Do not move her neck. Is there bleeding?"

"Yes," he answered, scanning. A red ribbon pooled beneath her hairline. Another trickled along her shoulder. He pressed a towel gently against the back of her head. "Controlling."

"Is she responsive?"

"Minimal," he said. "Eye flutter."

Inventory: airway, breathing, circulation. Don't count the sins in front of you. Count the seconds.

The siren sound grew, Doppler swelling, blue and red washing the stucco in violent pulses. EMTs moved through the gate with a backboard and a jump bag.

Questions came quick. Gloves. Commands. Collar click. Straps drawn tight.

"What's her name?"

"Jacksyn."

"How far did she fall?"

"Second story."

He watched their hands like a man watching a ritual he could not interrupt.

"Family?" someone asked him.

He opened his mouth. Closed it.

"No."

The stretcher rolled out. He followed until the gate, then stopped long enough to look back.

Didi stood by the pool, arms wrapped around herself. Diogo hovered beside her, silent, watching the ambulance as if it carried a verdict.

Didi took a step toward him, and her voice came out thin. "I didn't see you."

He stared at her, then looked away.

In the beginning, we learned to hide with leaves. Anything to cover what we had done.

Tonight, there were none.

He climbed into the ambulance.

Hospital

The ICU waiting area smelled faintly of antiseptic and old coffee. A television played muted weather over a map of Georgia.

Tiny raindrops marched across counties he had driven through a hundred times without noticing.

He sat forward in the molded chair, forearms on his thighs, hands laced so tightly his knuckles blanched.

He had cleaned most of the blood from his chest, but not all of it. A faint rust-colored shadow remained along his collarbone.

When the elevator doors opened, he didn't look up at first.

He knew her walk.

Didi didn't rush. She didn't cry out. She didn't search the room frantically the way people do when panic needs an audience. She stepped into the waiting area and stopped.

No makeup. No liquor. Just fatigue.

He stood.

"You didn't have to come," he said.

Her eyes moved past him, toward the double doors. "I know."

She sat across from him, not beside him. Close enough to speak without raising her voice. Far enough to make the distance visible.

"How is she?" Didi asked.

"Skull fracture," he answered. "Bleeding. They're watching the swelling."

Didi nodded once. Her fingers tightened on the strap of her purse.

He waited for an accusation. For fury. For a question that demanded the parts of truth he didn't want to speak.

It didn't come.

Instead, she said quietly, "You were always careful."

Not accusing. Remembering.

"I was," he replied.

Past tense.

A nurse stepped through the door. "Harrison-King?"

He rose automatically.

Didi did not.

"I'll wait," she said.

He turned slightly, as if expecting her to follow. She stayed seated, eyes on the doors, not on him.

He nodded and followed the nurse.

The ICU room hummed softly with machines that breathed in steady intervals. Jacksyn lay beneath sterile light, bandage threaded through her hairline. Tubing curved around her face. Her chest rose and fell in careful rhythm.

No stage lights.

No music.

No laughter.

Just consequence.

He stood at the foot of the bed and saw his reflection faintly in the distorted, thin glass of a cabinet door.

He had kept his eyes closed on the balcony.

He had known the rail was slick.

He had known risk when he felt it in his palms.

He had chosen it anyway.

Leafless was never about nakedness. It was about awareness.

And now he was fully aware.

He did not whisper an apology. Did not promise. Did not bargain with God. He simply looked at her and let the moment accuse him without words.

After a while, he stepped back into the hallway.

Didi was still in her chair.

She looked up. "How is she?"

"Stable," he said.

Didi nodded.

Silence again. A long one.

He could walk over. Sit beside her. Take her hand. Speak. Explain. Try.

He did not move.

Didi watched him for a moment, then gave the smallest nod—not permission, not forgiveness. Just acknowledgment.

Then she looked away.

That was when he felt it.

Not anger.

Loss.

Not the kind that arrives with slammed doors, but the kind that thins the air slowly until you realize you have been breathing something else entirely.

She had been standing beside him for years.

Tonight she was sitting across from him.

Not gone.

Just no longer aligned.

The nurse called from down the hall, asking him to sign a form.

He took a step forward.

Then stopped.

For a brief second, he imagined lowering himself into the chair beside Didi. Shoulder to shoulder, no defense. Saying something honest.

He did not.

Instead, he walked toward the nurse.

Behind him, Didi remained seated.

Alone.

Outside the hospital, wind moved through the ornamental trees lining the parking lot.

Their branches were bare.

Not broken.

Not dead.

Just exposed.

And for the first time in years, he did not reach for anything to cover himself with.

He simply stood there.

Leafless.

Afterword On Being Leafless

The title ***Leafless*** is intentional.

In Genesis, after Adam and Eve became aware of their nakedness, they covered themselves with fig leaves. The leaves were not simply about modesty. They were about protection. About hiding. About the instinct to cover what had just been exposed.

Leafless, then, is not about nudity. It is about what remains when the covering fails.

Throughout this story, the stage becomes a place of performance. Skin is currency. Applause is affirmation. But performance is not the same as exposure. One can be fully visible and still guarded. One can be admired and still unseen.

The Corporal believes discipline is his covering. Didi believes desire is hers. Jacksyn believes proximity might become intimacy. Diogo believes ownership gives him leverage. Each character hides behind something—training, beauty, ambition, power. But when consequence arrives, none of those coverings hold.

The fall is not simply physical. It is moral. Relational. Spiritual. It is the moment when awareness replaces illusion.

In writing this story, I was less interested in who was wrong and more interested in what is revealed when we can no longer pretend. Exposure is uncomfortable. Sometimes humiliating. Often clarifying.

In the beginning, leaves were chosen to conceal shame. In this story, there are no leaves left to reach for.

What remains is truth.

And truth, once seen, cannot be unseen.

Chapter Fifteen

Little Girl

"Jay, you need to get up. If you're keeping the car, Mama's gonna need a ride to work."

His sister stood in the doorway like she owned the whole hallway. Not tall enough to block light, not heavy enough to make a presence, but somehow she did both. She had that gift, the kind that came from being underestimated your whole life and learning how to weaponize it.

She didn't knock.

Of course she didn't.

Jay rolled over, pulled the sheet higher, and spoke without opening his eyes.

"Get out."

She leaned against the frame and smiled as if she had all day.

"I really wish you'd start sleeping in drawers. Or a robe. Or a towel. Something. Anything. 'Cause this right here," she waved at the bed like she was presenting a crime scene, "this is not godly."

Jay sat up, the sheet slipping just enough for her to make a sound.

"Shut up. Stop gawking. And get out of my room. And on your way out, learn how to knock!"

She didn't flinch because she enjoyed this. She enjoyed him.

As his vision adjusted, he finally looked at her. That petite outline and that light voice didn't match her age. Nothing about her matched what she was supposed to be. Turner syndrome had done its work early. It had stunted her growth, softened her features, and kept her looking younger than the calendar insisted.

Strangers saw a middle schooler. Jay saw his little sister, and he hated that the world treated her like a child. He hated that he sometimes did too.

"Maybe if you came in on time," she said, "you could get up on time. You only stay out late because you know Mama's stuck working doubles."

"I stay out late because I'm grown," Jay snapped, swinging his legs off the bed. "Now get out, *Little Girl!*"

That name landed the way it always did. Little Girl.

A nickname or a joke, sure. But also a reminder, as if her body's betrayal needed help doing damage. He used it when he was irritated. But he also used it when he was protective. And he used it when he didn't know what else to say.

She crossed her arms, chin lifting like she was his mother and his teacher at the same time.

"Jay," she said, slower now. "Who was that guy?"

Jay froze for half a second, then kept moving as if he hadn't heard her.

"What guy?"

"The older one in the Monte Carlo," she said. "Alonzo, Training Day style. He dropped you off near Covington and Redan last night. I saw it when I went to get a Coke."

Jay stopped pulling on his sweats and looked at her.

"I don't know what you think you saw."

"Oh, I saw it," she said, eyes bright. "I've seen you talking to him before, too."

She grinned, testing him, enjoying the way his irritation sharpened into something else.

"He's fine," she added, dragging the word out like candy. "Especially for somebody in his forties. I was just asking 'cause I might want to talk to him. You know I like older men."

Jay's voice dropped. Not loud, angry, or tight.

"Stay out of my business."

"Neither do I," she blurted. "I rode the bus home last night. Whoever you think you saw, it wasn't me."

Jay's eyes narrowed.

"And he's not interested in little girls," he said, letting the last phrase sting on purpose.

Her smile fell. Heat rose in her face. She hated that he could still make her feel small.

"I'm not a little girl," she snapped.

Then, because she couldn't help herself, she smirked again.

"I'll give you this though, you're getting smarter. Alibis and everything. Classic MARTA excuse. Nobody questions lateness in Atlanta. Blame the bus and everybody just nods like they were on it with you."

Jay grabbed his hoodie. She ducked out laughing as a pillow flew toward the door and hit nothing but air.

Mama appeared two minutes later. Coffee in hand, robe tied tight, hair wrapped like she meant business. Her curves moved with the confidence of a woman who had earned the right to be tired and still be respected. She stood in the doorway and looked at Jay like he was an invoice she had already paid.

"Boy," she said, "didn't your sister tell you I'm waiting? The pharmacist shows up before his tech; it looks bad."

Jay slipped the hoodie over his bare chest, still warm from sleep, still built like he lived in a gym. Mama's eyes dropped, then rose again with a slow headshake.

"You really think you're fine, don't you?" she said. "All that muscle. I wish you'd spend less time chasing chiseled abs and more time chasing a degree."

"I do my part," Jay replied, sipping her coffee like he owned it, then handing it back like he was doing her a favor.

"Covering tuition, paying bills. You're not disputing that."

Mama's expression softened, but only slightly. She was no-nonsense, but she wasn't unkind. She loved her babies the way women love when they've had to do too much alone.

"No," she said. "I'll give you that. You've been holding it down. I'm proud of you."

Jay blinked at the praise like it startled him.

Then Mama's eyes flickered toward the hall.

"And your sister," Mama added, quieter, "she's brilliant. But she's still very much a little girl in the head. Mouth too smart for her life experience. I've got time before she really gets boy-crazy."

Jay almost laughed.

"Don't be so sure, Mama."

Mama gave him a look that said don't start with me, then turned and walked out.

At dawn, Jay drove them both toward Covington and Redan. Mama tugged her glasses down, muttered goodbye. His sister demanded twenty dollars for her MARTA card even though she had a new one. That made the morning feel normal.

Jay sighed and peeled off a fifty.

"This is all I got," he said. "Take it, and I want my thirty back tonight."

Mama arched an eyebrow from the passenger seat.

Then she smirked. "Don't worry, I'll pay you back before your broke friend Marion tries to borrow it. He's consistent. You always end up covering for him."

Jay muttered, "Marion's my workout partner."

"Mmm-hmm," Mama said. "And he pays you back eventually, right?"

Jay didn't answer. Mama didn't need one.

His sister waved and hopped out, already talking about pizza as if the world owed her a slice.

"How about I use your change and grab something from Mellow Mushroom?"

Jay shook his head as she shut the door.

Then she saw the car.

A sleek black Monte Carlo slid into a parking space across the street like it belonged there. Glossy. Clean. Too intentional for a random morning. The driver stepped out.

Bald head. Salt-and-pepper beard. A body that didn't try hard but still announced itself. Broad shoulders, a confident stride, and that calm that made you feel as though you were the one moving too fast.

By the time she blinked, he was beside her.

"Well, good morning," he said, voice warm and practiced, like he had been saying it to her for years.

The scent hit first. Mint. Cologne and something clean underneath. His smile came next, controlled, the kind a younger woman could mistake for safety.

Her knees wavered. She hated that they did.

He touched her shoulder lightly, not gripping, not pulling, just steadying. Like a father who wasn't always around but showed up when he felt like it, and you learned to treasure the moments, anyway.

"You alright?" he asked.

She swallowed. "Yes."

He handed her a sealed bottle of water.

"Unbroken," he said, watching her eyes as if he enjoyed watching people decide.

She sipped. Her hands trembled only a little. The bus rolled up, doors hissing open.

He helped her stand, like she needed help even though she didn't. She let him anyway.

"I didn't need the bus," he called as the doors closed. "I just came to talk to you."

Her heart kept moving after the bus did.

Later that day, after computer lab, she took the side stairs out of Burruss. She liked the side stairs. Fewer eyes, less noise, and fewer people treating her like a child.

And there it was again.

The Monte Carlo sat in the lot like a promise. Like a question.

Curiosity beat caution.

She leaned close to the tinted glass, hands cupped to see inside.

"May I help you?"

She spun so fast her throat tightened.

He was behind her, smiling.

"Sorry," she said. "I didn't see you."

He laughed, easy. "Clearly. You were busy peeping."

Her cheeks burned. She tried to recover with attitude.

"Do you always lurk behind girls on campus?"

"Touché," he said, enjoying her. Then he tilted his head. "You got dinner plans?"

Her mind raced. Two encounters in one day. Too neat to be an accident. Too bold to be innocent.

She should have said no.

Instead, she smiled like she was grown.

"I'm a movie buff," she said, nodding at the car. "With that ride, I'm guessing your name's Alonzo."

He didn't flinch. "You'd be right."

"You're lying."

He chuckled. "Nah. Training Day hooked me. Took years and more money than I like to admit, but I turned this baby into Denzel's Monte Carlo."

She couldn't help it. She liked that, and she liked him liking that she liked it.

"Please tell me your last name isn't Harris."

"Filmore," he said smoothly. "And I'm not a crooked cop."

Her grin slipped into something more intrigued.

"So, Alonzo Filmore... are you asking me to dinner, or are you asking me to trust you?"

"Both," he said, and opened the passenger door as though he were opening a chapter.

Dinner at Marlow's stretched from appetizers to dessert. He didn't rush or push her, nor did he beg for attention like boys her age. He gave it calmly, like he had plenty.

She asked him question after question. He answered enough to satisfy, not enough to reveal.

That was part of the charm. The mystery felt like maturity.

By the time they left, she felt seen and studied at the same time.

"You should probably get home," he said at the car. "It's after seven. Won't anyone be looking for you?"

"Not on a Friday," she said. "Mama's slammed. Jay's... Jay."

He watched her say her brother's name. Like it meant something to him.

"I need to swing by my condo," he said. "You okay with that?"

Her better sense tried to rise.

Her desire stepped on it.

"I'm okay," she said.

The condo was a high-rise on 17th Street. Floor-to-ceiling windows. Skyline glittering. Everything clean and expensive, but too quiet.

She perched on the sofa, almost afraid to crease it.

Alonzo came back in fresh clothes, cologne renewed, confidence unbothered. He crouched in front of her, rested his hand lightly on her shoulder again.

"Relax," he said.

Her chest tightened. "I'm just... nervous."

"I thought time wasn't a factor," he replied softly.

"It's not," she said, then stumbled. "I just..."

Her sentence dissolved under the weight of his gaze.

He didn't touch her this time. He just watched her the way a man watches something he's already decided belongs to him.

The silence stretched long enough to feel intentional.

Then he stood.

"I should take you home," he said calmly.

She blinked, confused. "Why?"

"You should've checked in," he answered, voice measured, almost paternal.

It made her feel cared for.

It made her feel chosen.

She didn't know the difference yet.

On the drive back, she stared out the window, trying to settle what she felt.

Finally she asked, "What made you do that?"

"Do what?"

His smirk made her want to hit him and kiss him at the same time.

Before she could press, he shifted.

"How old are you?"

"Jay's nineteen," she admitted. "I won't be until December."

"Fair enough," he said lightly. "And I'm forty-four."

She laughed under her breath. "So math is not your subject."

He smiled as if he liked her mouth.

What unsettled her wasn't his age.

It was the way he said her brother's name earlier. Like it belonged on his tongue. At the curb, he idled and looked at her the way men look at the thing they've decided they want.

"I'd like to see you again," he said. "But you need to understand something. Discretion is non-negotiable. Not even your brother."

Her pulse raced.

"When?"

"Soon," he said. "I know how to find you."

As she stepped out, his voice followed her like a shadow.

"Be safe walking home."

Weeks passed, and secrecy became a rhythm.

She skipped a class here and there. She said that she was studying. She said she was in the lab. She learned how to be believable because she wanted what she wanted.

Alonzo took her on day trips. Shopping sprees. Little gifts that felt like proof she mattered. He didn't shower her every day. He wasn't present like that, appearing when he wanted to.

And when he appeared, it felt like a blessing.

To avoid suspicion, she left most of it at his condo. Except the frames.

Three pairs of glasses she loved too much to hide. Red. Tortoise. Leopard print. They made her feel grown. They made her feel seen.

Mama noticed the shift anyway.

"You and your brother still love each other," Mama said one afternoon. "But that love always had teeth."

Her mother didn't know the half of it.

One evening, sprawled across her bed, she clicked through an online cart. Jay appeared in the doorway. This time he knocked twice, as if trying to be better.

Then he sat beside her without asking.

He brushed her hair with his fingers like they were little again. He looked at her screen.

"Shopping again?"

"Just a jacket," she said quickly. "Weather changing."

Jay didn't laugh.

He pulled something from his hoodie pocket and set it in her lap.

Red frames.

Her breath caught so hard it hurt.

"Where did you get those?" she whispered.

"You left them in his car," Jay said, voice flat.

Her throat tightened. "What?"

"The same car he picked me up in yesterday," Jay continued. "Right after I did a job for him."

His eyes were darker than she had ever seen them.

"What are you doing with him?" he asked. "Don't lie."

Her voice broke. "We've been seeing each other. Since the night you saw us."

Jay shook his head once, slowly, like he was trying not to fall apart.

"I don't want you seeing him again."

"You don't understand," she pleaded. "Alonzo's a good man. He treats me like an adult."

Jay laughed, but it wasn't humor. It was pain.

"Look at me, *Sis*."

She tried. Her eyes kept dropping.

"Look at me."

Something in his voice changed. Not anger. Not yelling. Something worse.

She lifted her eyes.

Jay stood, unzipped his hoodie, and let it fall. Then he turned slightly and lowered his sweats just enough.

Her world stopped.

His back, ribs, and thighs showed deep welts and raised scars. Marks that didn't belong on a nineteen-year-old body.

Her brother, who worked out like he was building armor, had been carrying damage underneath it the whole time.

"My God," she whispered. "Jay... what happened?"

His voice cracked.

"Alonzo's clients happened," he said, and the words sounded like shame and rage braided together. "Sadists pay well."

She started crying immediately. Ugly. Shaking. Not cute.

"You're scaring me," she said.

"Good," Jay replied, not unkindly, but firmly. "Because you don't get it yet."

He sat back down and stared at the floor like he couldn't afford to look at her.

"You remember that girl who disappeared last year?" he asked. "They found her weeks later near that junkyard. Everybody talked about it."

Her stomach dropped. "Of course I remember."

"It's not unsolved," Jay said quietly.

Her body went cold. "What do you mean?"

Jay swallowed hard. "I was there."

She covered her mouth.

He kept going because once the truth starts, it refuses to stop.

"Marion met her first," Jay said. "He bragged about how grown she was. He got us invited to this party. No rules. No IDs. Everything out in the open. Drugs, couples, whatever you wanted."

He paused, blinking like the memory burned.

"I thought it was a dream," he continued. "Until it turned."

His hands trembled. He pressed them together as if in prayer.

"She stepped outside," he said. "Said she needed her bag. We followed. Two guys boxed her in. And then I saw him."

Her voice came out small. "Alonzo."

Jay nodded once.

"Calm," Jay said. "Smiling. Like it was a normal night. Like he'd done it before."

He took a breath that sounded like he was trying not to drown.

"He motioned for me to open a trunk," Jay said. "I froze. Marion froze worse. Then Alonzo checked her bag, nodded, and... gave an order."

Tears streamed down her face.

"They killed her," Jay said, voice breaking. "Fast. And then they cut what they needed to make a point. Alonzo filmed it. Steady. No flinch. Like he was making content."

She made a sound that didn't even sound human.

Jay's eyes went hollow.

"They shoved us into a van," he continued. "My car got destroyed. I watched it crushed like it was nothing. And the message was clear."

He turned to her.

"He owns us because we saw it," Jay said. "Because he has proof. Because he knows what fear makes a man do."

Her hands shook so badly that she couldn't wipe her face.

"And Marion?" she whispered.

Jay's jaw clenched. "Deeper than me."

Silence swallowed the room.

Then Mama screamed.

They ran into the living room.

The TV was on. *Breaking News*. Flashing lights. A drug bust. Assets seized. Two suspects wounded. One fatality. Then the photo filled the screen.

Alonzo.

Her chest tightened like a belt.

Jay froze.

Mama stood in the middle of the room with a hand pressed to her mouth, eyes locked on the screen like she was watching a ghost get confirmed.

Jay tried to steady the moment.

"Drug deal gone bad," he said quickly. "Happens every day. You alright, Mama?"

Mama didn't look at him.

She kept staring at the screen.

"When I heard the name," she said softly, "I didn't believe it."

Her voice shook, but she didn't fall apart. She was too practiced at holding herself together. Too practiced at being the only adult in the room.

"I been expecting this for years," Mama continued. "I just didn't think it would feel like this."

Jay swallowed. His sister clutched his arm.

Mama finally turned toward them.

And she said the word like it had been sitting in her throat for twenty years.

"Your father," she said. "Alonzo. He's dead."

Epilogue

The room held its breath.

Jay didn't move. His sister's hand stayed on his arm like she needed his bones to keep her standing. Neither of them looked away from Mama.

Father.

The word didn't behave like a normal word. It didn't land and stop. It expanded.

It rewrote the past in real time.

His sister's mind reeled through every gesture. The water bottle. The hand on the shoulder. The warmth that felt paternal only because it was occasional.

It wasn't affection.

It was familiarity.

Jay stared at the floor, jaw clenched, as if his scars were speaking louder than his mouth could. His body, the same body he built in the gym to look untouchable, had been carrying a truth he never wanted her to know.

Mama sat down slowly like her legs finally remembered they were tired. She didn't cry. Not yet. Her face was pale, controlled, the way it gets when a woman has held a secret so long it becomes part of her posture.

Outside, the world kept moving like it had no respect.

Cars rolled along Covington Highway. Someone laughed across the street. A siren wailed far enough away to ignore.

But inside that living room, life stopped.

Because the truth had finally come home.

And the Little Girl understood, with a clarity that felt like pain, that they hadn't been living near danger.

They had been living inside it.

Not in Alonzo's shadow.

In his house.

Built with his hands.
Protected by his absence.
Controlled by his touch.
And even dead, he still owned the air.

Chapter Sixteen

Chimera

Selene stiffened as his hand firmly cupped her breast, hoping her reaction went unnoticed.

The room was dark enough that she didn't have to close her eyes to imagine being somewhere else or doing something else. As she lay flat on her stomach, her face turned toward the wall, she breathed into the pillow while Ethan moved behind her. His touch was gentle and familiar—but distant and not welcomed.

She didn't move, at least not in rhythm with him. Her body cooperated a little, more out of habit than desire.

"Are you okay?" Ethan asked in a low tone.

"Just tired," she murmured into the dark.

When it was over, he kissed her shoulder, shifted to his knees, and climbed off the bed from behind her like it was nothing new.

More relieved that it was over than grateful that it had happened at all, she lay still. At some point, she'd pulled the top sheet over herself, wrapping it around her waist like it might offer comfort. Not surprisingly, it didn't.

Her phone buzzed on the nightstand. She gave a quick glance. *Maybe: Genexis Diagnostics*. This time, she didn't answer.

Her stomach tightened as she turned her face away from the screen and replaced the phone on the nightstand. Something was wrong, yes, but not with him. Not even with the sex. Expected and routine, it was something to get through. The hard part to explain was why she kept saying yes to something she never really wanted.

Closing her eyes, she tried to reconnect and feel herself, but again, something inside had gone quiet, like it was waiting to be revived.

She sat up just as Ethan's silhouette rose from the sunken tub behind the glass partition. Like everything else in the room, it was open, high-end, and easy to see through.

She exhaled as she braced herself, ready to respond with the usual lie. Ethan's silence wasn't cold, it was careful. He gave her space when he sensed something was off. And as much as she appreciated it, she low-key wished he'd press. At least this once.

As he stepped out of the steam, water droplets still clinging to his skin, his silence continued.

She listened to the soft rustle of the towel as he dried off, then the mattress dipped beneath his weight, followed by the familiar rustle of sheets and the click of his phone being placed on the charger.

No goodnight. Not anything.

Selene swung her legs over the edge of the bed. Feeling the chill in the room, she reached for her robe and slowly and automatically moved toward the shower until the envelope on the dresser caught her attention.

She'd tossed it there a few days ago, unopened, when it arrived earlier than expected.

Genexis Diagnostics. Plain white, no logo—just her name and address, centered and impersonal. It was all business. More than simple curiosity drove her decision to order the test. It was more like a dare to herself. She wasn't even sure what she was looking for. Something just felt off.

When asked earlier, she'd told Ethan it was just one of those ancestry things—laughing it off as a fun, historical genetic walk to help her understand her future through confirmed revelations of her past. But she hadn't mentioned the second part. The weird results from her blood test weren't discussed.

There was no mention of the way her stomach had tightened when the nurse looked at the screen, then back at her—cautious, confused, like one of the markers didn't match what she expected for a woman with Selene's profile.

Selene picked up the envelope and held it between her fingers. Still sealed and safe for now. She set the envelope back down, still unopened, and walked to the shower before she could change her mind.

The water ran hotter than it needed to. Selene, not moving, stood beneath the pulsating stream, letting the water hit the back of her neck before trailing down her spine. She didn't reach for the sponge, didn't lather; she just breathed. It wasn't about getting clean. It was about getting quiet. The kind of quiet that didn't come with Ethan's silence.

She finally stepped out and wrapped herself in a towel, walked back through the open room, and didn't look at the dresser. She already knew the sealed envelope was still there. She passed it without breaking her stride.

She dressed quickly and kept walking. Past the dresser, past the front door, past the part of her that wanted to turn around. The key was already in her hand, pressed tight into her palm. Her body had made the decision before her mind could second-guess it.

Selene hurried through the clinic's entrance. She sighed as the glass doors parted. Not having an appointment, she approached the receptionist's desk. The young woman behind the desk didn't look up right away. When she did, she smiled.

"Ms. Alexander?" she asked, politely, but with caution. "I remember you from last week. You're back sooner than I expected."

Selene nodded. "Yes, I had some follow-up questions."

The receptionist glanced at her screen, then back at Selene. "Do you want to speak with one of our nurses? Or—?"

"If someone's available."

"One moment."

She disappeared through the frosted door behind the desk, leaving Selene standing there, unsure of what would occur next.

A few moments later, a woman with a confident but open face, in pale green scrubs stepped into the lobby. Her badge read, *Maya D., Lab Tech Supervisor.*

She gave Selene a polite smile, then a second look. Something in her eyes shifted.

"Ms. Alexander," Maya said. "I wasn't expecting to see you today."

"Funny, I wasn't expecting to be here."

Maya nodded slowly. "Do you want to talk in the back?"

Selene followed her through a narrow hallway lined with clipboards and wall-mounted gloves. Inside the small consultation room, Maya motioned for her to sit.

"I don't usually do this," she said in a whisper. "But I recognized your name, and... well, I was surprised you hadn't been contacted yet."

Selene's jaw flexed. "About what?"

Maya hesitated, then continued. "Your results weren't flagged as urgent, but something about the genetic markers stood out. So, I flagged it internally, just to be sure it wasn't a processing error. I wasn't supposed to say anything."

"But here we are having this conversation."

Maya smiled softly. "Let's just say I'd want someone to tell me if it were me."

Selene looked down. "What exactly is there to tell?"

Maya tapped her fingers against the sealed folder resting on the desk. "Technically, I can't disclose results outside a formal consult. But if you haven't opened your copy yet, I'd recommend you do that soon."

Not trusting Maya's voice, Selene nodded.

Maya stood. "Do you have someone you can talk to about this?"

Selene thought of Ethan.

"I'm not sure yet," she said.

Maya didn't press. "If you need anything, just call."

She nodded, thanking her before stepping back into the light of the hallway and walking toward the parking lot.

Selene stepped into the daylight and squinted. She didn't go straight to her car. Instead, she wandered past the row of neatly parked vehicles until she found a patch of shade near the edge of the lot. She removed the envelope from her shoulder bag and ran her thumb along the sealed flap. One small tear. That's all it would take. Her phone rang. Startled by the sound, she blinked and pulled it from the same bag that held the envelope.

Ethan.

Of course.

She stared at the screen for a moment, started walking again toward her car, then answered, "Hey."

"You okay?"

His voice was soft and careful. The kind of careful that comes after you've been forgiven for something you didn't know you'd done.

"I'm fine," she blurted.

"You left before we could speak."

"Sorry, but I needed some air. I was restless."

Ethan paused. "Are you sure everything's alright?"

Her eyes dropped to the envelope still in her hand, her bag clutched in her armpit.

"I'm sure," she said, her voice thinning.

"Want me to meet you somewhere?"

"No," she said, in an even softer tone. "I just needed to clear my head."

"Okay. Just checking in."

"I appreciate that."

She hung up before the man on the other end of the silence could ask another question. She opened the door, tossed her bag and phone onto the passenger seat, and sat sideways in the open driver's door, envelope in hand. For a while, she didn't move. She just stared at the envelope, wondering about the content of the thick pages inside. Then, slowly, she peeled the flap open. Inside, there was a folded cover sheet, and a stapled summary. No fanfare or bold warning labels. Just black ink on white paper.

She sat on the curb and unfolded it in her lap, smoothing the pages with the flat of her hand.

Most of the content was numbers, ranges, and values she didn't understand, even though the interpretation was printed in the far-right column. The genetic markers and comparison ratios also confused her.

Then, a word she didn't expect. It appeared once in the report's body—then again at the bottom, bold and centered like a question.

Chimerism.

Even after she read it aloud, it didn't sound real.

She read the sentence again. "*Suggestive evidence of genetic chimerism. Clinical correlation recommended.*"

Her brow furrowed. *Chimerism?* She hadn't heard that word before. At least, not in any context that made sense now. Was that a typo?

She scanned the page again and looked around as if someone might explain it to her. But the parking lot was still.

It couldn't be a medical problem if Maya had only recommended a clinical consultation with a medical laboratory technologist, instead of an appointment with a genetic counselor. What did *clinical correlation* even mean? The phrase itself sounded so technical, even coded.

She still wasn't sure what she'd come looking for, but this wasn't it. Or maybe it was. Just not like this.

Selene sat in her car, the envelope now folded and stuffed between the seat and the console. Her phone lay dark beside her, the word still haunting her.

Chimerism.

She unlocked the screen, opened her browser and typed slowly.

"What is chimerism?"

The results flooded in fast.

"A rare condition where two sets of DNA exist in one person..."

"...can result from a vanished twin in utero..."

"...most cases go unnoticed until medical testing reveals inconsistencies..."

One phrase stopped her cold.

"Absorbed twin."

Her stomach tightened as she scrolled, each new article hitting harder—medical journals filled with strange cases, families stunned to learn they weren't biologically related to their own children.

"What?"

After several minutes of reading, one headline caught her eye—a woman whose DNA didn't match her own reproductive tissue. Selene lowered the phone to her lap. Her breathing thinned, shallow and fast. What did this mean for her? Was someone else living inside of her?

No, it couldn't be. This had to be one of those new-age labels used to explain away weirdness. Or maybe it was a glitch, a testing error. Maya had hinted that it could be.

Maybe she should wait, take her time. Talk to someone—get a second opinion. Her thoughts were rational. But her body disagreed. Her skin tingled. She gripped the steering wheel hard.

In the rearview mirror, the same face she saw every day stared back. And yet, for a moment, she didn't recognize it.

"Maybe the other *she* has always been there," she whispered, pressing the ignition button.

"I just never knew what to call her."

Her phone lit up again.

Ethan.

She didn't answer. She pulled away from the lot, not knowing where she was going, only what she was running from.

Selene didn't remember making the last few turns. She gripped the steering wheel tighter, realizing she'd passed the same gas station twice. The traffic was light, but she still felt boxed in, like the surrounding cars were moving too slowly and too rapidly at the same time.

Her jaw ached. She'd been clenching her teeth without knowing it. She looked up and realized where she was—Lenox and Piedmont. Near the mall. She needed nothing. Wanted nothing. But her hands turned the wheel anyway, guiding her into a nearby parking garage with little thought.

She pulled into a space and cut the engine. For a moment, she just sat there, staring ahead, the word *chimerism* still looping in her mind like a skipped record. Reaching into the console, she grabbed a roll of Lifesavers and froze. *Pep-O-Mint.* She didn't even like that flavor—never had. She always went for Tangy Orange. She unwrapped one anyway and popped it in her mouth, and bit down hard before the coolness could register.

It didn't help. Her phone buzzed again. Not Ethan this time. A different number. Local.

She hesitated, then answered.

"Selene Alexander?" The voice was female. She was polite, but clearly guarded, like every word was filtered.

"Yes?"

"This is Dr. Nadine Carver's office, returning your inquiry about the Genexis report. She has a few minutes available this afternoon if you're able to come in."

Selene hesitated. She hadn't scheduled anything, hadn't even made the call. She didn't know Dr. Carver.

"I—uh. What time?"

"Can you be here by 3:15? Dr. Carver just had a cancellation. We're in Midtown."

Selene looked at the clock on her dashboard. 2:42.

"It'll be tight with traffic, but I can make that."

"Great. Bring your lab report with you if you have it. We'll see you shortly."

The call ended before she could ask how they even got her number. She sat still for another moment and then opened her maps app and typed the name in.

Carver Internal Medicine.

Selene found street parking half a block away from the glass-paneled building with bronze letters that read Carver Internal Medicine. The lobby was modern, beige, and unnervingly quiet.

She checked in at the front desk, still unsure how this appointment existed. The woman behind the counter simply smiled and asked for her ID and insurance card.

A few minutes later, a nurse greeted her from the hallway, tablet in hand, and motioned for her to follow, leading her down a colorfully accented hallway. She followed, gripping her shoulder bag tighter than necessary.

"In here," the nurse said, motioning toward a small exam room.

It smelled faintly of antiseptic and something lemon-scented, like a cleaning wipe that hadn't fully dried. Selene stepped inside and perched on the edge of the paper-lined table.

"Let's just get a few vitals before Dr. Carver comes in," the nurse said. Her efficient tone was neutral.

She slid the cuff onto Selene's arm and pressed a few buttons. Selene stared ahead, eyes fixed on a framed photo of a flower field that felt too cheerful for this room. The cuff tightened. A few seconds passed.

"Your blood pressure's a little elevated," the nurse said casually, tapping the screen. "Could be nerves. It happens."

Saying nothing, Selene gave a polite nod. She hadn't realized how hard her foot was tapping against the floor until the nurse asked her to stay still for the pulse reading.

"You can take your shoes off if you'd like," the nurse added, still not looking directly at her.

Selene mumbled, "I'm fine," and stayed where she was.

Temperature. Pulse. Oxygen. All within seconds.

"Dr. Carver will be in shortly."

And just like that, the nurse was gone, leaving Selene in a room too quiet for her thoughts.

Selene sat stiffly, tugging at a loose thread on her sleeve as her mind raced. The envelope was still in her bag. The door opened gently.

Dr. Nadine Carver stepped in with a tablet in one hand and a warm but professional smile. She was tall, with locs pulled into a loose bun and her expression quiet and steady.

"Ms. Alexander? I'm Dr. Carver. Thanks for coming in on such short notice."

Selene stood, shook her hand. "I wasn't sure what this was about or how your office even got my number."

Dr. Carver nodded. "That's fair. Your results were referred to us through a network flag in the Genexis system. When certain anomalies appear, especially of a genetic nature, they sometimes route cases to specialists within our network."

"Without my requesting it?"

"There's an opt-in clause in the consent paperwork you signed. It allows consultation referrals under specific circumstances. Yours qualified."

Selene blinked. "Okay."

"I know it's strange. But it's not an error."

She took a seat across from her and tapped a few things on her tablet.

"Before we begin—have you opened your report?"

Selene nodded. "I read it."

"And the term 'chimerism'—are you familiar?"

Selene hesitated. "Not until today."

"Would you like a clearer explanation, or just to talk about next steps?"

"Both," Selene said.

Dr. Carver folded her hands over the tablet. "Simply put, *chimerism* occurs when a person carries two different sets of DNA. Usually from a twin that was absorbed very early in the womb. It's rare, but not unheard of. Most people never know. It's often discovered by accident—blood tests, transplants, fertility issues."

Selene exhaled. "So, it's real."

"It is. And in your case, the indicators were strong enough to suggest a second genetic signature—one that's distinct but traceable."

"Traceable?" Selene asked.

Dr. Carver nodded. "To specific tissues. It's possible that one DNA set dominates in certain parts of your body, and the other elsewhere."

"And that means what?"

"We can't say for sure without further testing. Some people experience shifts they can't fully explain. Hormonal, behavioral, even relational."

Selene sat back, stunned. "So, there's someone else inside me?"

"Not someone," Dr. Carver said gently. "Just another *you.* A different map, layered over the one you've always followed."

Selene didn't respond right away. Her thoughts were scrambled, looping phrases like *another map* and *layered DNA*. She swallowed hard.

Dr. Carver didn't press. "You don't have to decide today. But if you're willing, I'd like to run one more panel—something more targeted. It could give us clearer insight into how your markers are expressed."

Selene gave a faint nod, though she wasn't sure what she was agreeing to. "Okay."

"Take the weekend. I'll have the front desk reach out."

Dr. Carver stood and extended her hand again. Selene shook it, her grip softer than before.

"Thank you," she said, her voice dry.

"You're welcome. And Selene?" Dr. Carver paused. "You're not alone in this. I've had other patients face similar discoveries. It can be unsettling—but not unmanageable."

Selene didn't respond right away. She just stared at the floor, as if trying to trace the second version of herself hiding in the fibers of the carpet. Dr. Carver gave her time. When Selene finally spoke, her voice was low.

"Is there someone I should tell? I mean, does this affect anyone else?"

"That depends," Dr. Carver said gently. "Has it already?"

Selene thought of Ethan. His patience and softness. His confusion every time she shut him out for reasons she couldn't explain.

She nodded. "Maybe."

Dr. Carver didn't push. "If you need time, take it. We're not in a rush. I can refer you to a genetic counselor for further testing and guidance when you're ready."

Selene smiled gratefully. "Thank you."

The doctor stood. "I'll give you a few minutes."

When the door closed, Selene exhaled slowly, as if breathing for the first time all day. She reached into her bag and pulled out her phone. No new messages.

But the last one still sat there—*Ethan. "Let me know when you're ready to talk. I'm here."*

She stared at the words until they blurred.

Then, finally she typed, *"Soon. I promise."*

Selene offered a tight smile and stepped out of the room. The hall felt too bright now. The receptionist handed her a printout with possible follow-up dates, but Selene barely looked at it before tucking it into her bag. At the exit, her phone vibrated.

Ethan.

"Missed call."

Then: *"Just checking in, call me when you're ready."*

Then immediately, *"1 New Message—Just checking in. Call me when you're ready."*

Selene stared at the text. A lump formed in her throat. She wanted to tell him. To explain everything. But how do you tell someone you're two people in one body? That parts of you aren't yours—or maybe they are, just not the parts you recognize? She locked the phone without replying and kept walking.

She reached her car but didn't get in. Instead, she leaned against the driver's side door, letting the warmth of the metal seep into her back. The city moved around her—horns, footsteps, fragments of conversation. All of it distant.

Her hand hovered over her bag, where the follow-up dates waited unread.

She wasn't ready for another appointment. Not yet. But she wasn't running anymore, either.

She stood there for a while, arms folded, the hum of the city rising and falling around her.

Then, without checking the time or her phone again, she slid into the car, started the engine—and drove. Not home, and not to Ethan.

She didn't know where she was going, only that her body had already decided.

Twenty minutes later, she was standing outside a bar she didn't remember noticing before. It was tucked between a boutique cigar shop and an antique bookstore, barely lit like it didn't care to be found. She stepped inside.

Cool air hit her skin, followed by the scent of cedar and citrus. Low music played. It was something jazzy and old. She didn't take a seat at the bar, but leaned against it.

The bartender looked up, smirked, wiped his hands, and asked, "Looking for something?"

Selene hesitated. "I don't know."

Her words felt honest. More honest than anything she'd said all day.

"Then you're in the right place," a voice chuckled behind her.

It was a man's voice. Very confident and familiar sounding, the way strangers sometimes are.

She turned, and for a moment, something in her shifted. A shift not driven by desire or loneliness, but recognition. Not of the stranger, but of her. The stool creaked as she shifted her weight. She hadn't planned to sit, but once her body found the chair, it stayed.

He noticed. "You look like someone who just walked away from something big."

Selene gave a slow smile. "Or walked toward it."

He lifted his glass slightly. "Either way, here's to movement."

She clinked hers lightly against his.

He gestured toward the bartender. "Another round?"

Selene looked at her glass, still half full. "Let's see where this one takes me first."

He chuckled. "Fair. So, what brings you out tonight? You don't seem like the usual type."

She tilted her head. "What's the usual type?"

"People looking for a reason to be noticed." He paused, scanning her face. "You seem like someone trying to disappear."

Selene didn't respond right away. She cautiously maintained her silence before she answered.

"Maybe I'm both."

He nodded, accepting that without further explanation.

He didn't ask anything else right away. Just took a slow sip and watched her with the kind of attention that felt unhurried and unbothered.

Selene traced the rim of her glass with her finger. Her body felt lighter than it had in days, but her skin tingled, like she was just slightly out of sync with herself.

"You live around here?" he asked.

She nodded, then shook her head. "Not far. But I don't come out much."

"I can tell."

Selene smirked. "Is it that obvious?"

"It's not a bad thing. Just rare." He leaned in a little, elbows resting on the bar. "Most people wear a mask when they're out. You seem like someone who stays guarded. But just now, something real peeked through."

She looked down at her drink, swirling the ice. "Maybe I left it in the car."

He raised an eyebrow. "On purpose?"

She didn't answer. But her hand found her glass again. And her next sip was slower.

They sat like that for a few minutes, taking in the jazzy sounds.

Without assumption he gently asked, "You want to get out of here?"

Selene's breath caught. Her first instinct was to say no. Or maybe laugh. But something in her—some quiet pulse she'd never followed before—said otherwise.

"Where would we go?" she asked, her voice lower now.

"Somewhere quieter," he said. "Someplace that doesn't ask questions."

She hesitated. Then nodded slowly. "Okay."

They stood without a word. He placed cash on the bar, and she followed him through the crowd. As they reached the door, Selene felt an unfamiliar steadiness rising in her chest. It wasn't fear nor desire in the way she'd known it before. It was something else entirely. Something waking up.

Outside, the sky had shifted. It was no longer day, but not quite night. That in-between hour where the streetlights come to life and everything softens at the edges. Selene hadn't meant to stay out this long. She had planned nothing at all. But Ethan rarely pressed her about time. He'd long stopped asking where she'd been, sensing her need for space before she even voiced it. His messages were always the same—short, open-ended, patient.

She inhaled slowly and followed the man through the bar's front doors.

The air was heavy, thick with the promise of summer rain. A few drops visibly dotted the sidewalk.

They didn't speak as they walked. Selene kept pace beside him, the tension between them noticeable but quiet. He led her to his car. She didn't ask where they were going. She didn't need to. When he opened the passenger door, she stepped in without a word.

Inside, the cabin was dim, the leather seats still held the warmth of the afternoon sun. Faint instrumentals, smooth and unhurried, seeped through the high-end speakers.

He got in, glanced over. "You okay?"

She nodded. "You?"

He gave a slight shrug. "Didn't expect this."

"Neither did I."

They sat in stillness. A pause that should have been but wasn't awkward. It was just real.

Then she looked at him fully. "Take me somewhere quiet."

His hands flexed on the steering wheel before he nodded once. "I know a place."

The drive was quiet. Selene stared out the window, watching the city pass in snapshots, neon signs, silhouettes on sidewalks and the blur of traffic lights switching from red to green.

She should have, but didn't ask where they were headed. Her pulse had settled into a slow, deliberate rhythm. She wasn't calm, nor anxious, just alert.

They turned off a major street and wound through a neighborhood of low buildings and narrow one-ways. The neighborhood boasted older apartments, a few renovated storefronts, and a small discreet and unassuming complex tucked behind a wall of overgrown hedges.

He parked and killed the engine.

"We're here," he said.

Selene looked around. "Is this your place?"

He hesitated, then nodded. "Yeah."

Still, she had no questions. Just a nod in return. He led her up a flight of stairs and unlocked a door near the end of the hall. The apartment was small but clean and uncluttered. The scent of wood polish lingered in the air. A couch, a lamp and a bookshelf with spines facing out in uneven rows showcased one abstract painting on the wall.

She stood just inside the doorway, arms loose at her sides, scanning the room like she'd stepped into someone else's memory.

"You want something to drink?" he asked.

"No," she said softly.

He watched her for just a moment, then moved to the lamp, dimming it. The soft glow shifted the room into something warmer and quieter. Selene stepped out of her shoes.

"I don't usually do this," she said.

He raised an eyebrow.

"I'm not nervous," she added. "Just paying attention."

"To what?"

She turned to face him fully. "To who I am right now."

They stood there, the space between them charged. Then slowly and deliberately, she closed the distance.

He didn't move when she stepped closer. Selene raised her hand, just slightly, brushing her fingers against the hem of his shirt. He didn't flinch. Instead, his hand lifted to meet hers, and for a moment they just stood there connected by fingertips and something else neither of them tried to name.

When he leaned in, his lips didn't go straight for hers. They hovered. And again, Selene closed the gap. The kiss was soft at first. No rush, just a quiet confirmation that this was happening, and she was allowing it.

And then it deepened.

His hand slid to the small of her back. Hers to his chest. He pulled her in fully, and she followed without hesitation. She felt herself loosening, unfolding in a way that startled her. Her skin responded first, then her breath. Then something else. She didn't stop it.

It continued when he guided her toward the bedroom. It didn't stop when her sweater hit the floor nor when he asked nothing of her but her presence. For the first time in a long time—she *wanted* to.

And afterward, she lay still, one hand resting on her stomach like she was holding herself together. Not out of regret. But to feel who she was and who she wasn't. The one who came here and the one who never would have.

Morning came without apology. Selene blinked into the light spilling through unfamiliar curtains. The room was still. She sat up slowly. Sheets fell from her shoulders. She was alone.

There was no note. No lingering scent. No name to tie this to anything permanent.

She moved carefully, feeling that one wrong step might destroy whatever held her together. Her clothes were on the floor, folded neatly.

By 7:20, she was back behind the wheel, easing into traffic. Her phone buzzed in the console—Ethan again.

2 Missed Calls. 1 New Message.

"Still here. I know something's up. Just talk to me. Please."

She didn't answer. Not yet. Not until she figured out which version of herself would be speaking. Her GPS recalibrated as she passed the exit she *meant* to take. She barely noticed.

At a red light, she caught her reflection in the rearview mirror. Same eyes. Same face. But everything beneath it felt rearranged and rewired. Maybe this wasn't about losing control. Maybe this was about *recognizing* the one who had it all along.

The house was dim, not from nightfall, but because the blinds were still drawn. Selene stepped inside quietly, the door clicking shut behind her. The hush felt heavier than usual.

Ethan sat on the edge of the couch, elbows resting on his knees and his head in his hands. A soft light from a corner lamp cast shadows across his face. He didn't move or rush her. He slowly looked up.

"You didn't text," he said. His voice was calm, but firmer than she was used to. "I was starting to worry."

Selene set her bag down on the entry table. "I know. I wasn't sure what to say."

"I get that," he said. "But I still needed to know you were okay."

She nodded. "Thank you, I'm okay, and I didn't mean to shut you out."

He stood slowly. "You didn't shut me out. Not fully. But something's different. In you."

Selene hesitated. "There is."

"And is it *something* I'm supposed to meet? Or make space for?"

There was a pause.

His eyes locked with hers, searching, like he was trying to decide if she'd brought someone else home. Not physically, but emotionally and spiritually.

"Because it feels like there's someone else standing in the room with us."

Selene blinked. Her lips parted, but no words came right away. Then softly, "Maybe both."

He stepped closer but didn't reach for her. "Then let's start there."

He continued with an exhaustive sigh.

Her words lingered in the space between them like a breeze before a storm.

Ethan exhaled slowly, and his tone changed.

"Right," he said, backing up a step. "Because you've always had secrets, Selene. I just never thought I'd be the last to know you were keeping them from *yourself*, too."

She flinched. "It's not like that." She snapped.

"Then what is it like?" His voice cracked. "Because from where I'm standing, I watched the woman I love walk out the door, disappear into herself, and come back smiling like she's finally free—only I don't know who I'm looking at anymore."

Selene's eyes welled, but she didn't break. "Ethan, I'm not unraveling. I'm understanding. For the first time in my life, I feel like I make sense. Like everything I've ever questioned has a reason."

"That's great—for you," he snapped again, then softened immediately. "I'm sorry. That wasn't fair. I just—" he ran a hand over his face. "I've waited so long to be let in. Now it feels like someone beat me to it."

She moved toward him, stopping a foot away. "No one else is here. I swear."

"That's the problem, Selene. I *believe* you. But it still feels like I'm competing with a ghost. And I'm not sure I'll ever win."

They both stood in silence.

"You said you'd never leave," he added quietly, reminding her of a promise she didn't remember making.

Selene reached for his hand with a warm but unsure touch.

"I haven't."

He didn't pull away. But he didn't close the gap either.

"Maybe not in body. But part of you is already gone, Selene. I feel it."

She blinked back a tear and whispered.

"Then maybe it's time you met the part that stayed."

Ethan's eyes softened as he looked at her — not with anger, but something far more dangerous. Longing.

For a split second, she saw it — that familiar ache behind his gaze, the part of him that always reached for her first, even when she pushed him away. His lips parted as if he was about to say her name the way he used to, the way that made her believe he'd never leave.

She thought he was staying. But instead, he nodded slowly and deliberately. It was a gesture of finality dressed up as patience.

"I'll see you later," he said in a low voice.

She didn't try to stop him.

The door clicked shut behind him. Selene stood still, her breath caught in the space between hope and certainty.

Ethan stepped outside, the sun barely risen. He ran a hand over his face, exhaling hard, unsure if the ache in his chest was exhaustion or something permanent. That's when he saw him.

A man leaned casually against the passenger side of a dark gray sedan parked just a few feet away near another house in the cul-de-sac. Athletic build. He had his hands tucked in his jacket pockets. Calm. Too calm for a stranger watching a quiet neighborhood wake up. Their eyes met.

Ethan took a few steps before speaking. "Can I help you with something?"

The man offered a polite, almost amused smile. "Just waiting for someone."

"Friend of a neighbor?"

He shrugged. "Yeah, something like that."

Ethan studied him. There was nothing threatening about the man. No scowl, no rough edges. But something still didn't sit right. He looked familiar, and yet Ethan couldn't place him.

"Did you fold her undies and leave them on the bed—or are you wearing them?" the man asked in a low and teasing tone.

Ethan stiffened. "Excuse me?"

The man smiled wider but didn't clarify.

After another long pause, Ethan muttered, "Have a good morning," and turned toward his car.

"You too," the man said, as if they were old friends passing in a grocery store.

Ethan drove off. He didn't look in the rearview mirror. The man stayed exactly where he was.

Selene stood just inside the front door, watching the taillights of Ethan's car disappear down the street. She didn't cry. Not yet. The ache hadn't settled, only hovered.

When she finally stepped out, the sunlight hit her skin. She squinted into the morning haze and stopped short. He was still there. Leaning against his car like time didn't touch him, like nothing inside that house had shifted or cracked. As if he knew it would.

Their eyes met again. Selene exhaled slowly and walked toward him, each step heavier than the last.

"You just stood out here?" she asked.

He tilted his head, eyes amused. "Where else would I be?"

"You saw him leave?"

"I saw someone leave," he said. "Didn't know who he was. But I figured it wasn't me."

She crossed her arms. "You don't even know me."

He nodded thoughtfully. "Not yet. But I'm good at reading tension. That wasn't just someone you used to know."

"No," she said quietly. "That was my husband."

He quickly hid the flicker of surprise that showed on his face.

He straightened but didn't step away. "You could've told me."

"I didn't know I needed to," she replied. "Until this morning, I thought I was one person."

That made him pause.

"I don't follow," he said.

Selene hesitated. Then she stepped into the house and retrieved her bag from the table. She met him again in the open doorway. She reached in and pulled out the folded paper. The *Genexis* report. She didn't hand it to him, just held it between them like a fragile artifact.

"There's something in me. Two sets of DNA. One biological blueprint overlaid with another. Doctors call it chimerism. I call it confusing."

He looked at the paper, then at her. "So, what does that mean? You're two people?"

"I don't know," she said. "But this morning I woke up with a voice in me I'd never heard so clearly. It doesn't whisper anymore. It wants things and it *chooses.*"

His expression shifted—interest laced with something gentler. Not pity, but awareness.

"Is that what brought you to me?"

Selene didn't answer right away. Then, without blinking: "I think it was the version of me that doesn't ask for permission."

A slow smile touched his lips. "I like her."

Selene's voice softened. "She's reckless."

"And maybe she's real."

She laughed honestly. "You're really not going to ask about the man who just walked out?"

He shrugged. "I didn't come here to compete."

Her throat tightened. "You folded my clothes."

"Wasn't sure if I'd see you again. Thought it'd be nice."

"You folded *everything,*" she said, her voice thinning into something between humor and disbelief. "Even my underwear."

He grinned. "Figured someone should."

Selene shook her head, but her lips twitched.

"Ethan thinks I'm having an affair."

He looked at her with disarming calm. "Are you?"

Selene tried to decide if he was dangerous or just confident. His eyes, his posture, the way his breath didn't hitch even once made her wonder. She thought about the girl inside her—the quiet one, the dominant one. The one who was no longer satisfied with polite explanations and patient love.

"I don't know yet," she said honestly. "But if I am, I'm not the only one involved."

He nodded and twisted his face. "Fair enough."

Selene looked down at the Genexis report, then folded it again and slipped it back into her bag.

"Do you want to come in?"

He didn't answer right away.

"Only if *both* of you want me there."

Selene felt the words drop into her chest like a pebble in still water. She turned toward the foyer, not looking back, but she didn't close the door behind her.

He stepped inside, closing the door gently behind him. The silence that followed was familiar but awkward. The atmosphere was charged. Selene didn't bother to offer him a seat, she just walked ahead toward the kitchen at a deliberate and slow pace.

He followed without a word. The kitchen was still dim, the early sun barely touching the edges of the counter. She stopped near the island and turned to face him.

"I should feel worse than I do," she said quietly.

His expression didn't change. "But you don't."

"I feel... awake. Like I've spent years trying to fit into a shape someone handed me, and now I can feel the edges of something else. Something mine."

She paused. "I hurt Ethan. I know that."

"And yet?" he asked.

Selene blinked slowly. "And yet, I don't regret this. I don't regret *you*. Isn't that awful?"

"It's human," he said. "And maybe overdue."

She looked at him. "You sound so certain. Like you've done this before."

"I've done a lot of things before. But not this," he said. "Not *you*."

Her throat tightened. "You should know, I still love him. That won't change."

"I know," he replied, too easily.

"You don't have to name it. Just feel it."

She continued to observe his every expression, her eyes softer now, less guarded.

"You weren't just a reaction," she said, mostly to herself. "You were a magnetic pull."

He stepped closer, not touching her. "So what are you pulled toward?"

Selene didn't answer right away. Her fingers grazed the edge of the counter.

"Myself," she said. "The part of me I've never met but somehow already miss when she goes quiet."

"You're not quiet now."

"No," she said. "And I don't want to be."

A silence fell again, but this one was warmer. She reached out and placed her hand flat against his chest. Almost romantically, creating and owning this calm space.

"I can't promise anything," she said. "I don't even know where I'm going."

He covered her hand with his.

"Then I'll walk behind you. Just close enough to catch you if you fall."

She almost smiled. Almost.

His breath was still on her skin when she woke. The imprint of his presence on her shoulder, her thigh, her lips wasn't fading as quickly as she expected. Selene freed herself from his embrace and began the long walk. Selene stood in the bathroom, fingertips pressed to the edge of the porcelain sink. The mirror reflected her bare expressionless face. It wasn't unfamiliar at least, not entirely.

She tilted her head slightly, studying the curve of her jaw and the faint tension at the corners of her mouth. Her lips had been kissed, thoroughly. She remembered the heat of it, the press of hands that weren't Ethan's. But she was unnerved by the act itself.

It was how *natural* it felt.

She whispered, "Who are you?"

The woman in the mirror didn't answer. She just blinked, once, like *Selene* was asking the wrong question. Down the hall, the house was still. Ethan's absence clung to the air like cologne on yesterday's clothes. She could still feel his gaze from that morning—soft, sad, searching for a version of her that no longer existed.

Was she mourning him? Yes. But she was also relieved, free in a way. Still, she cried. She reached for the Genexis report on the counter. Her thumb brushed the corner of the page.

Two sets of DNA. Two cellular histories. Two stories trying to fit inside the same skin. Last night, she hadn't felt torn. She hadn't felt guilty. She'd felt seen. There was no adoration, but she was claimed.

Selene exhaled sharply and folded the report again. She looked back up at the mirror and ran a hand through her hair.

"Which one of us," she asked, voice trembling, "cried when Ethan left?"

The mirror stayed quiet. But for the first time, it didn't feel empty.

He sat relaxed at her kitchen table with his hands folded behind his head, like he owned the place. His posture demonstrated something more than arrogance, it was an ease of certainty. He watched Selene from across the room as she moved in a rhythm unfamiliar to her own body.

She wasn't flustered, but not confident . Not the Selene from the bar. Not the woman who said she didn't ask permission anymore. That version had vanished into the bedroom moments earlier, leaving this one barefoot and in a T-shirt.

He didn't speak. He liked the way his quiet demeanor made her fidget. To him, there was something beautiful about a woman trying to reconcile with herself—trying to decide which version deserved her loyalty.

Finally, she broke the stillness. "You didn't ask why I invited you back."

He tilted his head, not smiling this time. "I figured you were tired of holding it all alone."

She blinked and parted her lips, but no words came.

He leaned forward. "You think it's about me, but it's not. You're curious about what you feel around me because it doesn't feel like cheating. At least not in the way it should. That's what's confusing you."

Selene's hand trembled slightly as she set the mugs down.

"You say that like you know me," she said quietly.

"I don't," he admitted. "But I know what it's like to meet someone who shows you the version of yourself you didn't know you wanted to be."

She exhaled.

He leaned back, arms crossed loosely. "You're not trying to destroy anything. You're just not sure if the life you built was ever fully yours."

Ethan sat in his parked car just a few blocks from home with the engine off, hands clenched on the steering wheel. He had driven without direction. Not to escape, not really. Just far enough to stop feeling like a ghost in his own marriage.

He rubbed his eyes. Selene had looked different. Not just tired but transformed. Not like someone hiding an affair, but someone unveiling a new allegiance to herself. That's what made it worse.

He'd always tried to be enough. He wore his patience like armor. Now he wondered if his patience and understanding had made him invisible. And that man—whoever he was—hadn't even flinched. Like he knew he belonged there. Like he'd folded her clothes because he understood something Ethan didn't.

Ethan let out a bitter breath. "Did I miss something, or did I just refuse to see it?"

A memory surfaced. He imagined Selene curled beside him months ago, distant even in sleep. He had chalked it up to stress, hormones, her usual cycling moods.

He wanted to be angry, but he couldn't. He still loved her. That was the worst part.

She had looked back at him like she needed him and didn't—all in the same glance.

He picked up his phone, thumb hovering over her contact. But what would he even say?

"I want you to choose me... even if I'm not who you need right now?"

"I'll wait until this version of you fades again?"

"Come back to the life we built, even if part of you never lived in it?"

He tossed the phone onto the passenger seat and let his head fall back against the headrest.

The silence was heavy. If she came back he'd still wonder which version walked through the door.

Selene hadn't slept. She watched the sky change color through slats in the blinds. The night unraveled into morning like a confession she couldn't take back. The man had left just before dawn, quiet as he came. No words or promises. Just a parting glance that made her stomach twist.

Now, she stood in the kitchen barefoot, stirring tea she wouldn't drink. The doorbell rang.

Her chest tightened. She hadn't expected anyone. She peeked through the sidelight window and froze.

Ethan.

And behind him—coming up the walkway, coffee cup in hand—was *he*. Not together. Not yet.

Selene moved like a dreamer jolted awake. She opened the door before either man could knock. Ethan looked tired, lips pressed into a line, holding something in his hand. A notebook. One she'd left in his car last week.

"I figured you'd need this," he said.

"Thanks," she murmured, taking it. She tried not to notice the way his eyes searched her—face and neck, marveling at the way her sweater hung off one shoulder.

Before another word passed, the man reached the steps. He paused, then smiled, as if pleasantly surprised.

"Morning," he said lightly.

Ethan turned, clocking the man's presence. Recognition sparked—slow, uneasy. "You again?"

The man sipped his coffee. "Looks that way."

Selene stepped between them instinctively, palms half raised like a traffic officer.

"This is complicated," she said, her voice barely above a whisper.

Ethan looked at her. "He knows where you live?"

The man interjected, "You left your address on the invoice in your bag. It wasn't hard."

Ethan's jaw tightened. "You searched her things?"

"Folded her clothes too," the man said, smiling without apology. "She didn't seem to mind."

Selene closed her eyes, a flicker of shame rushed up her neck.

"Okay, stop," she said. "This isn't *whatever* you both think it is."

"No?" Ethan asked. "Because it sure feels like I walked out of my own house and into a waiting room."

The men's silent stares triggered something in her.

"I didn't plan any of this," she said. "I'm still trying to understand who I am—what I am. I didn't ask for a second voice in my head that isn't crazy, just separate."

She looked at the two of them. "But I'm not broken. I'm not confused. I'm just changing."

Ethan blinked, the pain in his eyes hollow and raw. The man nodded slowly, with an unreadable gaze.

Selene stepped back, leaving the door open.

"Either come in. Or walk away. But I won't choose today."

The door closed behind them with a quiet thud. Selene moved ahead without turning on the lights. The morning sun pushed through the blinds in pale slits. Ethan hovered just inside the foyer, shoulders tense, eyes flicking between the stranger and the familiar furniture that now felt foreign.

The man stepped in as if he belonged there, his gaze brushing the space. He slid off his jacket and draped it over a nearby chair slowly and deliberately, then turned his attention to Ethan.

"Nice place," he said casually. "Clean, organized, very considerate."

Ethan ignored the jab, though his jaw tightened. "Why are you here?"

The man tilted his head, hands tucked back into his pockets. "I was invited."

"By her," Ethan said, his voice graveling. "Not by us."

Selene exhaled. "Ethan..."

He held up his hand. "No. I need to say this. I've been patient. Supportive. I've held space, even when I didn't understand what I was holding it for. But this—" he gestured between them—"this wasn't in the vows."

The man raised his head. "Neither was chimerism, I imagine."

Ethan turned sharply. "You don't get to talk about things you barely understand."

"I read the report," the man replied evenly, eyes still on Selene. "You left it on the table."

Selene's heart thudded. She hadn't even realized he'd touched it.

Ethan's voice cracked. "You read it?"

The man nodded. "It's fascinating. She's fascinating. There's a whole map inside her most people will never see."

Ethan took a step forward, fists half-clenched. "And that gives you the right to...?"

"To what?" the man interrupted smoothly. "To want her? To understand a part of her that maybe you can't? I didn't write the rules."

Selene flinched. "Stop. Both of you."

They both turned toward her. She stood in the shaft of sunlight now, hair wild, eyes glassy but focused. Her voice softened.

"This isn't about you versus him," she said to Ethan. "This is about me trying to understand what's happening inside of me. I didn't ask for this."

Ethan swallowed hard. "But you didn't stop it either."

Her shoulders sank. "I didn't know how."

The man took a step closer, but not toward either of them—just deeper into the room, into the dynamic. "Maybe it's not something to stop. Maybe it's something to follow."

Ethan looked at him, broken and bitter. "You think you're the answer?"

"No," the man said, finally meeting Ethan's eyes directly. "I think I'm a mirror."

Total silence took over the room.

Selene's hand brushed Ethan's. He didn't pull away.

"I still love you," she whispered.

"I know," he said, eyes red. "But I don't know who I'm sharing you with anymore. Him—or her."

Another moment of silence.

He then looked at his wife as she stared at the man. The curve of her mouth, the fire in her eyes, the ache she hadn't hidden well enough. There was love. And there was something else. Something blooming. And not for him.

He stepped back, turned toward the door, brushing past the man with nothing left to say.

The man didn't move. He just stood there, watching Selene with the same calm.

"You didn't stop him," he said after a moment.

She closed her eyes. "He wouldn't have stayed for this version of me. Not forever."

The man nodded slowly, as if he already knew.

The door had barely closed when the silence shifted again, heavier this time. Selene didn't cry. She stood rooted in place, the light from the blinds slicing across her face. The man remained near the entryway, watching her but not approaching. There was no triumph in his posture. Just patience.

"I didn't want it to end like that," she said softly.

"I know," he replied.

She turned to face him. "He was good to me. Always."

The man didn't challenge it. "That's why it hurts more."

Selene nodded, her throat tight. "I didn't plan for any of this."

"But you felt it coming."

She looked down at her hands. "I just didn't know what 'it' was."

Selene's brows pulled together. She glanced at the man, who raised one eyebrow and gave a slow but knowing smirk.

"I'll get it," he said, already moving toward the door.

He opened it casually—but the man on the other side was anything but.

Ethan stood there, keys still clutched in one hand, his chest rising and falling like he'd run a sprint that started in his own rage and ended in reluctant resolve. His eyes darted from the man's face to his own front door, as if verifying the address. His jaw tightened, but when he spoke, his voice was level.

"Is Selene here?"

The man leaned against the edge of the open doorframe, studying him. "She is."

Ethan didn't look away. "I'm not here to fight."

The man nodded. "Didn't think you were."

Behind them, Selene stepped forward, stunned. "Ethan…"

He glanced at her. Not coldly—but not without pain. "I forgot my charger," he said quietly. "Or maybe I just forgot who I am."

No one moved.

Then Ethan looked at the man again, as if sizing him up. "I don't like you," he said.

The man's smile was brief. "You're not supposed to."

Another pause. The air was thick with it—an unspoken agreement forming like condensation on glass.

Ethan exhaled hard and ran a hand over the back of his neck. "But I can't lose her."

"She's not something to win or lose," the man replied, calmly. "You love her. But I recognize her."

Ethan's voice dropped to a low rasp. "You folded her clothes."

The man gave a soft shrug. "I noticed."

Selene stepped closer. "Why did you come back, Ethan?"

He turned toward her, pain softening just enough to make room for confession. "Because I know love when it hurts this much. And because I saw the way you looked at him. Like he spoke to the version of you I've never met."

She swallowed.

"I didn't come back to stop it," Ethan added. "I came back to understand it."

The man glanced between them. "So what now?"

Ethan looked past him to Selene. "I don't want to lose all of you. Not even the parts I've never met."

Selene took a step closer. "And what if those parts want you both?"

The man looked at Ethan, then back at her. "Then we figure it out. The three of us."

Afterword to Chimera

There are stories we tell about who we are, and then there are the stories our bodies tell without asking permission.

Chimera began with a medical curiosity. But the more I sat with the concept, the less it felt biological and the more it felt human.

How many of us move through life believing we are whole, only to discover we have been living as a fraction of ourselves?

Selene's awakening is not meant to excuse her choices. Nor is it meant to indict them. It is meant to ask a quieter question. What happens when the part of you that has been silent begins to speak with authority?

Some awakenings feel like liberation. Some feel like betrayal. Most feel like both.

Marriage, identity, desire, restraint. These are not fixed structures. They are negotiations between the selves we present and the selves we suppress.

But metaphorically, it is something far more common. We are layered. We carry competing impulses, inherited patterns, unexplored longings. Sometimes they coexist peacefully. Sometimes one overtakes the other.

Chimera is not a story about infidelity. It is a story about recognition. The kind that feels like discovery and destruction at the same time.

If the ending feels unsettled, it is intentional. Identity rarely resolves cleanly. It evolves.

And sometimes what feels like betrayal is simply the first time someone chooses to meet the version of themselves that has been waiting.

Epilogue

In the end, every story is a mirror. Some show us who we were. Others show us who we are still becoming. I have written these tales not to offer answers, but to capture the moments when clarity and confusion sit side by side, when love reveals beauty in one breath and cruelty in the next.

Each character who stepped forward, each silence that stretched too long, each confession spoken in half light came from the same quiet place, the part of the soul that longs to be known but hesitates to be seen.

If these stories have done their job, you have not simply read them. You have recognized something of yourself within them. That recognition is the real fellowship, the bond between teller and listener, writer and reader, heart and page.

I do not know where the next story will lead or whose truth I will help tell next. But I do know this. Stories will continue to find me, as they always have, in the quiet, in the chaos, and in the kindred spaces between.

Author's Note

These stories were never meant to be about perfection, not in love, not in intimacy, not in the ways we stumble toward or away from one another. They breathe in pauses and silences, in the words we almost speak, in the memories we carry like stones, in the shadows where longing and weakness stand beside hope.

If you felt yourself recognized in these pages, may you also feel less alone.

If you recognized someone else, may compassion rise before judgment and gentleness before certainty.

Because beneath every mask, every silence, every frayed thread of connection, we are all reaching for the same thing: to be seen, to be known, to be loved.

That, in the end, is the fellowship of kindred minds.

—*Jonathan Bellamy*

The Year We Wore Purple

A Story-Poem Honoring the Morris Brown College Class of 1970

Written and performed by

Jonathan Bellamy

May 16, 2025 — MBC Reunion Celebration

With gratitude to **Marilyn Massey**, whose invitation allowed me to give voice to this history,
and with deepest honor to the **Morris Brown College Class of 1970**,
whose legacy, fellowship, and support made this tribute possible.

Atlanta, Where the Heat Met Soul

In Atlanta where the heat met soul,
Where dreams were stitched in Black control,
Where magnolias bloomed and freedom rang,
And Curtis, Aretha, and Marvin sang...
The year was '70 — the streets alive,
Marchin' and groovin' just to survive,
From Auburn Ave to Paschal's door,
We prayed, we played, and we wanted more.
The skyline low, but spirits high,
You could feel the pride when we passed by,
We wore our fro's like crowns of flame,
Unapologetic, and unashamed.
And Morris Brown — oh, mighty flame,
The school that bore our grandest name.
A place where Black minds blossomed in power,
Where every chapel held the hour.
Of truth. Of grace. Of call and song.
Where even IF-- the night was long,
We knew the sun would rise on cue,
And bring the dawn of something new.

Freshman Steps and Purple Paths

Late August, Early September, 1966, we came through that gate,
Young, wide-eyed, walking successfully toward our destined fate.
No cellphones pinged, no FaceTime--faced,
Just composition notebooks, paper, pens, and an upward move -in favored grace.
Gaines Hall buzzed with sisterly pride,
"She's your roommate now — y'all better ride!"
No decor created by apps and plans,
We shared the room, we shared our hands.
The band rehearsed till morning dew,
Clarinet dreams and drills, we knew.
From Fountain Hall to Macy's Day,
We marched in time; we led the way.
I saw Greeks step and chants unfold,
With courage, pride, and letters bold.
They crossed the bridge in uniforms tight,
And we all watched, our hearts full of light.
In the Union, laughter filled the air,
Print shop ink and student flair,
Through work-study jobs, we still found time,
To dance, to dream, to spit a rhyme.
Homecoming? Oh yes, we did that right—
Sunday suits and dresses bright.
Herndon Stadium — yielded only standing room,
When the band dropped the low tones — ba-boom, ba-boom, ba-boom.
And man, when Bubbling Brown Sugar took the floor,
Every eye paused their blink, and every spirit soared,

The crowd erupted. The night was gold,
As tradition, talent, and the sounds of soul took hold.
And then one spring, with silent feet,
We lined the street for a King's last beat.
Hunter Street cried. Our hearts did too,
As we laid him down in skies of blue.

Crowns We Earned, Lessons We Kept

Now listen — the experience and journey was more than just the steps we took,
It's the heritage, the blackness, the knowledge tucked in every book.
In those halls, behind each desk,
We learned from professors who saw our best.
Ms. George — French, but vision clear,
Said, "Baby, where you're trying to go, that major won't take you near.
Business is calling — go stake your claim,"
And I walked that path, and earned that name.
One of the first, a woman bold,
With a Business degree and a dream untold.
While others said no, Mo Brown said yes —
And adorned me daily for corporate success.
I wore the crown of Miss MBC,
Not just beauty — but responsibility.
Representin' our college across the land,
With pride in my heart and grace in hand.
Delta Sigma Theta — I took that oath,
Pledged with passion, anticipating sisterhood laced with growth.
Chapter president — I stood my ground,
And lifted my sisters when life brought them down.
And yes — Ms. Omega Psi Phi,
Honoring my brothers flying the flag of athleticism and academics under campus sky.
It wasn't just titles or dances which were so sweet,
It was legacy — proud, profound, complete, elite, time-tested, graceful, and concrete.

I made the Honor Society list,
Topped it off with a scholarship twist.
Work-study by day, study hall by night,
Still walked across that stage in the light.
And what about that job I landed?
A Fortune 500 firm — my corporate identity was branded.
With an Education degree but business sense,
I flipped the script, cleared all hurdles on every fence.
But more than degrees and accolades fair,
It's the friendships rooted everywhere.
From Atlanta's kiosked corners to Brooklyn's doo-wop blocks,
The love emanating from the years at Morris Brown is a flow
that remains unlocked.

The Spirit of the Times

Now while we studied, marched, and played,
The world around us shook and swayed.
'Cause the reality of the testimony of being Black in 1970,
Meant speaking of black power, both its pain and prophecy.
Atlanta stood at history's gate,
The birthplace of a dream so great,
But King was gone — his voice temporarily stilled,
Yet his spirit of freedom spiritually roamed that West End hill.
We felt the rumble in our bones,
Of change that rang like saxophones.
SNCC had marched through campus green,
And Panthers walked where we had been.
Stokely came — sharp, profound,
Black and proud, boots on the ground.
The fire in our eyes got warm and wide,
As we reclaimed our names, our blackness, the pride in our stride.
Afros grew like protest signs,
Dashikis danced through chapel lines.
Naturals, no perms, no shame, no quiet tone,
We spoke in fisted rhythms all our own.
Music? Baby, that was breath,
It pulled us back from grief and death.
"What's Going On" — Marvin cried,
While Aretha taught us to spell with pride.
James Brown made the people move,
Soul Train gave us Saturday grooves.
We dressed in suede and platform shoes,
And painted life in Black folks' hues.
But even joy had sharper sides,
When brothers were drafted, mothers cried.

Vietnam pulled destroyed and pulled dreams away,
And left some prayers with no reply and some declarations of faith were hushed, nothing to say.
Yet through it all, we held the line,
At Morris Brown, like the Phoenix, we rose, sculpted and defined.
With every chant and class and beat,
We built a future from our seat.

Turning Points

Then came the day — the tassel turned,
The lessons lived, the knowledge earned.
A stage, a name, a thundering cheer,
The world ahead, both bright and near.
Some stayed rooted, some took flight,
Some left Atlanta overnight.
Jobs awaited, big and bold,
Or dreams not yet fully told.
One walked north to teach the youth,
Another marched to speak their truth.
One packed bags for NYC,
While one stayed put to earn a graduate degree.
A brother drafted, sent to war,
A sister started her own store.
A friend who'd always cracked a joke,
Now wore a collar, preached, prayed and from the pulpit spoke.
We scattered like a mighty choir,
Still burning with that Mo Brown fire.
And even as the times would shift,
We carried forth that "Brown-ite" gift.
Resilience stitched in every thread,
Each memory — captioned by the words we said.
The classroom, quad, the chapel pew —
Still lived in everything we'd do.
For every cap tossed in the sky,
A new dream dared to rise and fly.
And though we walked on different roads,
We bore the same ancestral codes.
So when the world would test our pride,
We stood with "Brown-ites" by our side.

'Cause no matter where our feet would roam,
We knew that MBC was our connecting spot, our home.

Reflections from the Now

And now, dear friends, we gather near,
With hearts that stretch across each year.
To honor all we've been and done,
To shine like that Atlanta sun.
We made it through — the highs, the lows,
With purple fire the whole world knows.
From trailer dorms to Fortune ranks,
From clarinets to credit banks.
We paved the path, we held the line,
And made our legacy divine.
We proved that the Black and brilliant blend,
Could fight, could rise, could lead, transcend.
Look around — we're still that flame,
Still bold enough to claim our name.
Still loud enough to chant our song,
Still Morris Brown, still standing strong.
So raise your voice, and clap your hands,
For all who marched and made their stand.
For those who came, and those we miss,
We seal their memory with a kiss.
And let the young ones hear us clear:
You come from greatness — stand, draw near.
The world may shift, the tides may bend,
But *Brownite* pride won't break or end.
So here's to gowns once tossed and worn,
To friendships that will not be torn.
To 1970, loud and proud —
We rise, we sing, we say it loud:

We are Morris Brown. And we still believe.
We still achieve. We still don't leave.
We walk with purpose, power, grace —
And joy is written on our face.

The Fellowship

Acknowledgements

First, I thank my parents—Rip (Pastor Clinton Bellamy) and Sister B (Mrs. Willie M. Bellamy)—who gave me both the voice and vocabulary, rhythm and reason.

My siblings—Charles, Reg, NeNe, Goot, Val, and Stocky—thank you for holding up mirrors that showed me who I was long before I understood it myself.

This book is, at its core, a love letter to the house that made me.

My church family at Grace Place Atlanta COGBF—thank you for reminding me that faith, fellowship, and storytelling all speak the same language, and that each has its own *amen*.

Phortune—thank you for trusting me with the name "Dad."

Ta'Leasa—thank you for allowing me to stand beside you as a father figure and guide.

Baby-Miracle—thank you for letting me be someone you can come to.

Loving each of you has been one of the quiet honors of my life.

Johnny, James, Timmy, and Gabriel—thank you for standing with me on a day that shaped 5,941 of my tomorrows.

Meka and Myra—your loyalty turned empty rooms into stages.

Shunda, and Allison—thank you for being among the first to tell me I was not just a storyteller, but an author. Your confidence in my voice arrived before my certainty did.

ARC-thank you for giving me the opportunity to memorialize the ultimate Diva. . .JDR

@GaryEarlWilsonJr—1980 made you a Millennial, but your comedic timing belongs to another era entirely. The world just hasn't caught up yet.

My West End Wall of Fame—Angela "Baby-Angie," Carla "Dear Yvette," Lisa (affectionately known in my world as "Dammit Lisa"), and Boyz II Men—thank you for the soundtrack, the laughter, the truth-telling, and the reminders that art, friendship, and faith are rarely separate things.

And to Alyssa—my "Lisa From Decatur"—thank you for shaping me in ways I did not yet have language for. You were the first person who made me fully comfortable in my own skin. That gift has stayed with me long after everything else changed.

To Smokey—who arrived with Phortune, and somehow became family—thank you for keeping the lizards away.

And, finally, to my friends, mentors, colleagues, and the quiet encouragers who carried me in seasons I did not have the strength to carry myself: you may not see your names here, but your fingerprints are on every line. If you ever offered a word, a prayer, a challenge, or a gentle nudge forward, this book belongs to you as much as it does to me.

About the Author

Jonathan Bellamy's story begins in Valdosta, Georgia, where faith, resilience, and artistry were woven into his earliest days. The son of a Pentecostal minister and a business education teacher, he learned early that every life holds both struggle and strength.

A writer, spoken-word artist, and ghostwriter, Bellamy has spent decades exploring the rhythm of language and the power of story. From his childhood recitations in Southern churches to stages across Atlanta and beyond, his voice has carried poetry, performance, and truth in equal measure.

As a professional ghostwriter and editor, he has helped authors, leaders, and creatives bring their own stories to life — works that blend insight, conviction, and authenticity. *The Fellowship of Kindred Minds* is his most personal project to date, a collection that reflects his enduring belief that words can illuminate the darkest corners of the human heart.

He continues to live and write in Atlanta, Georgia, where the magic of storytelling remains both his craft and his calling.

For more writing, upcoming projects, and events, visit www.jonathanbellamy.com

Photo Credit

Cover photograph by Amelia Jackson
Photography by Amelia Design
www.photographybyameliadesign.com

www.ingramcontent.com/pod-product-compliance
Lightning Source LLC
LaVergne TN
LVHW090556110826
845146LV00001B/150

9798218820657